EIDOLON AVENUE: THE FIRST FEAST

A COLLECTION BY JONATHAN WINN

Crystal Lake Publishing
www.CrystalLakePub.com

Copyright 2016 Crystal Lake Publishing

All Rights Reserved

ISBN: 978-0-9946793-4-5

Cover Design:
Ben Baldwin—http://www.benbaldwin.co.uk/

Interior Layout:
Lori Michelle—www.theauthorsalley.com

Editor:
Ben Eads

Proofread by:
Linzi Osburn
Sue Jackson
Jan Strydom

This is a work of fiction. Names, characters, businesses, places, events and incidents are either the products of the authors' imagination or used in a fictitious manner. Any resemblance to actual persons, living or dead, or actual events is purely coincidental.

No part of this publication may be reproduced, stored in a retrieval system, or transmitted in any form or by any means, without the prior permission in writing of the publisher, nor be otherwise circulated in any form of binding or cover than that in which it is published and without a similar condition including this condition being imposed on the subsequent purchaser.

For my readers,
who set the bar high
and expect only my best.

For Hunter,
who inspires with his strength,
who impresses with his optimism,
and who comforts with his friendship.

For Ben,
who helps without question
and applauds without hesitation.

For Joe at Crystal Lake,
who was the first to believe in me.

For my mom,
who stands on the Rainbow Bridge.
And for Cinnamon,
who now waits beside her.

This is for them.
Always.

PROLOGUE

There is a place on Eidolon
that stands five stories tall.
Beyond locked doors,
dreams dreamt no more,
the tenants await their fall.

And on this day
on "Eye-da-lon,"
which waits five stories tall,
vindication sweet
feeds the hunger replete
as the walls inside whisper
Let's eat.

APARTMENT 1A

LUCKY

Monday, 3:24 PM

IT'S SAID ALL of Shanghai wept when she died.

It's said over three hundred thousand marched in a funeral procession four miles long that blustery March day in 1935. It's also said that somewhere in the sobbing throng several women committed suicide. Their silent screen Goddess, Ruan Lingyu, ending her life with a fistful of sleeping pills at the too-young age of twenty-four spawning a grief only death could calm.

Whether or not myth wrestled with fact to become legend, and some claimed it did, everyone agreed this was a sad full stop to the short sentence of what might have been a glorious career.

A week later, in one of the many squalid shacks that still hug the outskirts of Shanghai, an early birth followed this now iconic end, the young mother's overwrought anguish shocking her into the delivery of a small, sickly daughter. A dangerous unlucky beginning for a dangerously lucky life.

Or at least that's what little Ruan Liu's family said.

Decades had passed since her calamitous arrival on the wild wind of a wet night. Decades since she'd slipped from the unending horror of Shanghai and into the gentle cruelty of Toronto, and Paris, and East Berlin. Lifetimes, really, each with their own name, history, tale to tell, since the eve of her twenty-fourth birthday when seven small sips of steaming tea sealed her fate and brought her end.

Now, safe in elusive anonymity, her life behind her, her ledger running with red, Ruan sat and waited.

Having already said how-dee-doo to the big 8-0, any sane person would think the ire she felt over her cursed beginning would've been tossed on the ash heap of memory long ago. But no. Her cool palms quieted the flush staining her cheeks only to feel the stinging heat of the past return. And with all she'd lost, the one thing that remained, the one touchstone, the still beating heart thump-thump-thumping in her chest, was anger.

And Ground Zero, as it were, happened the day she was born.

Against Chinese custom, her parents had named her after a celebrity. It didn't matter that it was a famously dead one or the emotional wounds of the girl's suicide still bled. They'd branded their babe with the bedeviled woman's memory, tying her forever to the endless anguish of a wandering ghost.

Then they'd watched, certain little Ruan, who'd christened herself Lucky—

the Killer, Lucky the Devil—

at the not-so-tender age of ten, would meet the same fate as the infamous Goddess: a life of struggle and sadness followed by an early exit at twenty-four.

But why think about that now? she wondered as she ignored the ghost *whispering* from the shadows, another cigarette shoved between her lips, the phosphorous flame jumping as she struck the match.

Lucky the Shadow, said the thing snarling from the corner.

Though the words cut like so many knives, she never paid attention to the voice. Her eyes watched the

EIDOLON AVENUE—APARTMENT 1A

storm fill the cracks on Eidolon Avenue below. She took a breath, steadying the thumping of her heart. Her hands trembled, the flesh withered and drawn, the skin pale. Like moonlight, she thought as thunder rolled. She took another drag, drawing deep, and then deeper still, the smoke swallowed and held until, her lungs screaming, she relinquished it in a reluctant brume of blue.

Her past revisiting her was no surprise. In those spaces tucked along the edge of clarity marched an army of memories. And with time running short, daybreak to dusk a quickening parade of regret and guilt, there was little else for an old recluse to do than tug emotional threads from a century's worth of unraveling quilts.

"Just go away," she said to the ghosts.

They stood near, melding with the matted carpet and cluttered coffee table. Their sightless eyes watching her slow decline, the failing memory and faltering eyesight, they waited. Or sat opposite, legs spread, imbrued arms splayed. Or crouched in the corner hurling half-truths, each accusation showering her like beads of blood to splatter and scar the perfect white of selective memory.

"Drink," Madame Xuo urged from the past. The wealthy woman with the painted face leaning close, smelling of expensive silk and dangerous secrets, the red slash of her lips curling in a macabre grin. "Drink, little—"

Lucky.

Why? she thought. Why didn't I stop at three? She wiped away the tears, the movement impatient and quick.

Like the ghosts sitting opposite, or leaning against the wall, or standing at the window watching their hungry brethren on the avenue below, that day refused to die. "That was the end," she said to the memory blackening the corner. "At twenty-four, that was the end. But who cares?"

You do.

Those ghosts who refused the grave drew closer. The Silent in expensive gold. The Favored with the heavy eyes. The heat, the red. The low table with the brew—

"It can fell armies," she said, her voice small.

as old as China itself—

"And raise kings."

waiting in a large cup, a dragon whipping around the delicate porcelain.

"Just stop."

These random pieces of memory were exhausting. Memories she didn't want to remember. That she couldn't remember. It was useless. Nothing but confusion and dread.

She stopped.

What have you done? it said from the corner.

She remembered.

Secret doors opening onto narrow halls the color of fire. A hidden world of servants crawling, or shuffling, or waddling. Their legs weeping stumps thumping the floor as they whimpered, the tears heavy and wet. Their reaching arms ending at the rounded shoulder with five knotted fingers and five scratching nails. Their greasy heads turning to look, to see, to find, the rounded, smooth skulls too large for their twisted, turned necks. The rancid smell of sick and sweat and blood and fear.

EIDOLON AVENUE—APARTMENT 1A

The nightmare steaming in painted porcelain her final bow and the birth of—

The Killer, the mysterious Chinese woman with no name and a numbered Swiss bank account.

The Devil, who would step, soft and quiet, from the darkest of corners to strike without hesitation or regret.

The Shadow, her cold eyes the last thing the innocent, the powerful, the unlucky would see.

How many did you kill? came the snarl.

Her stomach turned, the fetid burn of remorse in her throat.

Do they stand below, three hundred thousand deep?

The cigarette clenched between her teeth, she dragged long and hard, the acrid bite of the smoke little comfort.

March in a procession four miles long?

The Echo annihilated, she stubbed it out on the blackened windowsill, her trembling fingers balling into a fist.

It wasn't arthritis, though her joints ached. And it wasn't Parkinson's. Of that she was sure. She would have given the little she had left to slap either label, any label, really, on the tremor in her hands. Anything other than the one thing she knew it was. The one thing she feared the most.

Which is?

She laughed, the sound more a snort than a guffaw. "Well, it's not fear, you son of a bitch," she said.

No? said the voice from the corner.

"No."

It's time.

For a moment, the room spun. For a moment, she closed her eyes, the horror of the life she'd lived and the death she'd wrought rolling in like a thick, living cloud of unwilling memory. For a moment, just a moment, the army approached and the ghosts won.

"You can see me?" Lucky said, sinking into her chair, her voice small and weak.

Arms reached, their fingers flexing to find and grab and wrap around her neck. Tiny mouths opening to taste her flesh. To bite and suckle.

"How can you see me?"

Revenge spitting from painted red lips or snarling through yellowed teeth.

"Stop," Lucky said. "Please, stop. I'll be yours soon enough. And you, all of you, you slaughtered, forgotten nameless—

standing three hundred thousand deep—

can tear me limb from limb."

He stood among the cracks on Eidolon below. The memory of this man, the one she loved, the one she cherished—

The one you butchered—

"Yes—"

to save yourself—

"No—"

as you kissed his lips—

"Stop—"

red with blood—

his ghost fighting to find form. The eyes, the arms, the angry jut of his chin, not yet clear.

"Soon," she said, her hand too tired to wipe away fresh tears. "Not now, but soon."

With a blink, he was banished, the avenue once

EIDOLON AVENUE—APARTMENT 1A

again a familiar strip of cracked concrete awash in rain.

Across the room, a key slid into the lock, the dead bolt turning, the front door swinging open with a gentle shove.

Lucky relaxed. The trembling stopped. She took a breath. The hungry fingers left her neck, the seven mouths ceased their suckling, and the not-so-dearly departed, their true terror relegated to the realm of erratic recollection, departed once more.

A breath later, her red coat dripping with rain, her blonde hair as bright as the sun, her salvation arrived.

⌒∞⌒

"Of course, Bobby Lee always was a bit of a pill," her salvation was saying. "That's what Mama always said. 'He's a pill, that Bobby Lee. As wild as the day is long, God bless his heart.' And she was right, of course. But Mama was always right even when she wasn't."

Although the salvation standing in the kitchen loading up the cupboards with a week's worth of groceries had a name, to Lucky she was and always would be Evangelical.

"Are you hungry?" Evangelical would say over her shoulder, her arm shoved deep in the cupboard. "Are you cold?" Evangelical would ask, her voice an echo as she stocked the fridge with government cheese and cheap cold cuts. "Is there anything else you need?" Evangelical would continue, her brow knitting as, slow and steady, she folded her reusable grocery bags. Creasing only on the creases, the corners lined up just so, the whole painstaking ritual more tedious than a Roman Catholic catechism.

Silence, Lucky thought. If there's anything I need, it's silence.

But not wanting to wound this devout woman with the kind heart, she kept quiet, offering a small smile, the shake of her head answering No, I'm not hungry, No, I'm not cold, No, I don't need anything.

And so it would go. Every Monday afternoon around three, blonde, blue-eyed Evangelical, a young woman of contradictions, her tall Midwestern height and wide hips at odds with the sweet syrup of the South that stuck to her every word, would arrive bearing two bags of groceries and a week's worth of Gospel.

A loaf of bread with a bunch of John. Some macaroni and cheese with a chaser of Mark. A pint of ice cream followed by Luke and a bit of Matthew with a box of instant mashed potatoes.

Getting no response from her stoic charge, she'd then talk of family. The bags emptied and folded, Evangelical would sit, her head cocked to the side, her face looking somewhat skewed. Then, freshly brewed tea in hand, one cup offered, the other sipped, she'd bury the rest of the afternoon in breathless homilies and sly bromides.

And Lucky would listen.

"So, of course," Evangelical said as she sat, her thick thighs pressed together. "Mama being who she was, well, she never did take Bobby Lee over her knee which is exactly what Grandpa Will and Grandma June would tell her needed to be done." The blue of her eyes peered through her blonde bangs as she watched Lucky. "Yes they did, God knows, but Mama, she wouldn't listen, no siree, not to one word.

EIDOLON AVENUE—APARTMENT 1A

"But, really, you can't help but wonder how different Bobby Lee would have turned out, you know?" she said as she hoisted herself forward to collect her cup. "Or at least I do. What path would he have taken had she smacked his backside with a switch now and then. Because he went off the rails, that one. *Absolutely* off the rails. Until that day in a crowded bus station when the good Lord redeemed him and brought him home."

Two small sips as Evangelical grew quiet, the memory of her Bobby Lee a sudden storm darkening her light, her smooth brow wrinkling for the smallest of seconds.

"But, oh, I don't know," she said, the clouds lifting. "Can your past really determine your future? Do all those memories and mistakes and whatnot really butt their noses into one's here and now? And believe me," she said, the cup on the table to hide somewhere in a valley of unopened mail and yellowing newspaper. "I've tried talking with Pastor Dan about this, but he won't hear it. 'Well, what do you think?' he always says. 'I don't know,' I always say. 'That's why I'm asking you!' And we laugh. But there's never an answer. Or at least not one from him or anyone else I talk to.

"So, what do you think?" Evangelical said, waiting.

Lucky looked at her, this simple, sweet soul. Wise, yes, but still so naive and unsuspecting. "I think we carry our pasts with us wherever we go and whatever we do," Lucky decided to say, playing it safe.

She swallowed. Her voice felt strange. Trapped and scared. She looked down to find her fingers around her tea, the mug balanced in her lap. She didn't remember lifting it from the table, or carefully bringing the steaming Lipton close. She cleared her throat again, pushing down the years of lies scrambling to her tongue, eager to slip past her lips.

"Are you your past?" Evangelical asked. She leaned closer, her knees still locked together like a vestal virgin. "Is it still a living thing, your past? Or are you able to move on and leave it behind?"

"I am all I've done." She coughed, finding the rim of the mug pressing against her lips, the tea begging her for a sip.

No.

"And what's that?"

She put it on the table, pushing it out of reach, and leaned back. They grew restless on Eidolon below. She could feel them. Could feel their formless faces tilt skyward, their ghostly ears cocked and ready for her to lose her battle and for those words, all those words, to escape. She could feel them gather and grow, pressing forward, their bloodied mouths opening to laugh, or shout, or scream in rage at the lies that would fall from her lips.

But no. No lies. Not today.

"What've you done?" Evangelical said. Her smile sweet, the blue of her eyes clear pools of innocent wonder, she waited, her thick fingers with their pink nails knitted together on her lap as she sat. "Wanna talk about it?"

Lucky turned away, the catch in her throat snatching her voice and stealing her courage.

"It's good to talk now and then, you know," her salvation said.

A dozen now stood below as the long-dead Madame Xuo whispered from the past,

EIDOLON AVENUE—APARTMENT 1A

Strong as stone—
A dozen waited in the rain, finding their forms.
Cannot falter—
Remembering her.
Cannot fail—
Remembering themselves.

"We should talk." Evangelical's voice sounded strange. Distant. As if she was standing on the other side of a large door. A locked door that had no key.

It is forever—

"No," she said.

On Eidolon, their eyes wild, their teeth bared in bloodstained snarls, they gathered together and drew near.

"No?" Evangelical said.

"No."

Lucky pushed the past away. Why on earth would I say anything? she thought. What good could come from knowing what she'd done?

It would destroy the best parts of who Evangelical was. And she just didn't have an appetite for that kind of cruelty anymore.

"Are you alright?" Evangelical watched her. "Should I go?"

No, Lucky wanted to say. Shocking herself, she leaned forward, her hand out to touch the girl's knee, or pat her hand, or something. Offer some small something to comfort, like a normal person would.

Seeing you is a burden, the man with the knife said, the waves crashing beneath him.

She stood in the kitchen, Evangelical. "More tea?" she said over her shoulder, her hands reaching into the cupboard for two thick white mugs.

Lucky closed her eyes. That missing minute, Evangelical here and then suddenly there, haunted her. Her throat tight, she swallowed again. Found herself considering taking a sip, a small sip, from her tea.

She looked up to find Evangelical at the door, shaking the rain from her red coat, a bag of groceries at her feet, the second one still balanced in the crook of her arm.

No, that'd been earlier. She blinked, squeezing her eyes shut for a moment, just a moment, and opened them. Evangelical came close with two steaming mugs of tea in hand, past and present once again on the same page.

"We should talk," her salvation had said.

I want to, Lucky said in that quiet voice that only she could hear. But there was too much. Too much dust, too many cobwebs.

You have much to answer for.

Yes, the blood had dried and the flesh had been nibbled and the bones gnawed years ago. Nothing worthwhile hid in the past.

There will be other chances, the slaughtered said from the corner, the words slow. She knew why they were thick. She knew why they sounded wet.

Lucky looked to the window and squeezed her eyes shut. Stop it, she thought. Nothing of use waited under those stones left unturned. To speak now of what was then, it was pointless.

Her stories could only destroy.

Besides, she wondered, her trembling hands rising to cover her ears, who would believe her beginning began the day she died?

CHAPTER TWO

IN A SHINING villa in the center of Shanghai, her thighs burning, her back aching, and her knees rubbed so raw they all but whimpered, Lucky knelt, silent, waiting and more exhausted than any *almost* twenty-four year old should be.

The Revolution had arrived almost a decade ago on the heels of a brief, bloody civil war. The Communist storm which had darkened the horizon for years had finally crept in and swept out the poor, the infirm, the religious. And now, outside the city, in the rural areas, thousands were dying in what was feared would be an historic famine. The old and weak falling first. Small children left to starve in the fields under the watchful eyes of hungry prey. The trees plucked of their leaves and stripped of their bark, the birds silent in their absence.

But far from the devastation and desolation, Lucky worked.

Her father dead and her mother dying, the family had abandoned Bad Luck Lucky. Closed their hearts, closed their pocket books, and closed their doors, leaving the cursed girl to fend for herself. Scraps of food dug from gutters. The touch of strangers endured for the warmth of a blanket and a bowl of rice.

Then one hot day, the clouds building and the air thick and wet with a coming storm, the woman with the lopsided smile had appeared and Lucky's life changed.

Although still young, she'd now spent five years as an indentured soldier in the army serving Madame Xuo the Silent. One of many girls who scrubbed Madame's endless floors and polished Madame's precious silver and bent under the weight of the buckets of rainwater carried into Madame's house.

Her fingers would dig into her elbows, squeezing the ache away. And she'd grit her teeth and close her eyes, willing away the fever, the chills, the exhaustion as she wet the brush and lathered the rag and scrubbed away stains that didn't exist. Accepting her fate as if she was old and the best bits of life were far behind, she'd pick her way through her rice, her fish, her piece of fruit, and then lay on the floor hoping sleep would come.

But regardless the misery the hours held, each day would close with Lucky and her fellow recruits standing shoulder to shoulder to offer a low bow as Yin Ying, the favored servant of Madame Xuo the Silent, passed by on her way to Madame's very private quarters.

One never saw Madame. It was said she was small and her skin was the color of moonlight. That her feet were tiny and her steps were nimble and all her kimonos were expensive golden silk, her wealth so immense and her power so vast that not even Mao Zedong dared interrupt the life Madame Xuo the Silent had carved for herself.

A life Lucky had a very small part in. And after four

EIDOLON AVENUE—APARTMENT 1A

birthdays ignored, four birthdays having passed without a word, this, her fifth birthday under Madame Xuo's roof, her twenty-fourth year, was when the dreaded invite came.

Like much of Madame Xuo's life, her birthday teas were legendary. An event that lived in furtive fears confided in quiet corners. Yin Ying would approach to whisper in the girl's ear. A nod of the head followed by a small bow and the newly damned would join the mysterious favorite to trudge down the Great Hall, turn the corner and never be seen again. At least not in the house.

"They found her," the girl said, her voice low. "On the edge of the water, in the bay where the ships come in."

"It's true," said her friend, moving deeper into one of the darker alcoves hidden throughout Madame's bright, golden villa. A dream of light and beauty, it was, the scent of rare flowers carried on light breezes sneaking through large open windows.

"I heard she couldn't speak," a third said, standing close, her lips against her friends' cheeks. "That she stood in a flowered dress with her eyes closed, like she was asleep."

The first girl shook her head. "No, she opened her eyes, but they were black and wet, and when she opened her mouth, flies crawled from between her lips. And her nose, it bled, too, but the blood was thick and black."

They all nodded.

"She stood there," said the second girl. "Blind, her nose bleeding black and her teeth missing—"

"Her teeth were missing?" said the first.

JONATHAN WINN

"That's what I heard," the third girl said.

"How horrible."

"And then when the black started to run from under her dress and down her legs and onto the dock," the third said, "the sailors, even the ship's captain, everyone who'd gathered to help, they ran away. It frightened them. They were sure she was a demon or something."

"Yes," the first girl said with another nod. "Something worse."

Then, their whispers no longer quiet, their hearts fearing discovery, they'd break formation, abandoning their post to scrub the floors or gather buckets of rain water or gently wash Madame's delicate ceramic cups, the story of this unfortunate stepping wordlessly from the dock to be pulled deep into the churning water of Hangzhou Bay left for another time and a different dark corner.

Lucky waited, kneeling, the room hot.

No one spoke of this space. Until now, Lucky had never heard of it. A part of the house, but separate, it lay hidden and protected by ignorance. Thick walls that shimmered with the glow of flames and a low ceiling that remained in shadow. Coals that smoldered with a dangerous heat in a brazier along the edge, the boards beneath her knees cracked, splintered, and covered in dust. The low table in front of her buckled with a warped ripple in its middle. The air heavy and thick, each breath was clouded with the stench of incense and herbs and heated wood. Around her, the walls were large heavy panels painted red that stretched floor to ceiling, a large bright green and gold dragon slithering, dancing, snapping along the

EIDOLON AVENUE—APARTMENT 1A

baseboard, its bared fangs in an endless chase with its forked tail.

"You may look at Madame," the oafish Yin Ying said through thick lips that masked a mouthful of blunt, crooked teeth.

With a glance, Lucky thanked the familiar, but mysterious, servant who stood too tall, walked too heavy, and offered slow dangerous smiles from a lopsided face.

Although both she and Yin Ying kneeled, the servant at the end, her back to the brazier, Lucky on one side of the table, facing her host, Madame Xuo sat perched in a low chair on the other, her knees gracing the floor, but not kneeling for that's something Madame would never do.

On the brazier, the cast iron kettle came to a boil and Yin Ying, a thick pot holder wound 'round her hand, poured the water into small tea pots on the table—one for Madame, one for Lucky—until it overflowed to run over the black clay. The tiny lid clamped on, more water was poured, sealing and heating the pot while the loose tea inside steeped.

The ceramic cup beside her pot was larger than usual. Where most held no more than two swallows, hers could hold six, maybe eight. Delicate and precious, the outside was painted with a dragon, a smaller echo of the one slithering along the baseboards.

Although she had yet to accept Yin Ying's earlier invitation to look at Xuo the Silent, Lucky knew what she'd discover. The face painted white, the brows careful strokes of black. A shining dark wig gathered in a large round bun. The pale powdered lips cleaved from nose to chin by a thick slash of red. The kimono a predictable expensive gold silk, her hands, the color of moonlight, sitting on her lap, discreet and out of sight.

And driven by something strong and unapologetic, something she couldn't fight, Lucky lifted her gaze. First to the dragon wrapping around the cup and the fingers of steam rising from the clay pot, then to the dim varnish of the low table sitting between them, and finally to Madame Xuo the Silent.

Her eyes saw Madame. And as the silent woman sat, her eyes downcast, the painted, powdered lids heavy, her chin tucked to her chest, the shadow sitting behind her (which could have only been Madame's) rose to stand and stretch, its arms reaching wide against the glow of the smoldering coals flickering against the painted red walls.

CHAPTER THREE

NESTLED IN A pile cluttering the coffee table sat a discarded pouch of Lipton bleeding into the sunken oval of a porcelain saucer.

"It's good, isn't it?" Evangelical said. She lowered the mug into a nearby abyss, the porcelain finding the saucer and a watery pool of its own russet-hued blood with a gentle clank.

"It can fell armies," Lucky heard herself saying.

And raise kings, came the remembered words from Madame Xuo's red room.

The vengeful wraith of the woman with the white face and a slash of scarlet for lips waited opposite Lucky. From a small, low chair that had once sat in a distant past, she was near the window in the here and now, her eyes low, her tongue crawling with secrets and lies and things best left unsaid.

"I'm sorry?" Evangelical said.

Madame Xuo stared at Lucky, her knees not kneeling as they rested not on the grimy grey of a familiar carpet, but on ancient boards that were cracked, splintered and covered with dust. Nearby, Yin Ying stood too tall against the worn yellow of the wall, her breathing too loud as her wet lips broke into an eerie grin. She looked at the drops rolling down the window pane, then Evangelical, and then Lucky.

And her salvation sat, a stubborn remnant of her present refusing the determination of her ominous past. Evangelical leaned forward to take her tea from the low table between them, the warped wood holding two clay pots and two ceramic cups and small plates of roast duck, rice, fruit, small bites of candy.

Chinese funeral food.

Lucky paused and closed her eyes.

Outside, heavy clouds sobbed sheets of rain.

Inside, present relented to past, the room growing hot. A dragon snapped, slithered and snaked along the baseboards, the walls painted panels of red. Lucky on one side of the table, too young to die, the cup in her hands. Madame across from her, her knees not kneeling, her eyes downcast even as Lucky took her first sip.

The brew was bitter and thick, tasting of forgotten corners in high cupboards and a misplaced pride which knew neither embarrassment nor shame.

"It's very old," Yin Ying was saying, her back once again to the precarious heat of the brazier. "As old as China itself, they say. They also say it's so powerful and rare it can fell armies and raise Kings." She laughed, the sound viscid with slobber and bordering on cruel.

A second sip.

Did Madame's lips twitch? Lucky wondered. Was there the hint of a smile poking at the corners?

Lucky's face felt strange. She swallowed. Blinked her eyes. Found it odd that she felt heavy. Like stone. Empty stone. Like a corpse. One of those mummified Buddhists found hidden deep in a dark cave. The skin

grey and shrunken, the skeleton still sitting as if waiting for coins to clink in his bowl. She was a husk. A husk that lived and breathed. That had skin that was warm to the touch with flesh that moved. Her cheeks, her nose, the edges of her eyes, everything, were she
this unfortunate
to see it in a mirror, it'd ripple like the waves
pulled deep
in Hangzhou Bay.

A third sip, Yin Ying gasping, Madame's gaze still downcast.

She wanted to feel her face. Put her palms to her cheeks to feel the skin coming alive, snapping, slithering and snarling like the dragon riding the base of her cup. But she couldn't. It wouldn't be appropriate. She needed to be silent and discreet, her hands on her lap, her head bowed.

Her face was moving. The skin was alive, yes. Her fingers could feel it—for her palms had insisted on discovery despite decorum—but she didn't know what it was. And her neck. The flesh there, too, was pulsing, pounding, wandering. Moving in ways it never had and simply could not and should not. She blinked, her vision growing dark.

She reached for the cup. A fourth sip.

"Madame," Yin Ying said from the past.

"Are you okay?" Evangelical said in the present, her blonde hair too close, her forehead almost pressing against hers, Lucky's fists clenched in hers. "Are you alright?"

"No," Yin Ying said again. "No one's ever had more than three." The servant was weeping, sobbing, her shoulders shaking, the heels of her hands digging into her eyes. "Madame!"

Lucky was no longer in her body. She stood somewhere else, watching, wondering, curious. Afraid. She could see herself, too skinny and too scared and too close to dead as she took another sip. The cursed child at the end of a loveless, troubled life. She could see Yin Ying kneeling, panicked and afraid.

Of what? Lucky wondered.

Her hands were trapped. Evangelical still held them.

"The day I died . . . " Lucky said.

Too young.

She stopped, the words leaving her, her voice sounding old, the young Lucky still suffering somewhere in a past that still lived.

Are you afraid?

She looked around and saw the unfamiliar. She was not home. Eidolon had never blazed with this kind of heat. The walls had never been this red and a dragon had never raced around this room in a blur of green and yellow and gold chasing a tail it could never catch.

The shadow stood behind Madame Xuo.

A sixth sip.

"Madame, please!" said Yin Ying to Madame Xuo the Still Silent, the words choked with tears. "She should have stopped at three."

"I need only three," Lucky said, her voice sounding distant.

"I'm sorry?" Evangelical released her hands. A cool palm was placed on Lucky's forehead. The devout woman's breath smelled of Ritz crackers and weak tea. We had Ritz in the house? Lucky found herself

EIDOLON AVENUE—APARTMENT 1A

wondering, and then thought of the discarded pouch of Lipton weeping somewhere in a saucer.

"We need to talk," Evangelical was saying, but the table still sat low and the room was still hot. And the Lucky living in the past still held her cup of tea, one sip, the seventh, remaining. She couldn't feel her hands. She couldn't feel her lips. The memory of these things, knowing where they were and how they were supposed to work, is what guided her now.

The shadow stood behind Madame who had yet to drink her tea. Madame who had yet to move. Madame whose eyes had yet to raise and blink.

Madame who had yet to see.

From where she stood, the Lucky who no longer knelt, the one who stood in this all-seeing space, saw the flesh of the woman's painted face had split and cracked. And the skin of those lips slashed red had peeled to dangle on her chin. A layer of dust lay like a thick blanket on the dark wig and the gold of the kimono had faded, the hem worn and frayed.

She could see the cobwebs covering Madame, the spiders crawling from the nose to skitter across the cheek and burrow into the ears. Their brethren poking from between her lips to scamper down her chin and into the gold of her kimono. Could see the hands that were not only paler than moonlight, but lacked life. The flesh on this body that should have seen a grave decades ago, yet still sat erect as if awaiting the clink of coin, had shrunk to the bone.

Madame was dead and this red room was the deep of her dark cave.

Glancing into her cup, Lucky saw her final sip. Felt the sudden breeze. A wind that was like the gentle sigh of something lonely and longing. A sigh that ruffled the cobwebs from Madame's hair. That brought with it the scent of putrid dust and fetid flesh. That peeled flakes of dried skin from Madame that lifted and ducked and dove and swam through the air. That danced near the window and darted away from the rain and spiraled and swooped to land in Lucky's Lipton.

No.

This ceramic was delicate and stained a shy brown, the brew ancient. If she looked hard enough into the thick liquid, she feared she'd see her own reflection, though she knew that would never be.

And although it wasn't something she saw, whether she knelt here, numb and dumb and almost blind, or stood, a tourist, separate and mute, she felt the shadow come closer. Leaving Madame, it came, abandoning the painted husk in an impatient rush, the gold of her kimono rustling.

And by the time Lucky had lifted her head, she knew.

"The day I died," she said to a world of shadow and red and chasing dragons. She knew the window was still there and the ghosts still gathered in the rain on the avenue below. Knew this past which had lived could not live again despite the familiar ghost hissing from the corner.

Evangelical spoke, her voice slow, the unheard syllable muffled as if whispered from the depths of the darkest shadow waiting at the end of the longest hall.

Kneeling at the low table, Yin Ying near, head down and sobbing, she knew the shadow would wrap around her. Knew it would embrace her. Squeeze tight. Squeeze the breath from her. Squeeze until that final

EIDOLON AVENUE—APARTMENT 1A

exhalation was released, reluctant and slow, into the air for Madame to catch, and inhale, and suck deep, deep, deep into her lungs and hold until, with a gasp, Xuo the No Longer Silent would lift her eyes, lift her lips in a smile, lift her head, and say,

"Drink, little Lucky."

The final sip passed her lips. Her mouth numb, her tongue thick, she swallowed. Her last breath stolen as the world stuttered and stopped and lurched lopsided.

"The day I died," Lucky felt herself say again.

"No," Evangelical said. Lucky could smell her skin and feel her breath. Could almost see her and feel her. Found comfort in that.

In the past, Madame Xuo the Now Living Corpse rose to crawl over the table, smelling of dust and death and shrunken skin clinging to crumbling bone. "You're not dead," her salvation was saying.

From the past, Madame smiled, a slow baring of smeared red lips and yellowed teeth, as Evangelical pulled closer, her words tickling Lucky's cheek.

"Not yet."

CHAPTER FOUR

HER TEETH WERE *missing*, she heard someone silently say, a girl from a distant, remembered conversation.

Lucky's tongue felt thick as it moved. Her teeth were safe and sound.

She stood in a hall. A narrow hall. One with many doorways and an end that didn't end, the long space leading to an unavoidable dark.

The low table was gone. As was Yin Ying and the brazier. The dragon no longer whipped 'round the baseboards and the wiggling of her flesh had quieted.

The red remained. A haze that snuck along the floor, and climbed the walls, and ducked into the shadows hugging the ceiling.

Lucky blinked, and then blinked again. Fingers flexed and her chest rose in a deep breath. Her mouth tasted of sick. And a sour burn stained her throat, stinging her nose when she swallowed.

She'd drunk the tea. She remembered. She closed her eyes, the heat of the red room returning.

A dragon chased its tail. Two clay pots waited. Madame Xuo sat silent and watching and dead. Then alive, bending forward, crawling near. The shrunken

EIDOLON AVENUE—APARTMENT 1A

flesh stretching as her skeletal fingers gripped the edge of the warped wood and she pulled herself close, the kimono rustling while cobwebs snapped and dust fell and spit dangled from her smiling lips.

Then there'd been black.

And now red.

This red. The dark hall bathed in a dusty crimson glow, the low-ceilinged space like some ancient, forgotten tomb.

She wasn't alone.

Something bumped against her calf. Too tired and too confused, she didn't look. Not until four fat fingers wrapped around her ankle.

Below her, it crawled. A torso with a large head squatting awkwardly on slender shoulders, one arm reaching forward, the thick fist on her ankle, pulling forward, pulling near. The large mouth opening, the sharp stench of something spoiled and infected and threatening to burst rising from the nubs of yellow teeth.

Its nose was pushed flat, the lips pushed forward. Its hair heavy, greasy strands sticking to a flaking, grimy scalp. The legs two clubs jerking from the hip, each with a long, thick, yellowed nail jutting from the end that scraped the floor as it angled near.

Lucky wanted to scream. Wanted to run. But the hall was too red and the world moved too slow. And even as the legless thing with the four-fingered fist wrapped its mouth around her ankle to gnaw the flesh, the tongue sticky and wet as slobber slid down her heel, she stood quiet.

After another blink, the haze cleared and she could see clearly.

A moment later, she screamed.

Like a swarm of insects, they crawled, waddled and shuffled. Heavy skulls squatting on twisted necks. Crooked torsos without legs. Arms that curled and bent to grope in the dark. Five fingers stretching from where the shoulder ends and an arm should begin.

Anonymous souls, these with legs, their eyes blind under sheets of thick flesh, feeling their way as they crawled, the wet sound of bleeding, torn knees dragging against the wood. Others unable to move, or see, or speak, sitting trapped in an unforgiving stench of sweat, spoiled blood, weeping flesh and mangled muscle.

In the corners, they lingered, these unfortunates, the insistent beat of their hearts visible beneath their too-pale skin and shallow, sunken chests.

Sensing her near, they turned. Sightless eyes attempted to see. Squat noses pressed flat to slimy faces lifted to catch her scent. Thick lips smeared with sick stretched into torn, ripped and jagged grins. Half-finished forms dragged and turned and moved close.

"You still live." Weathered with age and weary, the voice came from behind her. "I don't believe that's happened before. Not after seven sips of tea."

Carefully turning, fearing she'd step on someone or something, Lucky discovered Madame Xuo the No Longer Silent.

Still small, still pale, her lips still cleaved with red and her brows still perfect strokes of unapologetic black, she stood, wrapped in gold silk, bathed in red, surrounded by the swarm.

"No one has had more than three sips," Madame said, her eyes meeting Lucky's. "Yet this was allowed. And now I know why."

EIDOLON AVENUE—APARTMENT 1A

They scurried away from Lucky, these things. Their fingers no longer reached and their fists no longer grabbed. Their mouths no longer tried to gnaw her calves or ankles or feet. Desperate and afraid, they fled to the safety of open doors and thick shadow and smooth wall.

"Turn," Madame said. "Look."

She did.

Her shadow waited.

It was dark, as all shadows are. But this was different. It breathed. It lived. It had small eyes that opened and blinked. There was an awareness. A hunger.

"This has walked with me," Madame was saying. "It has made me and my life safe. From sickness, from poverty. From hunger. Can you imagine a life without sickness or poverty or hunger, little Lucky?"

Lucky didn't respond, her gaze on the dark standing in front of her.

"As Yin Ying said, this has felled armies and raised kings," Madame said. "It is pure power and might. As strong as stone, *it cannot falter.*" The hem of her kimono rustled against the floor as she stepped forward. "It cannot fail. And should you embrace it and let it become you, neither will you."

Lucky turned her head.

It turned with her.

"The rules of life will mean nothing," Madame said. "You will live free from consequence. Climb as high or fall as low as you like. There is no limit. It will be your choice what you do with it."

Lucky watched the dark. Beneath the surface, something waited. She could almost hear it, almost see it. She came oh so close to catching whatever was trying to speak to her or reach out to her. Even narrowing her eyes and looking closely, she still couldn't catch it, the thing allowing her just the smallest glimpse of souls trapped and bodies broken and a writhing world of never ending anguish.

"But there is a price," Madame said, her voice dropping to a whisper. "A price determined by what you choose. A price that must be paid when your life, this life, comes to its close."

From the dark, a face came forward. A young girl with tearstained cheeks. Small and grieving, she pressed to the shadow like a hand to glass, the lipless mouth speaking words Lucky couldn't hear. She moved close, and closer still, pressing her own face into the dark. It was cool and calm. Like the blissful shade of a giant tree on the hottest of summer's days.

She liked it.

"Can you hear me, little Lucky?" Madame said.

Yes, she could hear the old woman. But the shade, the dark, it was calling her. It promised relief from pain, from work. It whispered of freedom and strength. Of power. Perhaps even of wealth and a life of smiles and laughter.

In the dark waited the end of being at the mercy of others.

"Whatever you choose cannot be undone. Once you agree, it is yours and it can never be lost. You can run and it will follow. And I promise you," Madame said as she took another step closer, "there will come a time when you will pray for release. You will beg for it to be over. But it never ends. It is forever."

She wanted to turn to Madame. Wanted to

acknowledge the words being said. But she couldn't. She wouldn't. The dark brought her closer. She could almost feel its breath kissing her lips and hear the beat of its lonely heart.

"Think," Madame said, the word sharp. Sharp enough for Lucky to turn and peer through the red haze to see Madame standing, the mob of misshapen souls squirming around her ankles, their arms thumping against her shins. Tears fell from the woman's eyes, the furrowed brow urging what her words could not.

"Please," Madame said. "Think of what you are choosing. Of what it might be. At the end.

"You are young. Too young. And I know you hope, as I did many years ago, that this will be the answer. But it is not—"

A hand the color of moonlight rose to stop the words, the flesh soon wet with a stream of blood that stole between her long, pale fingers. Madame closed her eyes and, taking a deep breath, wiped the red from her lips with the back of her hand before speaking.

"I have said all I can. But know this: there is nothing to fear from death, but much to fear from a life without consequence."

Lucky turned from her, her eyes once again on the dark.

There was a long moment of silence.

"Are you afraid, little Lucky?" Madame said.

Lucky shook her head. Leave behind a life of work and pain? Even now, her arms ached. Even now, hunger burned and her body wept. Even though her day had been quick and her work interrupted by the invitation to tea, there were years of pain weeping in every bone and muscle and breath. Her days, day after day, cursed with pain she'd always feel, no matter how long her life.

Freedom from this is what was being offered. This was the choice she had in front of her.

Why wouldn't I take that? she thought. Afraid?

No, she was not afraid.

"You will be," Madame was saying as Lucky stepped into the dark.

CHAPTER FIVE

BELOW HER, THE waves of Hangzhou Bay slapped the pilings of the dock. Around her, men worked, barefoot, the thick denim of their pants rolled up to the knees. Or stood, smoking strong tobacco rolled in cheap paper.

She needed help, but couldn't speak. There'd been a hall. A narrow space with a low ceiling and many doors. The light was red. The walls reflected red. The floor more glowing red. Even the shadows waiting at what could be the end of the hall—for the hall had to have an end, yes?—were red.

Madame Xuo had stood in a mountain of bodies. Arms without fists that flailed and hit. Crude legs that thumped the floor as they tried to crawl, and lift, and stand. Teeth too large for mouths that sliced faces in two. Gashes that still whimpered, still wept, still bled.

And Madame had spoken. There'd been a warning, and then blood. But the air, it was cool and inviting. There'd been silence, then. And knowing what the future held, she'd stepped into the dark, the shade, the shadow.

Yes, Lucky remembered.

Here, the sun was bright and the sky was blue.

Here, men rushed to and fro, piles of fish shimmering and flapping and wiggling as wheelbarrows bounced along the dock. They stood in groups, these men, talking as more ships came in, others running to retrieve the nets and fill the crates and stock the wheelbarrows and push past yet again.

No one stopped for the strange girl in the flowered dress.

She opened her eyes, but they were black, someone said from the past.

She blinked, her vision clear.

Flies crawled from between her lips.

She opened her mouth. Nothing but the sour smell of vomit.

Black started to run from under her dress and down her legs.

She glanced down. The wood beneath her bare feet was free of black and blood or anything else that might slip from her body and slide down her legs.

She was a demon.

"Hello," she said to the man, a young scrawny thing with hooded eyes and thin lips, who passed within inches of her.

He ignored her.

A second man, this one larger with the belly of a Buddha and legs like tree trunks, shuffled near.

"Hello?" she said again.

He passed by without so much as a glance.

"Sir," she said to the third, this one older with the bent back and frail legs of one who'd seen decades of work. But, perhaps deaf and exhausted, he, too, ignored her.

She stepped forward, out of the shade.

EIDOLON AVENUE—APARTMENT 1A

The shade followed.

Another step. The shadow kept pace. Tightened its grip. Refused to leave her.

A man stopped to light a cigarette.

"Hello, sir," she said. "Sir?"

The match jumped to life, the flame meeting its target, the man drawing deep before exhaling in a cloud of silver and blue.

"Sir!" she said as she drew close, face to face, the shadow now covering him.

He paused and looked down at the sudden dark staining the dock. And then glanced up at the sun, looking for a cloud that wasn't there.

A moment later, cigarette in hand, he turned and left, quickly moving to join the crowd welcoming a new boat to shore.

They couldn't see her, she realized. Her shadow, this new dark that was now a part of her, had made her invisible. A second step and it followed her again. For a moment, she feared she'd never feel the sun again. And then, remembering the blood pouring between Madame's fingers as they covered her mouth, she pushed the thought out of her mind.

She lifted her arm. It looked muted and pale, like moonlight, the boards beneath almost visible. She flexed her fingers and then made a fist. It felt normal. It all felt normal, save for the dark that would never leave her.

A man watched her.

Standing away from the crowd, he stood dressed in worn denim. Thin and older, a touch of silver to the little tufts of hair clinging to his head, he stared, his eyes shifting to the side as he noticed her looking at him.

Dragging her dark behind her, she marched over.

"Sir," she said, "You can see me? Yes?"

He looked at his sandals, and the dock beneath, and then finally the waves rolling in from the horizon.

"I'm lost," she said. "Is this Hangzhou Bay?"

No response.

"Please," she said. "Help me."

"I know what you are," he said, his eyes refusing her.

"You can see the shadow?"

His eyes still on the horizon, the waves, his brethren pulling the nets and loading the crates, he nodded and then spoke. "I know where this comes from."

"Madame Xuo," she said.

He shook his head. "Madame Xuo is no more."

"I just left her. I work for her and I was with her just—"

"Madame Xuo was found in a doorway near her home over a week ago. She'd been dead for many months. Maybe years."

"And Yin Ying?" she said. "Her servant?"

He shrugged. "All I know is the house is no more. The servants released. The windows shuttered and the doors locked." His eyes met hers. "Do you not know what you are now?"

She shook her head. All around her, men passed by, navigating clear of her shadow as if she was seen, though she knew she was not. "I know I'm not seen. That they don't see me," she said, glancing toward the crowd. "But you see me. Why?"

"It is not a gift. Seeing you is a burden. Knowing what you are is something I don't want. Something no one wants. Go away."

EIDOLON AVENUE—APARTMENT 1A

A man pushing a wheelbarrow of wiggling, snapping, jumping fish stumbled and ducked into her shade, the wheelbarrow coming to the briefest of stops in the dark as he adjusted his grip and righted the wheel.

The wiggling, snapping, jumping stopped, the fish coming to a final rest.

Her reluctant friend stood and moved away, pulling a large knife, the kind used to gut fish, from a holster wound 'round his leg. "I'm sorry," he said as he walked to the edge of the dock to go back to work.

She and her dark followed.

"Wait," she said. "Talk to me. Am I invisible? Can I be seen? What can this do?"

"Were you not told?"

She shook her head.

Standing at the edge of the slapping waves, he spoke. "Then this is new. It can be stopped. If you can, do so now. Save those who will die. Save those mothers and wives and children who will weep because of you. Save all those whose lives will be ruined because you chose to live and breathe and walk among us. End this, here and now, and you can save us all.

"Do you see?" he said as she moved to stand in front of him. "You have a choice." He held the knife out to her. "It is early. You can choose good. You can still do good."

She took the knife.

The dark grew.

"Families will thank you," he said. "Your death will answer prayers they've yet to pray."

She thought of her cursed birth. The cruelty of her parents. Her mother smelling of vomit. And falling into selfish sleep driven by too much drink. Of her father's fingers reaching, grabbing and gripping before pulling her close, too close, to destroy her innocence. She thought of the bend in her back and the burning scream of her muscles as she scrubbed an already spotless floor for the dead Madame Xuo.

A drop of rain slapped the dock. And another. Then another.

She realized that a life without power wasn't one worth living. Always at the mercy of others. Saying "yes" when your body cried "no." Hiding your exhaustion and terror beneath small smiles and low bows. Enduring smacks, slaps and kicks day after day after day.

No. He was right. That wasn't a life she wanted. Not anymore. Perhaps the journey wasn't even worth being blessed by a darkness with an appetite, a hunger, she could almost feel.

She didn't know.

The man watched her, his shirt growing wet from the rain. A rain that fell from a cloud that darkened only them. He took a drag from his cigarette. His eyes narrowed and he nodded.

Her father was in those eyes, that cigarette. Even that nod.

She swallowed her rage and tightened her grip.

It cannot falter, Madame had said. *It cannot fail.*

She thrust the knife deep, slicing in and then up and to the side.

"Go away?" she said, her voice low.

He grabbed her wrist as the blood ran.

"A burden to see?" She dragged the knife down to rip his stomach wider. "And what am I now?" Pulling

EIDOLON AVENUE—APARTMENT 1A

the knife free, the skin parted and his steaming, slippery guts slid free to dangle against his thin waist.

He looked at her and tried to speak, but could no longer catch his breath.

"Your family will thank me," she said.

She could feel her shadow grow.

He tried to blink, to remain awake and present, but his eyes closed.

Her body tingled as the shadow lengthened, reaching wide to cover the dock and darken the waves.

His skin lost its blush and, the soul captured and swallowed, his body collapsed on the dock and tumbled with a splash into the water.

She felt light and free. Powerful. Feared.

She moved to the edge, her eyes on the churning current of Hangzhou Bay.

A moment later, he rose to the surface. A moment after that, dead fish, dozens and dozens and dozens, all trapped in her shade, bobbed to the surface.

Her heart pounded and her breath came in short, shallow gasps. Sweat stained her brow. She wanted to kneel, to rest. But, no, she'd never kneel again.

I'm sorry, she silently said to the stranger caught by the current to bump against the pilings. But your kindness was cruel. It was unnecessary. I no longer have to endure the shame in silence. And now people can pay for their cruelty. They'll have consequences. I will not.

Except for the guilt, Lucky thought. As brief as it was.

There was blood on her hands. Blood that soon disappeared, the shade lifting it from her palms, her wrists. Even from between her fingers and under her nails. Her skin soon so clean it was as if there'd never been a crime.

She smiled.

A life without consequence, the wealthy, powerful woman said from the past.

Closing her eyes, she reached her arms wide, welcoming the dark and willing her shadow to grow and spread, the dock, the water, the boats soon under an umbrella of black.

And the men on the docks started to argue as more fish died and those who were older stumbled and fell and those who were healthy wiped unexpected sweat from their brows and those whose hearts were ruled by superstition fell to their knees to pray as the sudden darkness fell from the blue of a cloudless sky and Lucky the cursed, Lucky the damned, Lucky the unseen and unloved and powerless closed her eyes and allowed herself a small smile of pure satisfaction.

CHAPTER SIX

WEEKS PASSED.

She kept to the alleys and dark corners of Central Shanghai. Silent and still, she'd stand, testing the shadow. Watching its limits, seeing its strength. Encouraging its growth.

She'd watch it move as she did. Watched it stop when she stopped. She'd lift her arms and see it rise. Stretch her arms and watch it widen. She'd push her hands in front of her and grin as it stained the ground at her feet.

It sighed when she wept. It laughed when she smiled. And fed by her frustration and a lifetime of bitter sadness, it strengthened as their shared anger grew.

She learned that, with the move of a hand, she could make the stranger who walked like her father stumble and fall. She learned that, with a simple breath, she could make another stranger, a callous man with cruel eyes like the man from the dock, cough and reach for his throat, his face turning red as he struggled for air.

Week after week, she and the shadow grew closer, their bond deepening, the two becoming one. It became her and she, aware her choice was wrong and could only bring an end she'd regret, still welcomed it without apology.

Whatever price to be paid would be paid.

Later.

What she could not do with the move of a hand or a single breath is kill. To do that, she had to approach and commit the act herself. Trusting she would remain unseen and no consequences would follow, she'd grip the blade of the knife—the one she stole from the dock, of course—and with the smallest of motions slice once across the neck and then watch as the wound opened and wept.

Or stab the base of the skull, quick, and step back while the nameless would stop, fall on bended knees, and then topple forward, their hand pressed to the back of their head as they died in confusion.

Their families will thank me, she'd think, convinced these men were cruel by the lift of their chin or the way they narrowed their eyes. I'm answering prayers they've yet to pray.

For weeks, Lucky did this. Slaughtered, testing her limits and feeding her revenge, safe under the anonymity of her shadow. Killed, never eating, rarely drinking, the shadow giving her what she needed to survive if she would give it what it craved: the experience of a life ending. The shadow relishing the confused panic of these strangers as they realized this was their end. Those final moments of heartbreak and regret for all they were losing. Family, friends, dreams. The sweet simplicity of the stranger's last breath.

She and her shadow grew closer. And she learned.

Sometimes she was seen. When she'd stand at a

store window, hoping to catch a glimpse of her reflection, a stranger would pass and, turning their head, catch sight of the odd girl in the flowered dress and nod. Or in a crowd when someone, a man, sometimes an older man, would stop and, seeing her alone and unloved, offer her a small smile.

Those people she never killed.

But she could be seen. Especially when she was weary and her heart was lonely. With all she knew and all she'd first believed, there were doubts. Perhaps she was not invisible. Perhaps not even invincible. Perhaps she could fail. Or falter. Perhaps she'd reach too far or wide or stab too deep too many times and upset the balance between her dark and their light and the charade would crumble into a world of consequence.

She didn't know. But with Communism taking over Shanghai and having grown tired of killing the nameless for sport, she, like many, fled to Hong Kong where opium ruled and secret societies destroyed their enemies with an iron fist. Where someone with Lucky's gift would be welcomed and respected and perhaps feared.

She soon found herself in the crime infested Mong Kok district. Fruit stands crowded the street. Shops sat behind shuttered windows. The sound of children crying rose from behind closed doors. Somewhere a window broke in a tinkling shatter of glass. A woman shouted and then was silenced with a cruel slap.

From around the corner, as night fell, a young couple appeared. Tourists perhaps, their clothes too clean and their shoes too new for Mong Kok. Their eyes wide with fear, they all but ran down the street.

A breath later, a group of men, all in dark suits and

felt fedoras, followed, bats in hand. A moment after that, quickly circled and trapped, the screams began as the bats raised to bruise flesh and break bone.

After a lifetime of searching, Lucky had finally come home.

CHAPTER SEVEN

"WE NEED TO talk," Evangelical had said, sudden, premature crow's feet creasing the smooth corners as she narrowed her eyes.

On Eidolon below, the crowd had grown. They stood, finding their forms. Heads tilted skyward. Arms hung, the fingers flexing into angry claws. Blood inched from between snarling teeth to spill over lips and drip onto chins.

Inside where it was dry and warm, Lucky stared at Father. "You will call me 'Lucky.'" He sat opposite her, dressed in a suit that shone silver in the grey light of this rainy day, dark glasses resting on the bridge of his sharp nose. He ignored her, pursing his lips as he thought, his cheekbones sharpening as he briefly sucked his cheeks in.

Far from the past in which he'd lived and ruled, the watch on his wrist was still worth the salaries of ten families in Hong Kong. And the sheen of his still black hair, the oil making it look like a helmet squatting on top of his head, spoke of an American influence as did the American cigarette between his fingers.

"Do you remember?" she said to his ghost.

You believed it was ancient

"I said 'You will call me Lucky.'"
and all-powerful.
"I ordered you, of all people, to call me Lucky."
You could walk through life
"And what did you do?"
and destroy
A cool hand pressed to her forehead.
without doubt
"What did I do when?" Evangelical said, her fingers now pressed to Lucky's wrist as she quietly counted her pulse.
or pain.
"And you, Father," Lucky said, ignoring Evangelical. "You sat there and sneered. Looked at me like, what, like some kind of girl. A woman who couldn't kill you with a thought, a look, a simple command. A weak nothing because that's what we were to you, weren't we? Weak, useless girls."

Father sat still. Not speaking, not moving. Not responding.

"But you were wrong," she said as she sat back. "You were wrong and you died because you underestimated me, you stupid old man."

"Are you talking to me?" Evangelical said.

Lucky turned and caught her eye before looking back at the empty chair.

"No," she said, the word slipping out before she could catch it. "To Father."

"Your father."

"Oh no, never," she said, unable to stop herself. "The Father of Mong Kok. In Hong Kong. The Father of everything. He ran everything. In Mong Kok. But I left. Went to Canada, like everyone else. And then

EIDOLON AVENUE—APARTMENT 1A

Paris, East Berlin, Rome. Never went back to Hong Kong. Couldn't go back to Hong Kong. They couldn't make me go back. I wouldn't do it. It wasn't allowed. And I'd never set foot in Mong Kok again, that's for damn sure."

"Mong Kok? China?"

"Yes."

"So, home."

She shook her head, suddenly aware she might have been speaking and then realized, no, she wasn't that stupid. She'd never do that.

Evangelical waited for an answer.

"No, not home," she said.

"Then what is Mong Kok?"

Mong Kok was a land of firsts, Lucky thought. Thought, not spoke, her lips firmly closed. My first serious kill. My first brush with respect. My first taste of the power of terror. The first time someone bowed low to press their face against the concrete in apology rather than feel my wrath. My first realization that I could step from the shadow and be seen and feared and celebrated and applauded. My first fortune. My first . . . well, my first everything.

"Your first everything," Evangelical said. And then she smiled, slow and careful.

"I'm sorry?" Lucky said.

"Your first respect, and power, and realization. Your first fortune. Your first everything, right?"

Lucky stopped. Those had been thoughts. She was sure of it. Private thoughts. And she knew she hadn't spoken them aloud. Had made sure to keep her lips pressed tightly together. Had kept her tongue silent.

But did I? she thought. Had I slipped? Was I

sharing secrets best left unsaid? And if I'd done this now, without knowing it, had it happened earlier? And often? And to whom?

They grew restless on the avenue below.

"Tell me—" She turned to Evangelical.

A line of people faced her, tickets in hand. No longer on Eidolon, she stood in a large room. A cavernous space with a high, ornate ceiling. One of rounded stone, a colorful mural catching the eye. A room with ticket gates and people sitting patiently in rows of chairs and the clip-clop of shoes on polished stone and announcements ringing out over a PA system. The 922 to Dallas at Gate 5. The 482 to Orlando at Gate 3. People rising in response, suitcases in one hand, tickets in the other, ready to navigate their way to a new adventure.

Outside the rain pounded the parking lot with a sudden ferocity.

These were ghosts, Lucky thought. Ghosts I don't know. But ghosts, yes.

Across the room, the glass doors slid open with a whoosh, the stranger coming in seconds later. Blond haired with a round face, his eyes nervous, his knuckles white as he clutched his small suitcase, he stopped, his eyes scanning the gates.

He didn't see her.

Yes, she remembered now. The slip of paper. The picture. The wordless promise that the job would be done soon and done well.

She clutched the blade in her fist, the world falling into a quiet, familiar dark as she called her shadow and her shadow fell. This would be quick. The neck. A long cut. Two inches deep. And then no more. She'd be done.

EIDOLON AVENUE—APARTMENT 1A

"Lucky."

The voice came from behind. And he still stood, her job, waiting. Near, so near. The end of it all so, so near.

"Lucky."

She couldn't escape that voice. That familiar voice that didn't belong in this bus depot at this time when she was getting ready to do this last final thing.

"Lucky," came the voice again, this time a whisper. She turned.

Evangelical stood shaking the rain from her red raincoat, suitcase in hand, the sliding door closing behind her with another whoosh. She did not look at Lucky. She did not call her name. She didn't even see her as she strolled past to wrap her arms around the blond man, cupping his round face with her palms as she looked into his terrified eyes, her lips saying something Lucky couldn't catch.

"Lucky," came the voice again, the Evangelical from the past hugging the Nameless Job while her present fought to regain control.

She closed her eyes. Squeezed them shut. Took a breath, then another, and a third as she steadied the shaking in her hands. Opened her eyes to find herself home on Eidolon.

Evangelical sat near. So near. Her blue eyes watched her from beneath the blonde bangs. "Thought I was losing you, there," she said.

"Did I speak?" Lucky said. "Out loud? About Father and Mong Kok and Hong Kong? Were those words I said? To you?"

"Shush. You're getting worked up over nothing. Now, sit back and close your eyes."

Lucky did just that, her salvation's hand resting on

hers. Breathed in and out. Steadied her heart, quieted her hands and, feeling safe, relaxed.

Soon, the quickest of sleeps came.

Moments later, perhaps many moments later, her eyes opened.

Father sat opposite her, glowing silver in the grey light, his cigarette burning. Madame stood near the window, painted white with thin strokes of black above her eyes, her gaze on the souls crowding Eidolon below. Yin Ying, lopsided and stupid and breathing wet, leaned against the wall.

The whisper in the corner rested, the familiar eyes narrow as it watched.

And Evangelical stood at the front door in the kitchen, suitcase in hand, shaking the blood from her red raincoat.

CHAPTER EIGHT

IN A WAREHOUSE on the outskirts of Hong Kong, Lucky stood, fearless, unapologetic and ready for war.

She'd risen too fast. One of the first women invited to officially join, she'd turned them down. "You work for me," she'd famously said. And she was right. Her shadow made her untouchable. She could say no. She could argue with the Father and the Uncles, as the various leaders of this secret society that ruled Hong Kong and much of mainland China were called.

She could do what she wanted. Ignore tradition and duty. Sit first, sip tea first, stand to leave first. Walk out the door when she wanted. No one, not even the most vicious, the most powerful, could even think of challenging her.

Yet some did.

Years ago an example was made. An example of what could happen if you dared strike Lucky or scream at Lucky or treat Lucky like any other worthless woman. An example that, in hindsight, terrified Lucky herself. One so ominous that it sent a chill down her spine that lingered for years.

Around a table at the back of a restaurant, they sat. Business had been discussed. Apologies for minor infractions offered and accepted. Money exchanged and blessings for good health and much continued success bestowed. The meeting was over and, eager for sleep, Lucky had stood to go.

First.

Not from Hong Kong, it's possible the stranger didn't know who she was. New to Mong Kok, it's understandable he was more than likely unaware of what could and could not be done with Lucky. But, no doubt fortified by the kind of courage found at the bottom of an expensive bottle, he'd stood and screamed and lunged, grabbing her by the shoulder and forcing her to sit. To show respect.

Then he'd slapped her, once, across the face, and laughed.

The room had fallen silent.

It's said he was lifted into the air, his arms held out, his legs forced apart, his head jerked back. It's said he wept and begged and demanded to be let down, to be let go. He was a man, didn't she see?

Though stories varied, it's agreed that the stupid man who'd had too much to drink died the most horrible of deaths. An end so vicious and brutal, the restaurant could never be clean enough to be opened again. They say his skin was stripped by unseen hands and the muscle sliced to dangle like bloodied butterfly wings. Men who had slaughtered for decades stumbled for the doors before violently splashing the sidewalk with sick. Men who believed they'd seen it all found themselves weeping in shock, the brutality of this unforgettable night wounding their souls and chasing them into their dreams.

It was said there were those who were so scarred

EIDOLON AVENUE—APARTMENT 1A

by the savagery of this night that they never slept again.

And all agreed that as her shadow slayed and flayed and butchered, Lucky stood calm and quiet as the blood rained down. And when it was done, when there was nothing left of the drunken fool but strands of ligament and fragments of bone, it is said she walked to the door without a word.

After that, she'd been obeyed. Allowed to do as she pleased when she pleased, she rose through the ranks, yet stayed separate, never answering to anyone but herself. A slip of paper with a name, perhaps a photograph, and the largest of sums deposited into a secret account by Father himself, for only he'd been given that information, and the problem would be dealt with. Always with a knife. Always in public. Always fast. So fast, it's said throats had been slashed by an unseen hand while the victim was in mid-conversation, the wounded only knowing of their approaching death when the blood spilled down their chests.

Having lived a life without consequence, Lucky believed herself invincible.

As she stood in the warehouse facing Father, having not caught the scent of sacred incense in the air or seen the incantations on the floor beneath her feet, she'd yet to realize how very wrong she was.

CHAPTER NINE

In the warehouse, shamans chanted and priests prayed. Scented smoke filled her lungs and somewhere someone was splashing Holy Water. In the shadows, Father and the Uncles stood.

They were trying to take her shadow from her.

It was working.

She couldn't breathe. She couldn't move. She couldn't think clearly enough or quickly enough to fight. Every word they said lifted the dark. Every prayer they prayed peeled the shadow from her flesh. Every mutter and murmur and sigh stripped the shade from her soul.

And it was agony. Her insides clenched. Her skin shrank to the bone. She fell forward, her arms wobbling as they supported her. Her face tensed. As if her eyes were being pulled from their sockets. Her tongue was swelling and her mouth tasted of blood. Her teeth felt like they were being pried from the safety of their homes. Her head was filled with the sound of a great wind, or a great ocean. A keening cry from the earth and the sky as she felt her flesh drawn inward and down and her bones grow cold with an unbearable chill.

EIDOLON AVENUE—APARTMENT 1A

"You are nothing now," Father was saying. He stood, cigarette in hand. Safely tucked outside the circle where the priests knelt and the shamans bowed and those anonymous men who bent low, their faces to the ground, clutched burning sticks of incense in their fists, he watched.

She tried to move again. She failed.

"You believed it was ancient and all-powerful?" Father said. "You thought it would have no weakness? That it could destroy without doubt or pain?"

Lifting her head, she blinked, searching for him.

All she saw were robed silhouettes surrounding her.

Fight, she silently said to her dark. We can't lose.

It gathered strength, clinging to her. Wrapping so tightly around her skin, it turned her bones to ice.

The prayers increased, the water splashed, and the shadow lost its hold again, slipping further away.

She wanted to weep, but didn't have the strength.

"You have much to answer for," Father said.

I will give you anything, she silently said. If you can fight, if we can win, if we can leave and escape, I will give you anything. Anything for as long as you want.

It returned, swooshing in, gathering strength as it burrowed into her center.

Yes, she thought. Take from me what you will.

Her insides lurched. She was sure she was going to die then. The pain was too immense. It was too much. She could feel the end coming. It felt light. Like the most gentle of breezes could simply lift her away into the sky, into the air, into the night.

She couldn't swallow. Her throat was too tight. She couldn't breathe.

They'd come closer, the shamans and priests and strangers. Seeing their success in her struggle, they'd grown confident her end was near.

They were wrong.

It moved up her spine, the dark. Stripped from her what it needed as it rummaged through her body and dug into her flesh and stomped on her bones.

She fell, her arms giving out.

They stood above her. Holy water splashed and incense smoked and useless words from stupid men did nothing to quiet the anger her shadow was now feeling.

She rose, lifting on her elbows.

They drew back.

A moment later, it began.

Thrown and tossed, the shamans landed against the wall with a sickening crunch. The priests, those who ran, were tripped, their legs shattering with a crack before their skulls were crushed, the blood shooting from their noses and bursting from their ears and splashing from their mouths.

"Not Father," she said, her voice a hoarse whisper.

The other priests, those who prayed, knowing they'd failed and their ends were near, fell forward, the backs of their heads sinking under the weight of unseen footsteps that stomped and crushed.

The doors had locked, so the Uncles could not escape. This was who she looked for now. The callous men who would rather enrage an ancient evil than see a woman with power.

Let them die.

And make it hurt.

Jaws were stretched until they popped and split.

EIDOLON AVENUE—APARTMENT 1A

Eyes were plucked from skulls and necks twisted until they snapped. Bodies fell and blood ran and Father stood, untouched, in the middle of the carnage.

Lucky could breathe again. She flexed her fingers. The tightness had eased. The pain had ebbed. She rose to her knees. The agony of her shifting insides had lessened. She put the heels of her hands to her eyes and took another breath. All around, men cried and screamed and begged as they fell. The most powerful leaders of The Triad being slaughtered in the space of an evening.

This would make her infamous. And untouchable.

Taking her hands from her eyes, she scanned the room for Father.

He stood weeping.

She rose and stumbled toward him. Found her feet heavy and her steps slow and thick. A living skeleton lurching its way toward the pitiful man who waited in a sea of steaming red.

Seeing her, he fell to his knees.

The Father on his knees, she thought. She allowed herself a smile.

She'd won.

"Beg." Her voice was almost too quiet and no longer her own.

"Please," he said, his hands clasped to his face. "It was to save you. It was only to save you. You don't know—"

"Save me?" She felt weak, her head too light. She couldn't catch her breath. She feared she'd faint.

His hand was on her, helping her. She sank to her knees. His palms, gentle and soft, held her face. "Lucky, there is much about this you don't know. We only wanted to take it from you."

"But you said—"

"What was said was to it, not you."

She looked at him. Looked into his eyes.

There was no malice there.

I've made a mistake, she thought. A horrible mistake. And not just here, with this. She looked around at the flat skulls leaking red and grey. The chunks of flesh and bits of bone. The fathers and sons and husbands and lovers who lay twisted and torn, their eyes open, their mouths silenced mid-scream. But a mistake with the Madame, as well. The tea. Those seven sips. Welcoming this unknown dark in exchange for strength.

It was wrong.

"I'm sorry," she said. "I didn't . . . " She stopped, the enormity of this massacre too great for mere words. She grabbed Father's hand. "It can't be taken from me. You know that, yes? It needs to, I know, but . . . " She fell quiet as a silent fist punched through her chest, grabbed her guts and twisted, taking her breath away.

Father was speaking, but she couldn't catch the words. The ocean was in her ears again and a great wind rushed through her head.

"Father," she tried to say, but her tongue was too thick, her teeth pulling, her throat swelling. "I'm sorry. Please—"

"Lucky," he all but shouted. He was gripping her face. Shaking her. "Lucky."

She lifted her head and looked at him.

A shadow fell over his face.

His eyes turned red and blood bubbled from his mouth to run down his chin.

EIDOLON AVENUE—APARTMENT 1A

"What have you done?" were the last words he said as the dark tore her away from him.

And as Father fell, she was dragged back across the floor, pulled across the room, through the shattering glass of a window, down the street and up, up, up into the sky, into the air, into the night, sleep coming as the world grew cold and the black of the ocean spread beneath her, Father's worry echoing in her mind, again and again.

What have I done?

CHAPTER TEN

THIS WAS IN PARIS.

"She was small," they'd say. "Chinese or Japanese. Asian, definitely. I think."

"Her hair was sort of dark, maybe," the other witness would remember, the officer jotting the useless tidbit down.

"Was she younger? Older?" he'd say, pen in hand. "What age range would you say she was? Any idea?"

A shrug.

Twenty years after Hong Kong, twenty years after the leaders of The Triad had fallen in one fell swoop, twenty years after Lucky had entered the warehouse a victim and emerged a legend, she'd become the woman seen, but never remembered.

"Yes, it was a woman," one witness after another would say before stopping in confusion. "But I just can't . . . I don't . . . " and they'd give up, unable to clearly recall the assassin who'd stabbed and sliced and slaughtered in broad daylight.

Back in Hong Kong, the Triad was in chaos. Uncles on mainland China, in Canada, even in the United States and as far away as Eastern Europe were all angling to be Father now, everyone at the mercy

EIDOLON AVENUE—APARTMENT 1A

of bloody plots and cruel schemes and dangerous plans.

"I can't go back," she said to the dark from her new home. She'd woken to find herself in Toronto, in Canada, far from those who'd try to kill her on sight. "It was wrong, killing Father. I loved him. I miss him. He protected me." The dark moved. Pulled close to her. "He protected everyone. Without him, more blood will spill, more lives will be ruined. Brother will fight brother and father will kill son."

She closed her eyes and swallowed the regret sneaking up her throat.

A life without consequence?

What other lies had she been told? she thought.

The shadow wrapped around her. Cursed with a never-ending appetite, it was hungry. Knowing her reality, she knew what she had to do.

From her one bedroom apartment, she put out feelers to judge the situation. Learned she was no longer just Lucky, but something more, the carnage in the warehouse solidifying the myth already surrounding her. Within days, discreet introductions were arranged and silent agreements made. Lucky the Legend quickly became Lucky the Killer, Lucky the Devil, Lucky the Shadow.

Politicians eager to assassinate an opponent. Corporations desperate to kill the genius behind a rival patent. Greedy families hungry for more even if it meant wiping out the older generation. Anyone wanting a kill that was clean and quick.

For the right price, Lucky would do it.

And the shadow would feast.

Stepping out of invisibility, she chose to cloak

herself with the dark when she struck. Seen, but not seen was more exciting. More of a challenge. The details of her and her crime growing fuzzy, like a half-remembered dream, the more it was thought about and shared. Only the basics captured and recorded.

The authorities around the world forever on the lookout for a woman with two eyes, a mouth, a nose, two arms and legs, and darkish hair of indeterminate length.

She made a fortune.

For ten years, she ruled from her one bedroom in Toronto, leaving for bloody East Berlin when she grew bored and restless. Rome, London, Zurich, Amsterdam followed. An endless parade of butchered bodies and broken dreams trailing her as she, the assassin no one could see, stole away unnoticed and anonymous.

Her ledger in the black, always in the black, she then came to Paris where she settled.

And then stopped.

"My name is Samuel," he'd said. She'd taken his hand in hers and, together, navigated their way through the puddles dotting the rue Mazarine near Boulevard Saint-Germaine. He was Swiss. German Swiss, to be exact. "Dinner?" he'd said. She'd nodded. "A walk?" She'd smiled and agreed. More dinners followed. Phone calls and meetings. Laughter over afternoon cups of coffee. Shared smiles and lingering looks.

His scalp was smooth, his brilliance evident and unapologetic, and his voice could calm her with a single word. He stood tall and straight, offered easy smiles and patient approval, and had a touch that took her breath away.

EIDOLON AVENUE—APARTMENT 1A

"I love you," she said as they strolled the Seine. He smiled, his lips pressing close to linger on her cheek.

"Leave him be," she said to the shadow. The shadow paused.

"He is precious," she said as, bouquet in hand, she walked the hall to the judge who would pronounce them man and wife. The shadow stirred.

"What will it take to give him a long life in peace?" she said as she watched her beloved sleep, the comforter brought to his chin. "Whatever is needed, it's yours."

Two months later, the first child was taken from her womb.

CHAPTER ELEVEN

SHE COULDN'T STOP crying. The tears trailed down her cheeks and onto her chin, the tissue soaked and useless from wiping her nose.

"There will be other chances, yes?" Samuel said in his heavily accented English. He kneeled in front of her, his hand calmly stroking her thigh as she sat on the edge of the bed. "And if no, then, perhaps an adoption could be best, I think, no?"

Lucky shook her head. No. No children. She would never risk it. The seven children the shadow had stolen over the past four years hadn't been enough. She could feel it. The dark wanted something more. Something rich with experience.

Simple death isn't what fed this ravenous dark. It savored surprise and regret. The awareness of the end approaching. The panic growing as the limbs became weak and the vision clouded. The overwhelming stillness of the eternal silence as the world grew quiet. The darkness demanded tears, confusion, dread. The last moments of a life lived.

A child who was still safely in a womb, who'd yet to take its first breath, couldn't give that. It couldn't offer the experience the shadow was craving. A fetus

EIDOLON AVENUE—APARTMENT 1A

hadn't laughed and loved, discovered and cherished. It felt no loss when its soul was swallowed. Or at least not enough to satisfy an appetite eager for the succulent sweetness of final despair.

She'd been a wife for five years now. Lucky the Killer, Lucky the Devil, Lucky the Shadow was now Lucky the Cook, Lucky the Dishwasher, Lucky the Doting Wife and Eager Lover.

She would never be Lucky the Mother. And that was fine. As long as her beloved was safe.

Something told her he was not.

Drawing the sleeves of her cardigan down to her wrists, she pulled him in and held him close. "It's okay," she said. "I have you and that's enough."

He answered with a kiss.

"Brandy?" he said over his shoulder as he walked to the other room.

"Yes, in a minute. I'll be right there."

She stood and closed the door behind him and then removed her pants. In her cotton underwear, she walked to the side table by her bed and opened the drawer. A moment later, the small blade in hand, she closed the bathroom door behind her and sat on the edge of the tub, her feet on smooth white porcelain.

No more children, she said silently to her shadow. I will give you this and only this. I know it isn't much. I know you want more. But this flesh will be a taste until . . . well, until it is enough.

She held her foot in her hand and sliced the flesh from between her toes and along the instep. Bandaged and wrapped, Samuel never noticed her wounds if she wore socks, which she always did. Besides, the pain was bearable if it kept the dark distracted enough to prevent it from hurting him.

The slivers of skin held in the palm of her hand, her feet bleeding onto the white porcelain, she watched as the dark fell and the flesh disappeared.

Somewhere Madame was smiling. Somewhere Madame, who had warned her of a life without consequence, was nodding her head and laughing. Somewhere the little Lucky who'd been foolish enough to take seven small sips was stopping at three and welcoming death while the brazier glowed and Yin Ying slobbered and a dragon finally caught its tail.

Somewhere there was a Lucky who wasn't suffocating under horrible secrets.

"Here," she said as she pressed her palm to her mouth to quiet her sobs, her cheeks growing wet again. "This is all I have. This is all I am."

And the darkness drank her tears.

Samuel slept. The newspaper on his lap, the empty tumbler of brandy on the side table, he snored in the flickering light of the TV.

Outside, the moon sat high. The gentle swoosh of cars passing below stole through the open window along with the breeze, a hint of autumn in the chill and the scent of impending rain. Outside, Paris gently welcomed a quiet night.

Lucky stood in her underpants. She didn't remember leaving the bathroom. She didn't remember walking through the bedroom to open the door. She didn't remember walking down the hall and discovering Samuel here, asleep.

EIDOLON AVENUE—APARTMENT 1A

She didn't remember choosing to bring the blade.

Later, she wouldn't remember approaching her beloved and watching his chest rise and fall as he dreamt. She wouldn't remember lifting the knife. Or her hand, not her own, slicing his throat once, long and deep. She wouldn't remember him waking. Or realizing he'd been wounded. Discovering the gash and seeing the blood on his hand. Looking at her with such a look of exquisite sadness it punched through her fog and ripped her back into reality.

On those nights when the pain was greatest, she'd almost remember the bubbles of blood gushing from the cut as she pressed on the wound. Almost remember him trying to speak. To tell her he loved her. And ask her

Why? Why this? Why me? What have you done? Why?

On those nights when the agony was so relentless she begged for death, she'd torture herself with the memory of kissing him as he slipped away. The sticky warmth of the blood on his hand as his fingers gripped her hair.

And when the foundation of her delusion would crack and the guilt would rise like rancid sick, the warmth of that last sigh against her lips is what she'd punish herself with. His eyes, his kind, gentle eyes, losing focus as the end came.

She knew she could not speak. She knew she could not move. She knew there was a moment, a brief moment, that night when the thought of stabbing her stomach, in and then up and to the side, seemed logical and right. But the knife had been taken, the shadow insisting she feed it with the sharp misery of endless mourning.

She was not there, she'd insist to herself. This wasn't what she wanted to do, she'd cry. This killed me, she'd scream.

What she said was

"Make me forget. Him. This. All of this. Give me sleep and when I wake, I no longer feel. I'm dead. Make me dead. Inside. Do that and you will get what you want."

And forever broken and no longer strong enough to fight, she sank next to Samuel's chair and, too wounded for tears, allowed the shadow to lift and carry her into the deepest of sleeps.

CHAPTER TWELVE

"I STILL REMEMBER," Lucky said before taking a long drag from her Echo, the hungry ghosts swarming Eidolon below. "You lied because I still remember."

She'd fled Paris for America. Had given the dark what was promised. Fed its hunger. Had felt nothing, but still had dreams, nightmares, thoughts. Could still see her husband in tenuous shafts of light or the corners of steamy mirrors. Could almost catch his name when she first woke or when exhaustion forced her to stop and think and consider. The guilt was growing. The regret was strong. Had she the chance, the choice, to do it all again, she . . .

But no.

The thought was banished.

A year ago, she'd settled on Eidolon. Soon thereafter, her shadow grew silent. Its hunger no longer drove her. Her ledger black, she could breathe easy.

She glanced at the seething mass of vitriol clogging the street below. It stretched from curb to curb, one end to the other. Their bodies, torn and gashed and trembling, reaching as far as the eye could see.

"And where is your dark?" Evangelical said. She

stood in the doorway, shaking the rain from her coat. Then fast, too fast, she was in the chair, tea in hand. In the kitchen she now was, her arm shoved deep in a cupboard. Then gone, the lock turning as she let herself in. Then, again, in the chair, her hand reaching to press against Lucky's forehead, concerned her charge was running a fever. It was too fast. The past rushing, bleeding into the present. All of it too fast.

Lucky turned away to look out the window, her head confused and light and swimming. There were so many, she thought. So many dead. "I couldn't have killed you all," she said, her voice a whisper.

And below, in the rain, the crowd parting like the Red Sea, she appeared, her blonde hair bouncing, groceries in hand, her coat shining and wet. A moment later, the key turned in the lock.

Lucky took a breath and turned back.

"You didn't." Her salvation stood in front of her in a bloody red raincoat, past giving way to present. And this wasn't fast. This was real. With a smile, she plopped down in the chair, the red running down the shoulder, across the lapels and wandering along the seam before dripping onto the carpet. "We need to talk."

Lucky looked toward the strip of concrete below.

"You won't find your answer down there," the blonde said. "And, no, you didn't have to kill them all. For some, the death of those they loved was enough. Those wounds never heal. You know that."

Swallowing fast and hard, Lucky squeezed her eyes shut. Samuel came. Snoring in the chair. The empty tumbler of brandy. The newspaper folded open and resting on his stomach. The strips of skin offered and

EIDOLON AVENUE—APARTMENT 1A

accepted in the private hell of her bathroom. But not enough. Never enough. The blood bubbling from his throat as he tried to say

Why?

"Have you ever wondered where your dark went?" Evangelical, still in her bloody raincoat, leaned forward, elbows on her knees. "Didn't it seem odd that, after so many years of holding you tight, it'd suddenly let go?"

Lucky shook her head and shrugged. She reached between the cushions of her chair for her cigarettes.

"And them, down there," her salvation said with a nod toward the window. "Why there? And why now?"

Lucky ignored her.

Her heart thumping, she retrieved the cigarettes from between the cushion and the arm of the chair. "The blood," she said as she fought to steal the last smoke from the pack, her eyes on the window. "On your coat. Tell me."

"You really don't know, do you?"

She looked at Evangelical and then shook her head.

"The dark can't get to you here. Whatever's here, whatever is in this ground or crouching over this building, it's much stronger than your dark. Whatever's here is ancient. Relentless. So your dark can't get to you. It can't reach you or touch you." She smiled. A slow grin that crept from ear to ear. "But we can get you. We can reach you and touch you."

Evangelical grabbed Lucky's shoulder and, gripped tight, forced her to turn, to face her. "So why in the hell would I *tell* you why there's blood on my coat?" she said, her lips rising in a snarl. Her face was smeared red, blood soaked strands of blonde sticking to her cheeks and her forehead. "I'm showing you."

She grabbed Lucky's head between her hands and squeezed. "You're here, you can't get away and the time, finally, is right. I've waited forever for this. And I'm showing you."

The bus depot. Lines of people, tickets in hand. The rain pounding the pavement outside. The stone ceiling arching high above.

The last kill. The last job. The nameless blond man with the round face and thin lips. The one with the look of terror in his eyes and the knuckles clenched white. Evangelical, a younger Evangelical, happy and light as she strode through the swoosh of the sliding glass doors swinging her suitcase.

Memories. New memories.

The shadow called. The shadow falling. The world growing just dark enough. The people, those navigating their way to gates, tickets in hand, slowing and stopping. The quiet coming as time ceased. Evangelical and Bobby Lee—of course it was her brother Bobby Lee—frozen in a final embrace.

Lucky looked around.

The ghosts of Eidolon surrounded her. They'd found their forms. Heads with bullet holes in temples and throats slit wide sat on shoulders. Torn lips bled as they stretched into spiteful grins or angry sneers. Eyes awash in tears blinked and narrowed and stared. Men, women, children. Infants. Old and young and all the colors of the human rainbow, they stood watching her.

There is a price . . .

Father appeared as did Yin Ying.

A price that must be paid

The stranger from the dock, his intestines in hand, joined them.

EIDOLON AVENUE—APARTMENT 1A

when your life,
Madame Xuo, perfect, polished and as pale as moonlight, stepped forward.
this life,
And the whisper, the familiar whisper, moved from the dark and into the light.
comes to its close.
Lucky wanted to speak, but the lump in her throat stole her words.

Gates were called. People moved. Luggage was carried or rolled behind on wheels that jumped and squeaked. The low rumble of living conversation returned to echo off the walls. The ghosts were gone. Evangelical stood, Bobby Lee's hands cupping her face.

Before she knew it, she had moved behind him. Before she could stop it, the knife had slashed and sliced. Before she could catch her breath, Bobby Lee had turned and, seeing nothing but dark, turned back.

This was when Evangelical had screamed.

Lucky had forgotten.

Bobby Lee had fallen, his hand to his throat. The red sloshed between his fingers as he gripped Evangelical's arm, then her shoulder, and finally her neck as he pulled himself up and out and away from the pain. She sobbed in disbelief. And knowing it was useless, she screamed.

She lifted her head and looked right at Lucky.

"I see you," she said, her voice rising to a shout. "I SEE YOU!"

And then she stopped. The world stopped. Bobby Lee lay dying. Evangelical's face red and streaked with grief, her eyes dazed and in shock as they looked at her.

Strangers, confused and shocked, trapped as they stood, or bent, or kneeled to help.

"That's the moment that killed me, Lucky."

She turned to find Evangelical sitting in the chair. The bus depot was gone as were the rows of chair, the crackling of the PA system. The cup of Lipton balanced on her knees again, Eidolon had returned.

Four—Father, Madame, the man from the dock, and the ghost from the corner—remained, standing shoulder to shoulder.

Evangelical took a small sip. "I was done after that. You didn't need to stab me. You didn't need to kill me. My Bobby Lee dying in my arms was enough. The fear, the desperation, in his eyes. It was enough.

"No," she said, placing the tea on the low table between them. The one with the warped middle, the steaming pots and the small plates of funeral food. "It was not enough. It was too much. It would have been easier if you'd stabbed me. Would have saved me weeks of sobbing. Of suffering a pain so great I'd howl with grief. An agony that had no end and no answer. It would have saved me overdosing.

"And that would have saved my father discovering his only child, his last child, face down in her own puke. It would have saved my family the nightmare of burying me on a beautiful summer day." She stopped, her hand rising to lay flat against her forehead, the imagined cool of her palm perhaps calm and comforting. "And maybe, just maybe, my folks would have lived their last year in peace instead of pain. Maybe, just maybe, he wouldn't have turned the gun on her and then himself. Maybe, just maybe, there would have been a happy ending. That's what

EIDOLON AVENUE—APARTMENT 1A

they deserved, you know, my parents. A happy ending."

"I'm sorry," Lucky said.

"Really?" Evangelical said. "You're sorry? Your cruelty caused ripples, Lucky. Ripples that became waves. Waves of sorrow that destroyed souls and shattered lives. That robbed people of happiness. Saying 'I'm sorry' does nothing, absolutely nothing, for that." She leaned forward, her elbows on her knees. Her blue eyes blinked from beneath her blonde bangs. "There are no words that can wipe the red from that ledger. And you know that."

"So I die," Lucky said, her hands trembling, the cigarette still unlit.

"Here." Evangelical plucked it from Lucky's hand, shoved it in her mouth and, lighting it, handed it back to her. "It's your last one, isn't it? Enjoy."

Lucky took a long drag, her eyes on The Four waiting.

"Come," her salvation said as she stood, her hand out to her. Lucky rose to join her. They went to the window.

"Death is too easy for you," Evangelical said, her breath warm on Lucky's cheek as she stood behind her, her arms wrapped around Lucky's chest, her chin resting on Lucky's shoulder. "To stab you, or slay you, or flay you, well, what does that do?"

They grew restless below. Ambled toward the building. Their bodies colliding as they fought each other to reach the wall and crawl toward the window and press against the glass.

She moved away from Evangelical. Crept behind the chair, her hands gripping the back. Madame stepped forward to stand next to Evangelical. As did Father, and the man from the docks, the ghost from the corner joining them. The Four now Five, they watched her.

Lucky closed her eyes as she took another drag, sucking the smoke deep, the Echo reduced to a cylinder of glowing ash.

She opened them.

The walls were red. And they stood tall, Evangelical, Father, the man from the docks and the ghost from the corner. Shoulder to shoulder, they waited and watched. Everything was tall. And narrow. Lucky felt strange. Her skin was moving, her insides shifting. She licked her lips and found her tongue was thick. She felt like she wanted to kneel, or lay, her legs feeling weak and small.

"The Nameless Dead need more than that, Lucky," Evangelical was saying as the light turned dusty crimson. "Every cut, every slice. Every tear and sob and cry. Something quick and simple comes nowhere near to repaying that debt."

The four of them were now so tall, it was as if she was lying beneath them, their faces looking down on her. And her body was nothing but pain. Aches and creaks, pops and cracks. A relentless wave of tense muscle and burning flesh and breaths that were much too quick and much too shallow.

"A life without consequence has a price," Evangelical said.

The shadow came. Spread itself across Lucky. The sudden heat followed by an almost unbearable chill laying flat against her flesh to sink into her bones.

Yes, Lucky thought. Take me. Save me. I'm yours.

EIDOLON AVENUE—APARTMENT 1A

A breath later, it was gone. Lucky looked up to see it slip down the hall, up the walls and along the ceiling, spreading wide to stretch from side to side as it stood tall before collapsing into a skeleton still wrapped in expensive gold, the silk rustling as the dark burrowed underneath.

Something bumped against Lucky. She turned to look.

She knew that face. She'd loved that face.

Oh god no.

Twisted and stretched, he crawled next to her, his arms missing, his feet beginning at the hip, his flesh torn and scraped and bleeding.

"I'm sorry, Samuel," she tried to say, but the words wouldn't come, her teeth too big for her mouth and her tongue too clumsy and thick.

This wounded thing no longer the ghost hissing

Lucky the Killer, Lucky the Devil, Lucky the Shadow

from the corner, he inched along the floor, seven sleeping lumps, her aborted beloved, wiggling from his naked spine, the skin parted and peeled, as they suckled his flesh.

Hearing her, and then seeing her, he lunged, his teeth bared. They sunk into her shoulder, driven by the endless anger of a love betrayed. His razor-sharp teeth tore the flesh and chewed the muscle, his body growing plump as he feasted on her guilt.

She screamed and tried to get away. But she couldn't move.

The angry Nameless Dead drew near, a pile

three hundred thousand deep

worming her way in a line

four miles long.

At the end of the hall, Madame's skeleton carefully stood. In the dusty red light, Lucky could see the flesh grow. Pale and white, it slithered from the bone and snapped around her limbs, reaching up to her neck and the smooth of her skull. The kimono fell and rose as the darkness pumped fetid air into her dry lungs. Fingers stretched. The head circled on the neck. Hands rose to find the black wig with the high bun still on the head and turned it, adjusted it, made sure it was sitting just so.

A moment later, the eyes opened to blink and look around and see. The moment after that, the chin quivered, the long fingers rising to press against her dried, peeling lips.

A door opened, Yin Ying soon lumbering toward Madame Xuo the Living. The favored servant approached the woman and whispered in her ear. The tears came then, Madame's face trembling as Yin Ying took her by the arm and, together, turned with her to walk down the hall, the throng swarming them. Ravenous teeth champing at their ankles. Arms thumping their calves. Yellowing nails scratching their flesh, the beads of blood shoved into slobbering mouths to be licked and sucked and savored. Sightless eyes on slimy faces turning, their noses lifting to catch the scent of hope, of freedom, that waited outside the hall.

Madame and Yin Ying reached the door.

It opened.

"Wait." Throwing her one arm forward, Lucky, legless and wounded, struggled to pull herself forward, her fingernails scratching wood. Samuel clamped to

EIDOLON AVENUE—APARTMENT 1A

her shoulder, her seven aborted beloved wandering along her back to stab and dig and burrow beneath the flesh, pulling her skin back to suckle the naked bone of her spine, she watched Madame as she, Yin Ying and the dark moved through the door, slipping free from this seething storm of endless torment.

―

They say the house still stands somewhere in the middle of modern Shanghai. They say that Madame Xuo, now very old, sits, silent and never seen, still sipping a brew as old as China itself, shadowed by a servant who stands too tall, walks too heavy, and offers slow dangerous smiles from a lopsided face.

And, it's said, trapped behind the walls of an infamous room of red panels and splintered wood, live dangerously unlucky souls, forever haunted by their sins, their blinded eyes and broken bodies on an incessant search for a freedom always out of reach.

Much like the dragon whipping along the baseboards chasing a tail it'll never catch.

APARTMENT 1B

BULLET

Monday, 3:24 PM

Five blue. Seven red. Four yellow.

He blinked the sleep from his eyes. Lifted his head from the mattress. Saw the shit hole on Eidolon Avenue he called home. The TV with the cracked screen sitting on the plastic crate. The yellowing walls with the rust colored streaks running from ceiling to floor. The scattered pizza boxes and cheeseburger wrappers. And his friends . . .

five blue, seven red, four yellow

sitting on the cheap ass coffee table.

That's right, he thought. They were all there.

Five blue. Seven red. Four yellow.

He stretched and turned to the window. Kicked the sheet away from his legs. It was raining. And late.

Fuck.

Hated that job anyway.

And FUCK his foot hurt.

He sat up and turned his leg.

What the fuck?

A new tat. A snake. A small snake. A fuckin' cartoon-ass fuckin' garden snake or something. Some punk ass shit a prom queen flyin' on Molly would get before getting fingered in the back of some quarterback's Chevy.

And it wasn't even good work. It sat above his ankle bone like, what the hell, two inches long maybe? Not very thick. Lines sloppy. Mouth closed. No fangs.

Straight and lifeless and fuckin' boring. And the coloring was all fucked up. It was sorta green, but . . . fuck me, yellow? Kinda yellow-green-blue? Who the fuck knew.

He could do better work while shaking off a five day binge. Hell, he'd done better work shaking *from* a five day binge.

And fuckin' hell, I'm on one now, he thought as his guts clenched.

He fell back on the mattress and closed his eyes. Didn't remember getting that tat. Didn't remember much. Last night a blur. Yesterday a blur. Day before that and maybe before that, all of it a fuckin' mess of random shit. He thought of stretching, then realized his body hurt too much. That he was too tired. And his mouth tasted like funk and fuck and pussy and shit. And the tat felt fresh. It still itched. Still kinda hurt. More than usual. Like a fresh sunburn that'd just been smacked or something.

Fuck. If he had someone, someone special or something, he'd feel better. Probably. They'd help. Or at least talk with him. Help him figure out what the fuck was up. Who the fuck knew? Maybe not.

Whatever. Damn bitches were never worth the trouble.

Shit, his head was fucked. What day was it? It'd been morning and then night. He remembered. And . . . ah shit, man. Think.

Right. He'd left Eidolon really early. Yeah. Not yesterday. The day before? Shit, no clue. There'd been pancakes. At some dive. Sat near the door. Dined and dashed. That's what you did when you were flat-ass broke. That, and had a mouth that tasted like funk and

EIDOLON AVENUE—APARTMENT 1B

fuck and pussy and shit. 'Cause you did that, too, when you were flat-ass broke.

"One fifty," the small, scrawny dude with the spike through his nose had said. "It's final, Bullet. You ain't gettin' shit done until we get our one fifty, capice?"

Capice this, dickwad, he'd wanted to say. But he'd counted back from ten. Everything was cool if he could fuckin' count back from ten.

He'd gone to the tat shop. Later. Yeah, that felt right. After the pancakes.

"You're flyin', alright?" Spike had said. "Come the fuck back down to earth, man, and get us our money, capice?" And then he'd crossed his skinny-ass arms across his fuckin' Metallica tee like he was ready to throw down or something.

Punk ass poser.

His knuckles hurt. He opened his eyes and held his hand in front of his face.

Yeah, he'd punched something. Fingers scraped. Knuckles swollen. Black and blue and sorta yellow and, fuck me, red? Broken? He flexed his fingers. Nah, this was a wood punch, not concrete. Not flesh or bone. Wood.

"It's shit," he'd screamed at Spike, his fists clenched. Fuck counting back from ten. "It's fucking shit, man. I just want it fixed. It'll take two fuckin' seconds!"

Spike had held his hands up. Dude looked scared. Fuckin' petrified. "Come down, man, and then—"

"I'M DOWN." Pow.

Right. The counter. He'd broken their counter. Cracked that fucker right down the middle. Heard the damn thing snap, everyone in the shop stopping what they were doing to look over.

Shit, yeah.

He smiled.

He'd left then. Or they'd thrown him out. Makes more sense. Took a piss on the wall around the corner. Some bitch with a stick up her ass rushing by and clicking her tongue. Some dude standing near fake texting while taking too long a look.

Whatever.

"I just want it fixed," he'd yelled. His body was a canvas, you know? It was art. Fuckin' tats were his life. Everything was inked. Legs, arms, head, neck, back, thighs, whatever. Everything had something on him. And when he added some new shit, it had to look right. Blend in. Make sense. Be the right size. Right dimensions. Sit on the skin right. Be the right fuckin' colors.

Red wasn't just red, you know? There were shades of red. But this new shit? It wasn't right. They'd fucked it the fuck up. This red, right here, it was more brick than blood. It was too soft and orange, or something. The devil's eyes had to pop. He wanted them to pop. With blood.

Fuck it. Whatever.

"Cool tats," she'd said. It was afternoon. Late afternoon. The sun wasn't as bright. The shadows were long. And the shop had tossed his ass out. Went around the corner to take a leak and then puke the pancakes up by a dumpster.

Shitty stomach couldn't keep anything down these days.

"Cool tats." Those were the first words from the girl with the forked tongue. "I'm Eve." She'd stood near, her eyes sleepy and dark.

EIDOLON AVENUE—APARTMENT 1B

"Of course you are," he remembered saying. He wished he had a mint.

Coming closer, she'd dragged her thumb through the puke along his bottom lip. Stuck it in her mouth. Sucked and then smiled.

Fuck yeah. Twisted chicks. Love 'em.

"I do tats," she'd said. Goth chick with a Daddy's Girl Gone Bad vibe. Hair fifty shades of black. Bangs chopped with a razor. Big eyes rimmed with black. Skin whiter than rich kid coke. Dark blue smeared on her lips. Metal in her ears, nose, chin. Her small bright teeth chewing dollar store blue from her stubby nails.

Tiny and thin, her nipples poking from a thin tank that ended right below her tits, she stood there with a skirt the size of a band aid and legs like a fuckin' Halloween skeleton. The kind you'd stick in your yard and take down right before Thanksgiving. Only this one wore thick blue socks and battered combat boots.

What he wouldn't give to see those boots up by her fuckin' ears.

"You do tats?" His stomach had moved again.

"Yeah."

"Where?"

"Where do you want it?" She took the fingers from her mouth and stuck 'em down the front of her skirt.

He puked.

"Fuck that shit," he said as he turned over and pushed his face into the mattress. The rest was just dark. Clouds and confusion. Walking nowhere. Talking about nothing. The feel of her arm around his waist last night. Her thin hair in his fist as she gripped his cock through his faded jeans. The sound of sirens. The whirling flash of red in the dark. The chill in the air.

His face hot. His bones cold. His muscles seizing. His heart racing. The air like knives stabbing his lungs as he tried to breathe. Trying to act like everything was okay when he knew something was very wrong.

"It might rain," he'd said as she pulled him onto Eidolon Avenue.

It's cold, his mother said.

Shut the fuck up, man, he thought as he turned and pushed his face into the sheets. Thought of his five, seven, four friends waiting nearby. Thought of her.

He'd fought to focus that night, the fuckin' lock on the fuckin' door moving as he'd tried to shove the fuckin' key in.

Don't get sick.

"It might rain," he said again to the dark.

"It will."

"What?" He tried to look at Eve, but she felt far away. And there was a group of people on the other side of the street just standing there looking at him. The sight of them, it dug into his guts. They weren't doing anything, but, fuck me, the fact that they were *there* was wrong. His eyes stung with tears. There was a lump in his throat. His heart was gonna beat out of his chest. I don't want to die, he said to himself. He stopped.

Die? Fuck, man. Chill.

She'd waited, the key turning in the lock, the dented metal door opening with a shove. They walked down the hall and up the stairs to his first floor apartment, her arms still around him. She smelled of piss and old sweat and some hippie shit. Patchouli maybe? Probably. How could he not notice that?

It made his stomach move. Again.

EIDOLON AVENUE—APARTMENT 1B

Fuck. He pushed himself away from the mattress. He needed to get up.

―――※―――

Flies circled an island of shit and toilet paper and puke floating in an ocean the color of dark piss. The toilet was plugged. Had been for weeks. Some bitch snorting coke like an '80s college kid. Blonde and thin. Too thin. She'd dropped her cell phone down the can.

"My phone!" she had said. She looked at him, one eye swollen and puffy and bruised bright red, her face pitted with acne scars. She stomped her foot, her baby tits bouncing above her ribs. "Get my phone!" Blood the color of copper had seeped from between her teeth and dribbled onto her bottom lip.

He'd grabbed her by the hair and dragged all ninety pounds of her to the mattress on the floor. Ripped her cheap ass panties off. And between the punch, punch, slap, punch, bite, slap, punch had gotten one more in before throwing her ass out the door.

"MY PHONE!" were her last words as she landed in the hall.

He had to get up, he thought, his face still in the mattress. "What the fuck is up with my head?" he said to no one as he turned over. "Shitty fucking life full of shitty fucking memories. Fuck."

He swung his legs over the side. Leaned forward. He'd just been up. Had been in the bathroom, he thought.

"Wait, was I?"

Yeah, the plugged toilet. Miss Emma with her bony hips and eye swelling red and lost phone.

His heart thumped in his chest. His head was fuzzy

and light. Kinda dizzy and shit. He needed to eat. No fuckin' food, though. Cupboards bare. Floor sticky and cold underneath the piles of cheeseburger wrappers and pizza boxes. The furniture he hadn't sold or traded for
five blue, seven red, four yellow
busted up ages ago. Except for the mattress and the coffee table holding his sixteen, colorful friends. The ones waiting for him to scoop 'em up and swallow 'em down. Not yet, though.

It wasn't time.

He stood. Fuck, his thighs burned. They ached. His knees felt wrong and weird. Like swollen water balloons that were going to explode or something. Sorta like if he were to stab 'em with a knife, they'd send arcs of blood or puss or something everywhere. And his calves, his shins, they were weak. Like he was some old dude who'd fall over any second. Fuckin' getting sick.

Damn dirty bitches . . .

He looked down.

Two snakes sat on his leg. Two.

There'd been one, he thought. That's right, isn't it? Yeah, one. Earlier. Small. Not even two inches. And green. Or a green-yellow-blue-who knew the fuck what-color. But only one. Just one.

He was back on the mattress, his leg out, his ankle turned up.

Fuck.

They were, fuckin' shit, over, what, five inches long, ankle to knee. One on the front, the other moving up his calf. Were the mouths sorta open? Fuck. Hard to tell. But it almost looked like the small tip of a red tongue stickin' out. Blood, not brick.

EIDOLON AVENUE—APARTMENT 1B

And the skin around them looked swollen and dark and burned. And kinda fucked and round. Like a bubble. Like the feeling in his knees. He pressed it with his finger.

SHIT! Fucker stung. Fuckin' hurt. Bad.

He sucked the air in between his teeth, his eyes growing wet. The bubble went down and then, a second later, swelled up bigger. What the fuck? This had never happened before. In all his time, after all that fuckin' work, it'd never healed like this. With all those fuckin' tattoos—

"Is that the devil?"

Last night. Freaky Eve with the forked tongue had sat on his lap, the both of them here, on this mattress. Was it last night? Maybe. Whatever. She'd held his arm close, her black eyes scanning the sleeve of painted flesh inked from wrist to shoulder. A tapestry—fuck, he loved that word—of a lush garden. Green trees. Thick grass. Brown trunks. Mountains in the distance. The blue of a perfect sky that could never in a fucking million years exist. And demons hiding. Peeking from behind the leaves. From around the trunks. Even looking out from the ground itself. Like corpses rising from the grave, their eyes and hands and sharp claws pushing from the dirt.

Fucker had taken forever to do. But, damn, the bastard got it right. Colors, scale, size, scope. He fuckin' loved that piece. Too bad Tattoo Dude got shot up with a shitload of bad smack.

Sucks.

"I like his eyes." She'd watched the devil scrambling from the earth, his eyes large, his tongue forked, his fingers bleeding and raw and reaching.

"Yeah?" He wanted to kiss her. Wondered if her blue lipstick would taste like anything. Wondered if it'd taste like blue, whatever that tasted like. Thought of blueberries. He hated blueberries. Made him shit like a fuckin' Smurf. But he still wanted to kiss her. Didn't give a fuck if she reeked of old sweat, piss and patchouli.

"Brick, not blood," she said.

He laughed. "Yeah. Good call. You think it's alright?"

She nodded and shifted her boney ass on his lap, her tits drifting too fuckin' near his lips, his mouth, his teeth. He counted back from ten.

"Man, I was gonna have the fucker fix it, but I dunno. Might keep it now."

"Keep it." Her hands cupped his face, her short nails rough against his skin, her fingers cool.

"Owe 'em money anyway."

Shut up, man, Smart Skippy, the dude with the bright yellow hair, had said once. *Bitches don't like 'em broke.*

"You want a tat from me?" Her breath reeked of tacos and toothpaste.

"Hell yeah. Where do you work?"

"Where do you want it?" Her eyes narrowed, her teeth biting her bottom lip.

Fuck yeah.

He laughed and reached around to grab her ass as her arms slipped around his neck and her tits pressed against his chin in the dark of night.

Morning rain snuck in through the window and ran down the wall. Flies dive-bombed the toilet. He stood in the bathroom. The floor was cold and wet and grimy around his toes. The full-length mirror on the door stood in front of him.

"Cool tats," she'd said just hours ago.

He just remembered that, he thought as he looked at his reflection. Tall and ripped, from his big feet to the top of his buzzed head, he was art. From the green of the garden on his left arm—

"The trees feel alive—"

to the seascape on his right. The crashing waves. The swimming mermaids with their big tits and snapping tails. The green fish and blue sharks and hidden caves with their golden treasure. The enraged octopus squatting on the back of his hand to wrap around his wrist and forearm, its tentacles tearing the sailors in two

"It feels alive—"

and the flaming nightmare of the Gates of Hell on his broad back reaching from his waist all the way to his neck.

She'd wanted to see.

He'd peeled off his shirt and turned. Her fingers had brushed over his skin.

Fuck yeah.

She was quiet. He could hear her breathing as she'd caressed the demons running down his back. Her hands discovering the screaming souls twisting and turning and tearing in two as they writhed across his muscular shoulders and fell onto his tight lats. Her palm caressing the dark, heavy doorway, the fiery, screaming, endless nightmare of hell peeking from his spine.

Her blue lips had kissed the devil then. Found him near the small of his back. Horns and hooves and snarling teeth. Greedy paws clutching a flaming pitchfork, his razor sharp tail whipping the wind. Her lips found him and, her forked tongue licking his skin, had blessed him.

Holy fuckin' hell yes.

He turned and brought her into his arms. His hands had gone right back to her ass, her tiny body crushed against his.

"This room is alive," she'd said before he shoved his tongue in her mouth.

Goddamn, that hurt. His ankle twinged and stabbed and burned. He looked down.

The two snakes were now three.

The FUCK?

⁂

He blinked. Closed his eyes. Opened them again. Shooed away the flies and looked in the bathroom mirror. The floor was wet. Everything smelled like slimy shit and fucked up puke and cold rain. And there were now three snakes on his ankle.

He looked and, fuckin' shit, yeah. He was seeing three. Three fuckin' snakes winding around his calf, his shin, and on past his knee halfway up his thigh. And the motherfucker hurt. The skin was still swollen and red. The bottom half of his whole leg an angry sunburn that reached all around and down to his foot. A throbbing rash that crept between his toes and itched. That stung when he touched it.

That moved when he touched it.

The FUCK?

"Stay still," she'd said.

His skin was moving. He laid his palm flat against

EIDOLON AVENUE—APARTMENT 1B

his calf. Fuck, that shit hurt, man. But, yeah, the skin was vibrating. Kinda buzzing or something. Underneath. And, hand to holy god, he wasn't flyin'. He knew that.

The pills were on the coffee table. Five blue. Seven red. Four yellow.

He knew that.

Five blue. Seven red. Four yellow.

He'd counted and they were safe and his fuckin' skin, his leg, it was moving.

"Stay still." Her hand had wrapped around him, holding him steady.

The needle had stabbed in the dark. He laid on his bed last night. Eve was down below somewhere on his leg—his waist?—inking him up. He didn't remember where she'd gotten the needle. Or the color, those little plastic pots that stained his flesh. One minute he'd been grabbing her ass, crushing her tiny body to his, ignoring her stench while sneaking his fingers past her skirt and into her panties, and the next she'd been drilling him with a needle. He couldn't feel it. He couldn't feel anything. Knew he should, but didn't. He couldn't even see her, it was so dark.

How in the sweet fuck was she workin' on me in the dark?

The sun's not even up yet, his mother had said.

Shut up, man, he thought.

He swallowed hard, fighting the urge to slam down those

five blue, seven red, four yellow

and just make her go the fuck away.

She'd stood in the door, his mom, her hand on the frame, her tube top sagging too low and her shorts riding too high. This was back in the other house. The last house. The one they squatted in, out in the woods 'cause they were dead ass broke. The one with the busted windows covered in plastic and the vines that poked through the floorboards like desperate fingers. This was right before she'd stepped off the porch and out of sight. Before he'd left her face down in the dirt while he slid a backpack over his shoulder and hauled ass down the road.

Shut the fuck up, man, he thought.

Eve had slid on top of him in the dark. His hands lifting her skirt, he'd felt the needle stabbing his skin and her fingers holding his foot. But then he tasted blue and breathed patchouli and piss and her legs had straddled his stomach. All at the same time. Her tongue in his mouth and her hand holding his ankle.

What the hell?

Somewhere he remembered lifting her, and carrying her, and slamming her against the wall. Her head butting his and blood shooting from his nose. Her laughter as she bit his chin, her forked tongue licking the blood from his lips. He thrown her against the coffee table, he thought. It'd broken, the cheap ass wood splitting. He body slammed her, laying on top. She'd grabbed his head. Pulled him close. Had smeared her face in the red as he'd hauled out his cock and shoved it in her.

His stomach moved.

Fuck! He needed tp. Fuckin' toilet paper was under the sink. In the kitchen. Too wet in here. It'd get soaked. Get ruined. Everything got fuckin' ruined in here.

He made it the few steps down the hall into the

EIDOLON AVENUE—APARTMENT 1B

kitchen before stopping. His legs felt raw and red. The bleeding heat of hundreds of tiny needles pricking him. Tunneling into his tendons. Probing the muscle and gouging into the bone. His guts felt sloppy and loose. His knees like they were gonna fuckin' pop outta the joints.

He glanced down.

What the FUCK?

The snakes looked back at him from his waist. Tail to tongue, the three of them stretched from his ankle, up his leg, darted under his boxers, and ran all the way past his hip almost to his rib cage. Their mouths were open and they had sharp fangs. Their eyes were blood, their bodies large and wide and shiny. They even cleaved through the tats covering his legs, the Chinese characters—fuck if he knew what they meant anymore—moving to the side. Like, the snakes were pushing them out of the way. Slicing right through them and moving them to the side.

But no fucking way. That was impossible.

The skin was raised and sorta red. But there were big spots of white with, what the hell, dark underneath? Like, strips of black or something? He pressed his hand against his thigh, his hip, his stomach.

Shit, that hurt. Like fire. Way too hot. And it still buzzed. Still vibrated. He could feel it. Something living in his guts. He wanted to push on his skin again. See if it deflated. Made it feel any better. Cool it down with his hand. Thought he needed ice. But there was none. The freezer on the fuckin' fritz. And he didn't want to touch his skin again. Holy shit, he'd never had a trip this bad. Never crashed this hard or flown this high. Fuckin' hell. What if his skin broke and split open and puss or white ooze or who the hell knew what leaked out?

I'm sorry, his mom had said.

He could see her then. The forest around them, the sun not even up. She, face down, her tube top ripped and shredding. Her skinny legs spread and her ass falling outta her shorts. The vines around her ankles, her fingers in the dirt, reaching for the porch that was too far away.

Fuck no, he thought. Go away.

He grabbed the tp from under the sink and turned back to the toilet.

Let me brush my teeth first, his mom said. She cut in front of him to walk down the hall to his bathroom.

The fuck? He stopped as she walked away. His heart pounded. His head felt light. And his skin, on his legs, his feet, his stomach, the small of his back, fuck me, it felt like it was going to tear apart. Come off in huge sheets of raw flesh. He could almost feel it stretching and pulling and ripping. Getting ready to split and slide away.

Fuckin' hell, he'd rather be scratching himself to shreds in hobo rehab under a fuckin' bridge than do this. Knockin' his head against concrete as his body freaked the fuck out. Crappin' his pants and shooting puke out his nose. Anything but this fuckin' Eidolon trip.

"Mom."

She wasn't yet bone. She could still keep dinner down. Still had teeth. Her arms had track marks, but no red scabs. Nothing was cracking or falling apart or leaking out like a fuckin' creek or something. All white and yellow and green and gross.

EIDOLON AVENUE—APARTMENT 1B

"Mom?"

She stood at his sink. Flies buzzed around her as she dragged a dirty toothbrush across her teeth. Leaning forward, she spit frothy blue into the sink.

"You can't be here, Mom." He couldn't breathe. His chest squeezed tight. His face grew hot. His eyes filled with tears. He blinked and closed them. Squeezed them shut, real tight. Breathed deep. Count back from ten, bro. Count back from ten. Opened them again.

She still ignored him. Acted like she couldn't see him. She spit again. It was kinda red as it slid into the sink.

She stopped, her head down, chin tucked against her chest. She held the toothbrush in her fist. Balanced herself against the sink, her hands gripping the porcelain. Her knuckles looked swollen. Like they hurt. Her tits looked flat in her tube top. The skin was kinda blue and pale . . . or something. Her wrist looked too thin. And her legs looked wrong in her shorts. Like those fuckin' Holocaust pictures Mizz Martin showed in class once. Back in, what, 7th or 8th grade? Something like that.

"Mom?" Shit. He sounded like some fuckin' weak punk ass poser or something.

She belched. A deep sound. The sound of something wet in her throat. With bubbles and spit and the threat of rancid puke. She gulped and then sighed, her head down, her eyes fixed on the sink. Was she crying again? Fuck. Her face was in shadow. A blob of spit slipped from her mouth and hung off her bottom lip. And it just fuckin' hung there taking forever to hit the sink.

"You're dead, Mom." His knees were being sliced

open from the inside. The tips of countless razors carving slow, small strokes underneath his skin. Scalpels jamming between the joints and digging between the bones and scooping out the marrow. Slices of muscle being peeled from the inside. Everything just fuckin' hurt EVERYWHERE.

She spit into the sink again, her slobber hanging sorta red and yellow and green. No blue. And it was thick and wide, refusing to budge or fall or move.

His head was going to explode. His eyes stung with tears. Fuck. Count back from ten, motherfucker. Count back from ten, count back from ten. Everything was fuckin' a-okay if you fuckin' count back from ten.

This wasn't real. She wasn't there and his skin wasn't tearing open and there were no fucking snakes. It wasn't real. He wasn't flyin'. His friends—the blue red yellow—they were still waiting. For later. On the coffee table. It wasn't time. Not yet. All of this shit, it was some kinda fuckin' lie or nightmare or hallucination or something.

And that calmed him down for a moment. Until the drool hanging from her mouth lifted, arched its back, whipped around her neck, opened its eyes and hissed.

"HOLY FUCK!" He hit the wall as he stumbled back and turned.

"SON OF A BITCH!" He stopped, his body screaming. Every bit of skin feeling like it was being peeled away, inch by fuckin' inch. Everything raw and red and on fire. The bones grinding and popping and cold as ice.

Blinded by pain, he tripped into the living room and fell on the floor. "SHIT!"

He was sobbing now. The searing heat wrapping

EIDOLON AVENUE—APARTMENT 1B

him in a skin-tight blanket of red hot lava. He could barely breathe. He could barely think. There was just pain. An agony like he'd never felt before. And he wanted it to be over.

Now.

Crawling on hands and swollen knees to the coffee table, he grabbed a mug, praying there was a swallow of something at the bottom.

There was.

It was time, he thought, as he shoved

five blue, seven red, four yellow

into his mouth.

―※―

"Why 'Bullet?'" Eve had said. It was dark. Too dark. Like, a weird kinda dark that felt thick and somehow wrong. He could hear her and smell her, feel her in his arms, but he couldn't see her as they stretched out on the mattress.

"Pop always said I was dumber than shit," he'd said. "That I musta been born with a bullet to the brains or something. And it just stuck."

She pulled away.

"He was an asshole, but it's cool." He felt her scootch across the mattress.

She'd stood to go.

"Gonna jet?" he said.

She didn't say a fuckin' word as she dressed.

"Maybe we could, I don't know, hang again, or something." Well, shit, didn't that just sound fuckin' pathetic.

Chill, man, Skippy once said. This was before smart dude had choked on a Glock and taken a bullet down the throat. *Bitches don't dig desperate dudes.*

Whatever.

"Where can I find you?" He stood and stretched. Tried to see her in the dark before she left. Saw nothing.

"Yo, Eve, where you at?"

Still nothing.

"You wanna hit me up? Let me give you my cell, yeah?"

Silence.

What the fuck?

He didn't hear her walk across the apartment. Or open the door to leave. Didn't hear her go into the bathroom or anything. But she wouldn't answer and he couldn't even fuckin' feel her in the room.

The fuck?

"Eve?"

He looked for a light. Was careful to step around the broken coffee table. Hated the thought of anything stabbing into him, even if it was some small ass splinter or something. His foot touched his boxers. Bent over to pull 'em up. Felt the muscles in his back and hips scream.

Fuck! How hard had he drilled the bitch? Damn. He was too fuckin' young to feel this fuckin' old.

"Yo, Eve, where you at?" Hands out, like he was blindfolded it was that fuckin' dark, he found the wall. Inched his way across it to where the light switch should be. Couldn't find it. "Talk to me."

"What about your mom?" she said. Out of fuckin' nowhere, her voice had just been there. Like, right against his skin, his face, his lips.

EIDOLON AVENUE—APARTMENT 1B

"FUCK!" He jumped back. "Fuck, man. SHIT. Son of a fuckin' bitch. Shit. Scared the fuck outta me." He laughed. "Holy christ, Eve. Why didn't you answer, babe?" He reached out and found her standing against the wall.

"Tell me about your mom," she said.

"Nah, man. Another time." His hands found her shoulders, her neck, the curving slope of her small breasts. She was naked. And cold. Too cold. "Here." He moved to bring her into his arms. Hug her tight. Warm her up.

She backed off.

"You left her," she said. Her voice sounded strange. Hollow. Like, not coming from her or something. Sorta like when someone talks from the other end of a door or whispers at the end of a very long hall. That kind of hollow. "On the ground. In the woods. You left her."

He stopped, not sure what to say. "What?"

"Minutes after you left, they found her."

"Who? What? Wait, wait, wait, hold on a minute, here. What are you talking about? Who found—"

"Was she dead?"

"Huh?" His throat hurt. Had burned hot with each swallow. And his nose and the space between his eyes thumped. He felt sick, his skin feverish and aching. "Fuck, babe. Yeah, I think so."

"And if she wasn't?"

"The fuck? I don't know. She was sick, you know? I was, shit, what, seventeen or something? Fuck!" He reached for her and found the wall. She moved. Reached wider and had found her face, her shoulders. "What was I supposed to do? Huh? You tell me. What the fuck was I supposed to do?"

"She saw herself fall." Her voice sounded weak and far away. "Saw herself leave the porch and trip over the broken branches and fall. Saw you find her and saw you leave. Saw you run. Didn't see your tears—"

He strained to hear her, almost pressing his face against the wall. But that hadn't made sense. "Babe, please—"

"Because you didn't cry."

"Don't do this-"

"She saw them come."

"Stop." He moved to her again. Found her, her face cupped in his hands. "Why you doin' this, huh? How do you know this? The fuck, Eve? What is this? Why?"

His lips had found her. He pressed his mouth to hers, hard. Kissed her quiet, her forked tongue sliding along his teeth and slipping

five blue, seven red, four yellow

onto his tongue.

He stopped as she'd pulled back. Held her face in his hands as she'd gone into the wall. Like, as flat as the wall itself. Became the fuckin' wall. Disappeared into the goddamn fuckin' wall.

What the—?

"Eve?" He felt the wall. Had reached wide. Found only more wall. Reached low, high. Found nothing. Groped like some broke-ass blind man in the dark only to feel the smooth cold of flat fuckin' wall. "Babe?"

He found the light switch. The lights had flickered on.

Nothing. She wasn't there. He looked around. The coffee table wasn't broken. He could taste the pills in his throat. Had felt his nose where her head had butted him. Nothing. No blood. Looked at his fingers. No red. Nothing.

EIDOLON AVENUE—APARTMENT 1B

The fuck?

He looked at the mattress. Covers as tangled as ever, but no sign of her. No sign of them screwing. Nothing. No needle. No ink. Nothing, man. Like she'd never even been there. His head felt fucked up. Cloudy. Woozy. His skin had kinda itched or something. Felt cold on the inside. Every breath had hurt. His guts had turned. His head pounded. He could feel his intestines shifting and moving. Could feel them dropping. Like he'd be squirting shit any second. And the inside of his ears itched and his eyes burned. He closed them. Squeezed them tight.

At some point, he sat down. And then laid down. At some point, his eyes closed, the taste of five blue, seven red, four yellow on his tongue, his mind struggling with Eve just becoming the wall.

The fuck?

***

He smelled rotten wood first. Wet, rotten wood. Damp dirt. Dust and grime. The feeling of something crawling underneath his head. Beneath the floor boards and through the dirt, a hidden something just inches away.

This was the old house. The last house. The abandoned one in the woods. After Pop skipped town, the fucker, and Mom got too sick to work.

"Five bucks for a hand job?" she said. "Too fuckin' old and sick and tired for that kind of shit. Won't even get us McDonald's."

So, flat ass broke and hungry as fuck, they fled. Headed out of town and found a shack. "It'll do," she said as they broke down the door and stood in the one room hut. "Get wood for the fire." She looked at him as she'd opened the rusted, metal door of the wood burning stove. "Go!" And knowing she was sick and dying, he left to gather wood, whatever the hell that meant.

He screwed his eyes shut. Held his breath. It's a dream, he said to himself. I'm on Eidolon. She's dead. The shack is gone. That happened and it's in the past, you know?

Chill, man, Skippy with the fucked up blond hair said. Cool dude. Gayer than Christmas, but cool. Always fuckin' with his hair and shit. Whatever. *Just chill.*

Fuckin' shit was fucked up. He brought his knees to his chest. His guts were moving. Jumping and turning. Reaching and wiggling. Bumping into each other and getting all tangled up in knots. Even pushing against his skin. Like he could put his hand on his stomach and feel 'em slithering. But there was no fucking way he was going to push on his skin. Fucker could break and split open and, oh hell no, no way.

He opened his eyes.

Instead of the shit hole on Eidolon, he saw the shack. Windows covered with heavy plastic. Rotting wood. His mother sitting on the floor, her back against the wall. It was early morning. Still dark. She wore a stained, ripped tube top and shorts that were too short. Her lips and the flesh around her eyes were yellow. Her arms were pale and thin and scarred with weeping scabs, two on each forearm, three more on her chest. Patches of flaking white and seeping red that puckered and cracked and split when she moved. And the nails

EIDOLON AVENUE—APARTMENT 1B

on her hands had turned blue. Five spots of blue at the tips of her long fingers.

He caught her scent. The smell of curdled blood and sick flesh. The stench of crumbling teeth and a bladder that leaked sour piss. The skin on her fingers had shrunk to the bone, the knuckles round and swollen. And her body was turning white, too white, and looked cold. Every breath from her made his eyes water and his stomach jump.

He blinked. The shack shimmered and bent, Eidolon peeking through for a moment. The TV, the coffee table. The stained walls and his five blue, seven red, four yellow. But I've taken the five blue, seven red, four yellow, he thought. How many times? How many have I taken? How many were there?

Shit. No fuckin' clue, man.

He watched as the shack tried to return. He blinked. Pushed away the past. "Fuck no, man." He closed his eyes. "Go away." Took a breath. Opened his eyes again.

The shack. Still early morning. Moonlight shining through the broken windows. She laid on the floor. Pressed her face to the rotten wood as she sobbed. Her thin shoulders rising. Her body freakin' out. Head knocking against the floor. Fists clenching. Hips rising and falling. Bloody brown smeared on the back of her thighs. Laying in her own piss. Drawing her knees to her chest and then straightening her legs. Over and over. Knees to chest and then straight, her toes flexing as she groaned and sobbed and puked and shit.

"I'm so sorry," she said. The words were spoken into the wood. "Shitty stomach can't keep anything down."

Get up. Get up and go away. Just leave. You smell. You're sick. Too fuckin' sick. And I don't know what the fuck to do with you. So, just get up. Get the fuckin' hell up and go away and die.

She rose to her knees. Eidolon came back for a moment. She kneeled on his carpet. Her hand lunged for the plastic crate, the TV as she struggled to stand. She stood and doubled over, thick orange piss sliding down her leg to spread in a puddle at her feet. The yellow of the walls matched the yellow of her lips. "I'm sorry," she said again. She sounded weak. Tired.

"Go," he said, his teeth clenched. He closed his eyes. Pushed his face into the mattress. Wished away the pain in his hands, his guts, his legs, his skin. Wished away the nightmare of his whore of a mother taking too long to die. Counted back ten, nine, eight, seven, six—

"I'm dying," she said.

"I know," he said into the mattress.

She breathed, the sound rattling in her lungs and wheezing from her throat.

Five, four, three, two—

"It's cold." She was crying. He could hear the snot in her nose. Could imagine it running onto her top lip. He squeezed his eyes closed. Could still see her in his mind. Her hand to her stomach, standing in an orange puddle, hunched over as if in pain. Her hair thin and greasy. The sores around her mouth leaking down her chin as she grimaced and sobbed. Her eyes sunken and sad. "I need air."

"Then go," he said, his face still in the mattress. Fuck, there was no way he was gonna look at her.

EIDOLON AVENUE—APARTMENT 1B

"It might rain." Her voice came from the dark. Outside. On the porch. "Don't get sick."

He counted back from ten again. Smelled dirt and wet wood again. Felt the trees and the hills and the leaves waiting outside. Fuckin' surrounded by trees and hills and leaves. "The sun's not even up yet," he heard her say. He heard her stumble. Heard the boards creak and the breeze rustle the plastic nailed over the windows. Felt the chill in the air. Knew strange things, things with teeth and claws and appetites, waited in the dark behind the trees, around the trees, up in the branches of the trees.

Fuckin' nature.

The door creaked open. The slow shuffling sound of her bare feet on the porch. A pause. More sobs. A deep breath that rattled and wheezed and clicked in her throat.

He opened his eyes.

She stood in his hall, the bathroom in front of her. Took a step off a porch that didn't exist on Eidolon. She took another step. Her hand grabbed air as she stumbled and paused and fought for breath.

He couldn't take his eyes off her.

Fuck man, if this is a fuckin' dream, if I'm flyin', then let it happen. Let it finish. Once it's finished, I'll wake up and Eve with the blue lips and forked tongue will be next to me and bitch whore mom will be dead and I can go on with life.

Knock.

He lifted his head. The floor had bounced with that knock.

He sat up. She still stood, her back to him as if she was gathering strength for the next step.

Knock, knock.

It sounded like knuckles against wood. But it wasn't. Was it against the floor?

Knock, knock, knock.

No, it was the wall.

Knock, knock.

No, the floor and the wall.

Knock.

He looked up. The ceiling fan was swaying. Was it up there, too? He stood up to look. The room fuckin' spun. He sucked the air through his teeth. His neck felt like the flesh was peeling away in big, bloody strips. His back, the skin on his back, was hot. Too hot. Like roasting on a spit hot and then being carved clean on the edges of fuckin' samurai swords. He stretched his fingers and almost cried. If he had the courage to look he'd probably see the skin pulling away from the nails. See raw flesh and blistered knuckles and holes gouged into the top of his hands and his palms. The skin buzzed and snapped.

The fuck?

He looked.

Small snakes slithered on his fingers and whipped around his hands. Over the top. Around to the palm. Between the fingers and underneath the nails. But not on the skin. Fuck no, they were *in* the skin. Like tattoos. Living tattoos. Red, green, blue, white tattoos that were living *in* his fuckin' skin. But under the flesh like worms. Worms with fangs. His skin moved in ripples when they moved. Itched and clenched when they wrapped tight around the bones. Burned when they pushed out to inch along his nails. Attacking the octopus on his wrist and tearing it in two. Squeezing

EIDOLON AVENUE—APARTMENT 1B

the mermaids into a bloody pulp and twisting the sailors until their heads popped off. Upending the ships and splashing into the waves.

"Mom," he said aloud, though he wasn't sure why. He took a step, his knees popping and creaking, his legs like a fuckin' bonfire. He looked down as the floor thumped with another knock.

There was no more skin. His legs, his feet, everything was gone, replaced by snapping, snarling, twisting, turning snakes. But fuck no. No way. What the fuck kinda fuckin' trip was this? He wasn't flyin', but, FUCK, his arms, his hands and fingers and feet, all these snakes were fuckin' living tattoos. Embedded in his fuckin' skin. They wound around his toes. He could see them cleave through the Chinese lettering on his shins, up his knees, onto the inside of his thighs, and around the back of his legs. Dart up his hip and along his stomach. The little fuckers even wandered along his chest and dug into his pecs. Were he to lift his hand, they'd be on the back of his neck. Could sense them on his face, the tips of his ears, the top of his head. He could even feel them spilling from the Gates of Hell on his spine.

But fuck no. He was flyin'. He must be flyin'. *Count back from ten, count back from ten, count back from ten, motherfucker. Just count the fuck back from ten.*

He stumbled to the bathroom to look in the mirror, the glass jumping as the walls shook with another knock. Head over his shoulder, he turned, and turned again. Couldn't see anything.

FUCK!

Snakes. Nothing but snakes. He was made of snakes.

How the hell? Sobbing, he turned away and leaned back against the mirror. *What the fuck, man?* He couldn't stop the tears. *What the fuck? What is this? Was it a dream? A nightmare? I'm not flyin', man, but wake up, bro. Wake the fuck up.*

WAKE UP!

He lifted from the mirror. Felt something wet. Something tight. Pulled away to stand. The skin of his back remained. Already in pain and lost in emotional chaos, he didn't feel it sticking to the glass and pulling free from his muscle. Didn't feel it separating from his spine and his ribs, his collar bone and shoulders, as he turned to face the mirror. Hadn't noticed the slimy sound of ripping and tearing. Didn't know he'd left his flesh behind until he saw it hanging, a bloody swathe of discarded skin, shining and wet. Dozens of veins snapped and broken and pumping blood down the door. Snakes crawling like maggots through pink flesh. Dripping spider web strands of who knew the fuck what clinging to him as he stood and turned and stopped.

The FUCK?

He couldn't catch his breath. He could feel the blood rushing down his ass, the back of his legs, his ankles. Could feel the steaming puddle gather around his feet.

He couldn't fuckin' see right. He blinked as he looked down. Blinked again. Wanted to rub his eyes, but was afraid to raise his hand and touch his skin. Couldn't handle the thought of more flesh creasing and cracking and falling.

Covered in blood, his blood, *they* landed in the pool of red at his feet. All sizes and colors. Small, large, medium. Black, green, some blue, they pushed from his exposed muscle, from under his ribs, around his hips, the hollow under his collar bone and the top of his spine to fall like drops of rain in a squirming, jerking pile, their bodies tangled, bouncing as the floor knocked again.

"Mom?"

He heard a phone ring. From underwater. From the can. He looked over at the pile of shit squatting on a mountain of toilet paper and chunky yellow puke, all sitting in a cloudy pool of dark piss.

It rang again.

"This room is alive." Eve stood near, nipples jutting from her tank. Her forked tongue licked her lips. "It found her. It brought me and now it wants her to find you. To see you. And she does. She sees you. She suffered because of you. Was terrified because of you," she said as she drew close, her eyes on him,

five blue

short fingernails stroking his cheek. "And she hasn't forgotten."

"My phone," Miss Emma said from behind him. He turned his head. She wrapped her arms around him, her hands sliding between the snakes, her fingers lost in their tangled, shimmering bodies as she rested her face on the raw weeping muscle of his back, the blood staining the

seven red

bruises on her face where he'd punched, punched, slapped, punched, bit, slapped, punched as he'd gotten another quick one in before tossing her skinny ass out the door.

"Get it, man," Skippy said as he twirled

four yellow
strands of platinum hair in his fingers. His dead friend looked toward the toilet. "It's for you."

He belched, the taste of five Eves, seven Miss Emmas, and four Skippys on his tongue. His friends. Yeah, he was flyin'. He must be. This was all some fucked up stupid crazy flyin' dream.

Why are you here? he wanted to say. But his tongue wouldn't work. It was too thick and jumpy. And his lips twitched and burned. His vision was fucked and it was hard to breathe. He kept wanting to take the skin off the mirror. To turn around or something. Lean into it and push it back in place maybe. But that was crazy. It was all crazy.

He laughed, the tender flesh of his lips splitting as he smiled.

The knocking was growing. From the floors, the walls. The ceiling jumping. Insistent. Consistent. Never. Fuckin'. Ending.

They watched him. Eve with her blue lips. Miss Emma with her red bruises. Skippy with his yellow hair. Just stood there, all quiet and shit. He thought of that group the other night—last night?—on Eidolon. With Eve at the door, her arm around his waist as he'd fought to put the fuckin' key in the fuckin' lock.

I don't want to die, he'd thought.

Chill.

The phone rang.

The walls cracked, rips running floor to ceiling. He thought of Mom with her bleeding scabs. How they'd crack and weep red. The floor jumped beneath his feet. He wanted to sit, but was afraid he'd tear and split and weep, too. The ceiling was buckling and breaking.

EIDOLON AVENUE—APARTMENT 1B

Dropping tiles and dust. Dangerous small splinters that would stab if he stepped wrong. The flesh of this apartment, the skin, it was ripping apart. Like *his* fuckin' skin and hers at the end before she fell in the dirt and died. And the knocking, it wouldn't stop.

Through the slab of flesh still stuck to the mirror, all he saw were snakes. He couldn't see himself anymore. Just snakes. Everywhere snakes. He'd lift his arm. Snakes. Stretch his fingers. Snakes. Moved closer to get a better look, his hand smearing the mirror bloody red as he wiped away the skin, and saw tiny snakes running rings around his pupils and swimming in the whites of his eyes. He swallowed. It still burned and felt thick. He ran his tongue along his teeth. Felt long, skinny snakes climbing from his gums.

FUCK!

If he opened his mouth, would his tongue be forked? Like Eve's? He opened his mouth.

In the dark, he could see the roof, the inside of his cheeks, his tongue, the gums around his teeth, even down his throat, everything was the shiny squirming of living dark.

He swallowed. It felt thick. He took a breath. It was shallow.

He felt the cold of the toilet bowl against his arms. He was kneeling. Shooed away the flies. Felt the rain on the floor cooling his knees, his shins and the tops of his feet. Ignored the thought of that wet filth sticking to the snakes. Could still hear the muffled, wet ringing of the phone. He sighed and hoped he'd wake soon. Smelled the shit and the piss and the puke and decided it wasn't so bad after all. Thought of Eve dragging her thumb on his lip and sucking the vomit from it.

"Cool tats," she'd said. Yesterday? Who the fuck knew anymore.

He slipped his arm into the toilet. The water was chilly, the shit slimy and wet, the puke sticky and chunky and muddy. His fingers broke through the toilet paper. It stuck in long torn streaks to the snakes infesting his flesh, their slippery bodies sliding under it and around it before shaking it free. He reached further, deeper. Groped. The dark piss swam between the snakes. It burned. Like alcohol on an open cut. But this was along his hand, between his fingers, up his forearm to his elbow. A burn eating him in one big bite.

"I thought she was dead," he said to Eve. She still stood near, her lips still blue, her nails still blue, her hair still fifty shades of black. "She was dead. I swear it."

He found the phone. Gripped it. Lifted it through the toilet paper, the puke, the piss, the shit. Wiped it clean. As clean as he could get it. Looked through the brown, red, green, yellow to find the button to answer it, the cell glowing bright with each ring.

Ignoring the flesh creasing and cracking and weeping as his elbow bent, he pressed it to his ear. "Hello?"

The ceiling buckled and snapped like thunder, this great yellow cloud vomiting snakes, their slithering bodies pummeling the floor like a fuckin' hail storm. The gaps in the walls ripped and split, more snakes falling free to race along the broken boards. And the floor thumped and splintered as still more snakes tried to rise, to break free. With a deep groan and the sharp snapping of wood, the ceiling fell, the walls caved and the floor heaved. An ocean of snakes rolled forward to cover the apartment and slither their way toward him.

EIDOLON AVENUE—APARTMENT 1B

"FUCK!" He jumped up, jumped back.

"They found me." His mother's voice crackled from the phone. "Spiders, bugs, beetles. Snakes."

The seething wave rushed near. He closed the door. Slammed it shut.

"Mom!" He pushed against the mirror, the discarded flesh of his back hanging inches from his cheek.

"They made their home in me." Her voice was clear and calm. The voice of revenge. Of an anger that was patient and deep. "I was still alive, Bullet, and they crawled down my throat and in my ears and through my eyes and up my nose."

The door was bending. The snakes were pushing. His feet were slipping. The snakes on his arms and around his fingers were tightly coiled, their tails snapping. Their bodies rearing back and lunging under his skin, their fangs drawing blood as they tore the muscle and poked through the flesh.

"You left me." She was loud. So loud. From this tiny cell phone dropped and laying in pieces on the floor, her voice had taken over the room. Like the voice of God. "Why did you leave me? Do you know what that's like? To have them push through the scabs. To climb from torn skin. Slide out my ass, out my-"

"Fuck no, man! Stop!" The door was inching open. He could feel them on the other side. Could see them in his head, a massive storm of slick, slippery black. "I didn't know, Mom. Please."

"I wasn't dead," she said. They were starting to sneak through the cracks. Searching for their brothers living in his skin and on his flesh, these tattoos that had come to life and now covered every inch of him.

"More things came. Bigger things." Her voice was calm, but it cut through the slapping of bodies slithering in pools of blood and the slow creak of a door breaking. "Tore me apart. Peeled the skin away.

"I watched them. Saw them run into the woods, dragging my guts in the dirt." More snakes spilled in. More creatures. Strange, long things with heads that were too large and eyes too round. Tiny arms that looked human with even smaller fingers that gripped and grasped and reached. Tiny teeth behind lips that were too much like his. Sighs that smelled of sulphur and ash. Things that stretched their necks to see and draw close.

With the snakes, they slithered to gather around his feet, his knees. Crawl up his legs.

"Do you know what that's like? To be left to that?"

"No!" The door split in two, a wall of snakes, of other things, rushing in. And the living tattoos, they broke free. Burst from the cracks in his skin and popped those islands of white on his flesh to rear back, shining and wet. They were all over, from his neck to the soles of his feet. Their bodies rustled as they dug into his ears. Smacked his teeth as they pushed between his lips. Made him cough and gag as they slid across his tongue and dove down his throat. Felt like a fuckin' shiv made of fire as they stabbed into the cracks surrounding his eye balls.

"You will," she said. The cell phone sputtered and clicked, the light growing dim as the battery died. "You will."

Weighed down by snakes, lost in a pit of jerking, twisting dark, he was on his knees, his head resting on the toilet seat. Felt the world growing quiet.

EIDOLON AVENUE—APARTMENT 1B

I'm sorry, he thought as he fought to dig the little fuckers from his eyes. Jammed his fingers in his mouth to catch 'em and yank 'em out. Damn near shit as their fangs gripped the inside of his nose as he tried to pull 'em free. *I didn't know what to do, man. I was scared. I ran. I'm sorry.*

They were sliding down his throat. Their scales scratching, the bodies wrestling as they pushed down. He gagged and then gagged again, the taste of slithering black burning the roof of his mouth. His lungs moved as they lurched and tore through his body. Pushed aside his guts and squeezed his heart. Plunged through the gashes in his skin. Wormed their way through his brain, his head, under the skin of his face. He couldn't breathe. He couldn't think. He couldn't see. And right before he felt the sharp *pop* of his ear drum splitting, all he heard was the never fuckin' ending thump, thump, thump of crawling snakes.

He rested against the toilet. Closed his eyes as they jammed his throat. He couldn't swallow. He couldn't cough or gag. Hell, he'd shove his fuckin' fist down his throat and try to puke 'em up if he thought it'd work. But it wouldn't. I'm sorry, he silently said before all thoughts of his mother and his colorful friends—Eve with her five blue, Miss Emma with her seven red and Skippy with the four yellow—left him for the last time with his final breath.

From the hall he watched. His mother, healthy and clean, stood, her hand in his. She smelled of clean soap and washed clothes. Smells he'd never associated with her, but which he loved. Steps away, he saw himself kneeling next to the toilet in a pool of bloody puke. *What is this?*

It's the building. Her eyes found his.

What is? He turned to her.

This, it wasn't you. She smiled. *It never was.*

Together, they turned to go.

He glanced at the dead Bullet's ankle, the face that was no longer his resting in the island of shit and toilet paper and puke floating in an ocean of dark, cloudy piss.

There was nothing there. On his leg. No snake. Nothing at all. Nothing but familiar ink. Dead, useless ink. Chinese characters spelling fuck knows what on a lifeless foot resting in a pool of vomit spiked with the remnants of pancakes and five blue, seven red, and four yellow pills.

APARTMENT 1C

CLICK

Monday, 3:24 PM

THEY'D MADE LOVE, once, when she was warm. Now she sat at the kitchen table, her silence speaking volumes.

"I'm sorry," he said for the umpteenth time.

Nothing.

He'd discovered her an hour ago at the foot of the stairs in the lobby.

Hair a soft brown, eyes large and kind, skin pale and freckled. She'd sat facing the mailboxes, lost in thought, her lithe body, despite the rainy afternoon, in a sleeveless sundress, her small feet in strappy sandals.

Although he saw her many times before, strolling the park or sipping coffee in the cafe, he'd never approached or spoken with her. There'd never been the chance.

Until now.

And she was perfect.

Then again, they always were in the beginning.

Not wanting to startle her, he approached cautiously.

Seeing him, she stood. "Oh my goodness." Her heel caught the hem of her dress. "I'm sorry." Balancing on one foot, her hand gripping the railing, she fought to wrestle it free. "Just let me—"

"Here." He offered his hand. She took it, the heel free—the captivating stranger soon standing on her own two feet. "I've seen you around, but I don't think we've met." His hand held hers.

"Yeah, you used to be Colton Carryage, right?" She paused and offered a small smile. "That sounded rude. I'm sorry. I didn't mean to make you sound like some kinda has-been or something—"

"No, it's okay." He offered his pearly whites in return. "And I still am, by the way. Colton Carryage, I mean. Not a has-been."

She laughed.

Still holding her hand. "You new to Eidolon?"

"No, I'm just here to see someone." In the harsh fluorescent light, her skin looked ashen, her hair almost blonde. "And, between you and me, I hope they show up soon. I've been waiting forever and I basically drank a barrel of water at lunch."

He longed for the feel of her blonde hair gripped in his fist and the taste of tears against her pale cheek. "As long as you don't mind navigating around packing boxes, you're more than welcome to use my restroom, if you like."

"Um, wow. Thank you." She nodded. "That's very kind."

He'd started up the stairs.

"It's a shame you're leaving Eidolon so soon," she said as she followed.

"How do you know I'm leaving?" He turned back to her.

"Just a hunch. You said packing boxes, right?"

"No, no, you're right," he said. He felt something, then. An alarm bell. A warning. The hair rising on the back of his neck. A fist clenching in his guts. A lump building in his throat. Ignoring it, his eyes scanned the

EIDOLON AVENUE—APARTMENT 1C

freckled cleavage, the thin arms, the bare shoulders in the sundress. "You're good."

༺❀༻

She seemed so small standing in the hall to the bathroom. She paused, her eyes on the cramped room, the packing boxes, the yellowing walls, the rain pelting the narrow kitchen window.

"What's it like?" She turned to him. She'd yet to use the restroom.

"What's what like?" He wondered if he should offer her a glass of water and then realized the cups were packed in a box somewhere.

"Being famously handsome." She crossed her arms over her chest, her tits rising in the thin sun dress.

He laughed.

"I'm serious." She came close. "You and your family, you guys are, like, bold faced names, you know? It's not like I look up every day and see 'The golden son of a favored Senator,' or whatever it was The Post called you."

"Ah, The Post."

"'The favored soon felon, the son's light dimmed.'"

He laughed. A sharp, short burst of sound. One that wasn't happy, but was, instead, meant to interrupt and stop.

"That was after, you know—" A quick shake of the head as she fell silent.

"I know." His arms crossed over his chest.

"I'm sorry." She closed her eyes for a brief moment. "What is it with me and my . . . damn, what do you call it? TMI?"

"Yeah, TMI. Too much info."

"Ugh. I know. I just get all OCD when it comes to finishing a thought."

"Or a quote from The Post."

"Right. Forgive me." She uncrossed her arms, her fingers soon laced at her waist.

"Done." He grinned through gritted teeth. "Journalism major?"

"Nah, just a nobody. A nobody who's curious what it's like to live that charmed silver spoon Ivy League life."

"It isn't like that. Not anymore."

"Of course." She stood in front of him. "And what's that other thing like?"

He paused. The bedroom door was closed, he reminded himself. She was a stranger to him. He'd never spoken with her. She knew nothing. He almost sighed with relief. "I don't know." He shrugged.

"Is that why you're leaving?" Her hand reached out to fleck an imaginary piece of lint off his shirt, her palm pausing to lay flat against his muscular chest.

"No, not really." He stopped. Rain pelted the window. For a moment, the day grew darker. Again, the hair rose on the back of his neck. The tips of his fingers tingled and buzzed. Now that she was close, now that she was no longer a vision in the distance, some beautiful gift yet to be unwrapped, he realized there was a strange *something* about her. Not dangerous, but off. Something that made his throat tight and his skin crawl. That made his cheeks flush. "Family's called me back now that Dad's out and we're circling the wagons, so to speak."

"You think that'll help?" Her breath was warm against his neck.

EIDOLON AVENUE—APARTMENT 1C

"*They* think it will, so . . . " He stopped and closed his eyes. She was so close the scent of her lingered in his nose. The scent of something simple and chaste. And clean. His mouth watered. He swallowed, ignoring the warnings ricocheting through his mind like errant bullets and the warmth crawling down the back of his neck. "Once people see he's innocent I-"

"Despite the overwhelming evidence."

"Everything will be fine." He stepped back quickly and moved toward the door, ready to see her out. "Everything will be back to what it's supposed to be."

"Of course. A charmed life once again." She stopped him.

He realized he wanted her. Had work to do but was bored. Wanted, instead, to fan the flames of her desire, give hope to her fantasies, and then break her heart. Be cruel. Callous. He gave a small smile, the chin ducking to the chest, the eyes, nice and slow, looking up at her. He sighed, his powerful chest rising.

She smiled.

Worked every time. Especially if you were Colton fucking Carryage.

Her fingers slipped between his. "I like your place." She gave his hand a gentle squeeze. "Is that your bedroom? Over there?" She glanced at the closed door across the room.

"Yeah." He looked down. Her eyes were on him. She was small. Smaller than him, at least. And light. The perfect height. Perfect weight. Despite the warning, despite the alarms, he was going to do this. It'd be quick. Brief and angry. He could overpower, invade, pummel and punish and still find relief. From failure, disappointment, humiliation. Could still, in her, taking her, making her his, remember who he still was despite everything. Reconnect to his power, his privilege. A quick release and then peace. A moment from now, he could wrap his arms around her, pick her up and carry her to the couch.

But no.

He tilted her face to his with the tip of his finger. "So, now what?"

"You tell me." She waited.

He laughed.

"Well, I do have time, you know." She smiled.

"Yeah?"

"Yeah." She watched him. "And you are who you are."

He grinned. "Yeah, I know."

"And how many times am I going to be this close to—"

"Colton fucking Carryage, right?"

She laughed. "Right."

He moved closer, his lips near hers. "You wanna see it?"

"See what?" She waited, her eyes on his. Challenging him. Teasing him.

"You know." He kissed her. Her lips were soft, her breath sweet. In her lips he found the unspoken promise of soft, secret places. "My bedroom. Is that what you want to see?"

She laughed. "*The* Colton Carryage's bedroom? Um, *yeah*."

"You sure?" He breathed her in. Clean soap and soft skin. Innocence and desire. Want. No fear. Not yet. He kissed her again. Her body leaned into his. "Answer me. I need to hear the words."

EIDOLON AVENUE—APARTMENT 1C

She remained silent, but her lips, her hands, her body told him she was growing hungry. For his touch, his body.

"Yes or no. Do you want to see the bedroom?" His lips brushed against hers. "Say it."

"Yes." Her voice was almost a whisper.

His mouth curled, baring his teeth in a quiet burn of brilliant white. "Close your eyes." She did, his tongue finding hers as his hands slid down to wrap around her throat.

⚯

She sat at the kitchen table, saying nothing.

"Ya snapped it, didn't ya." Brody leaned forward. Chiseled jaw and dark eyes, his teeth too white, his frat bro was all bulging biceps and bottled tan. "Gonna shove her next to the ice cream?" Bro laughed and then lit a joint as he strolled to the window, his eyes peering at Eidolon below. "Predictable fucker, just like always."

"It wasn't something I planned, you know?" he said.

"Right," his bro said. "She'll end up with the meat in the walk-in."

"Fuck you." He turned away and closed his eyes.

"Awww," he heard Brody, smelling like Axe body spray and sweaty feet, whispering in his ear. "Bro here's gonna cry. Big ol' pussy just like his pop-pop."

Wrong again, asshole, he thought.

"You know what we do to big ol' pussies, right, bro?"

"Shut up, dick head." He clenched his fists and took a deep breath. A moment later, he opened his eyes. "Don't listen to him." He looked at her across the table.

"I'm not like my dad. I'm . . . " He stopped, not sure how to finish the thought.

She sat silent.

For a moment, he considered touching her. Stroking her skin. Tracing his fingers from the bruises on her throat through the freckles covering her chest down to the discreet slope of her small breasts.

But he didn't. "I'm not like him. And you're nothing like the others. That bothers me. I don't know why." He sat back, crossing his arms. He sighed.

Whatever. He'd already had her once. Had tasted her regret, her fear. Felt her underneath him. Toyed with the warmth of her tears. Usually, there was a second time. Sometimes a third. Before the chill of the flesh became too cold and the limbs no longer bent without breaking.

But not today. He couldn't.

Still, there was nothing as thrilling as that *click*.

The one that quieted the racing heart and silenced the fingers digging into his flesh, pulling him close, pulling him near. The one that hushed the breathless moans and wordless pleading. That kicked their quickening desire from its peak and gave them, instead, the stumbling confusion of a sudden end into a world that was forever dark.

All with a simple *click*.

He hadn't even learned her name.

Ah, now, *that* made her like the others.

"That's not true," he said to her.

"Another study partner?"

"No, Brody. I didn't even meet her until—"

"Some student aid slacker?"

"Shut up."

EIDOLON AVENUE—APARTMENT 1C

"Probably dumb as shit and just as desperate."
"Fuck you."
"Pussy."

"She's not like the others!" He ignored him. Focused on her. "She's not." His head hurt. "She's different. Somehow." He breathed deeply and watched her. "I just don't know how yet."

She still wore the sundress, though it now sat wrinkled above her hips, a nipple peaking from where a shoulder strap had slipped. Her arms hanging slack, her head tilted back, chin up, she waited, her legs open.

"Whore," Brody said from his perch near the window.

He swallowed and looked away. It felt obscene, the way she was exposing herself, her panties laying scrunched somewhere on the floor. It made his throat tight with disgust. And desire.

"I knew their names, you know. At some point in the beginning." He swallowed again. "Really. I did. I just forgot them because, you know, who cares, right? Tits. Freckles. Teeth. That's who they were, in the end. Big Tits. Red Freckles. A mouthful of huge Teeth. So that's what I named them. And this one?"

He looked back at her. The dull brown of her shoulder length hair. The skinny arms. The mouth smeared with lipstick. The jaw slack and drooling. The cheeks still shining with sweat. Her head sitting at an awkward tilt on her broken neck. "Well, her tits aren't anything to write home about and she can't be Freckles—" he said.

"Freckles?" his bro said.

"Yeah, man, Freckles. She had freckles, so . . ."

"Fuck, man," Brody said, laughing. "For real?"

"Anyway, there's already a Freckles," he said, ignoring his friend. "And this one, her teeth are just ordinary, boring teeth, so . . . " He thought of her downstairs sitting on the steps. The surprise that shouldn't have been. The sweet looking girl he'd spied so many times, but had never charmed. The gift who, not even an hour ago, had slammed him with his past. Who'd humiliated him with the rumors and lies about his once-charmed life.

The nobody who'd seen not the handsome young playboy and college quarterback with broad shoulders and killer abs, but instead the loser who lived in a dump on Eidolon Avenue.

"Why would she do that? As if I *want* to remember any of that?" He felt the color rise in his cheeks. His thoughts slow, his tongue thick, he clenched his fists and fought to remain calm. "Why would she, this person who didn't even *know me*, be so mean?"

"She's a bitch."

"I know, man."

"A slut."

Colton smiled. "Ain't that the damn truth."

"She had it coming, you know?"

"Damn right," he said, leaning forward, his elbows on the table.

"Can't trust a ho, my friend," Brody said, joint in hand, as he turned away from the window and slid down the wall to sit on the floor. "Rule numero uno in the Bro Code, shit head."

"I know, I know, I know." He looked at her. Thought again of her lips on his as she'd gasped when he'd shoved himself deep, her hips pulling back in shock, her palms pushing him away in panic. He smiled.

EIDOLON AVENUE—APARTMENT 1C

"She was too easy." The smile faded. "The others were worth my time. I charmed them. They trusted me." His hand snaked across the table, the fingers coming close to, but not touching, hers. "With them, there was fear. The fear that comes with being vulnerable. With wanting something they'd thought they could never have. What they'd remembered of me—the hot guy, the quarterback, the money—all of that blinding them to how far everything's, like, totally fall—"

"Can it, shit head."

He stopped. "Right." A deep breath. "Thanks."

"I gotchu, bro," Brody said as he stretched his legs and crossed his ankles.

"And this one?" He considered touching her as she sat, peaceful, her head resting against the back of the chair. He remembered her scent. The tang of light sweat and the cloying stench of cheap vanilla. "Here's the deal, man: she didn't know her 'place.' Who the fuck is she, right? I've met Presidents. I've driven cars worth more than she makes in a year. Fucked bitches *way* hotter than her. To slam *me*? To treat *me* like some kind of nothing *nobody?* That kind of stupidity demands a response. Needs to be balanced. I have to. It's like the Universe or something demands it of me. How else will people like her learn respect? Or learn what's right and appropriate?" He laughed, a short staccato that punched the air. "If I do nothing they just stay uncouth, uncivilized animals or something."

He leaned back. "But there's always a fight, at first. And I need that, you know? I need that fear, that fight, that sense of regret. I need them to know a lesson is being learned and that I'm the one teaching it. That power and feeling of importance? Of strength? Nothing like it, bro. It's so fuckin' sweet."

"Still a big ol' pussy like your pop, though." Brody said, stretching his arms above his head with a loud groan.

"But I'm not, dickwad. With a *click*, I end 'em. I take their fear, their terror, their weak little fists punching me as they cry, and, like a *fuckin' god*, I end it. Can you do that, Brody?"

Nothing.

"You can't, shit head," he said, answering himself. "But I can. And I do. And each time, I get a little bit of me back. Of who I still am. And, holy shit, hand to god, that right there, the little bitch laying there helpless while I *overwhelm her*, while I *teach her,* while she learns *respect*, that's what makes me nut." He leaned forward again, elbows on the table.

"But this one, here?" He looked to Brody, the six foot five jock with the chiseled jaw and billion dollar family at odds with the tattered carpet and sagging couch. The creased packing boxes and the rain falling outside. His bro a kick in the gut reminding him of all he could lose. Of all he's lost. Of being an outcast. Of being alone. No friends. No family. No money.

He swallowed and then continued, his eyes back on her. "But this one here, man, she kissed too quick, spread her legs too quick. Said 'yes' too quick. Didn't even raise an eyebrow when I grabbed her neck." He stood to leave. "I don't know. The whole thing is just off, you see? I'm telling you, there was nothing 'right' about her. She was wrong. It's all wrong. She was better when she was some anonymous nobody in a sundress."

EIDOLON AVENUE—APARTMENT 1C

Brody stood and headed to the closed bedroom door. "They always are, my friend."

He thought of her in the park, off in the distance. Or at a table across from him in the cafe, sitting, no book, no coffee. Just sitting. Or under the awning at the corner store in the rain, standing silent. Always in a sundress, her eyes on him. And then glancing away. Teasing. Tantalizing. Untouchable.

Couldn't remember seeing the little bitch in anything else. The image of her in a t-shirt and jeans somehow impossible to conjure.

"She really was unnecessary." He looked at her again, searching for her name. "So that's who she is. There's Tits, Freckles, and Teeth. And now this one. Unnecessary."

And leaving her at the kitchen table, he turned and walked to the bedroom, his bro in tow.

Two windows sat at the end of the small room, the sad stretch of Eidolon Avenue waiting below. Before that, along with the hardwood floors and dingy white walls scarred with long stains the color of rancid yellow mustard, there was nothing except a mattress shoved against a wall and a large deep freezer humming in the center. The kind with the lid that opened on the top, its wide base surrounded by bouquets of flowers and fragrant potted plants. A freezer made for heavy sides of beef and other large cuts of meat. And since Tits, Freckles and Teeth were laid out on the floor, it was empty.

"Should've hauled them out sooner," Colton said, looking at the bodies.

"Yeah?" Brody said, sitting nearby.

"Yeah, buddy. You blind? They're still frozen, dipshit." The skin was still white, the lips blue. And Teeth, her eyes were still open and pale and clouded. Their arms and legs had started to marble, the veins long dark lines creeping from shoulder to hand and hip to toe. More thick rivers of black peeking from their armpits to wander along the ribs. And Tits, the first *click*, her stomach had started to swell, the skin turning a gentle shade of green.

"Fuck, man, you see that?" Brody said with a laugh.

He smiled. "I wonder what it'd be like to screw that?"

"Oh snap, dude." Brody moved closer, his eyes on Tits. "For real?"

"Yeah, for real. Like, would it be like a balloon or something? Would the stomach deflate when I pulled out?"

"Would your dick come out green?" His friend squatted next to Tits.

He laughed, ignoring the desire buzzing in his hips. "Good one."

The dead waited near coils of rope and jumbo-size silk laundry bags. Soon their elbows would be drawn in, knees drawn up. Heads tucked to chests. The whole package wrapped and tied tight.

He knelt next to Tits. A skinny girl with honey-blonde hair, her body small and light and completely forgettable, the two awkward melons jutting from her chest at odds with her thin arms, miniscule waist and xylophone-like ribs.

"It was supposed to give me confidence," she'd said as she sat on his couch three months ago, her shirt

EIDOLON AVENUE—APARTMENT 1C

laying next to her, her bra on top of that, her arms crossed over her new acquisitions. "But they just feel weird. And wrong."

"You're beautiful." He'd convinced her he was a medical student, an easy lie to tell. And she believed him, her worry about the small red scars tucked beneath her breasts overriding her nerves as buttons were unbuttoned and fabric was pulled free and fingers fumbled with the hook of a bargain basement bra.

He slowly reached up, his hands taking her arms away, his fingers caressing the silicone swollen skin and delicate slashes of crimson as the blush rose in her cheeks. "Everything about you, it's beautiful."

"You think so?" She looked at him, her eyes welling with tears.

He nodded. "Uh huh." And then he moved close to kiss her cheek, the monster living inside him snapping and snarling at its chain, desperate to be coarse and cruel.

Soon, he'd promised.

"It's getting late," he said, shaking off the memory as he stood over the bodies. "Sun will be going down soon."

Now he grabbed the long-dead Tits by the ankles and dragged her away from the others. Unlike them, she was naked, her flesh so pale it'd turned a darker blue, save for the green of the stomach and the patches of purple near the armpits and clouding the feet. He tested her arm. It was stiff and cold, but still moved. "Fucked up, man."

"Not our problem, dip shit," Brody said as he walked to the window.

"Fuck it," he said. "And fuck you, man. Whatever. I can snap the elbows and break the knees. Pop the hips out of their sockets. Everything will bend. It'll be fine."

He dropped the corpse, Tits' head hitting the floor with a sharp knock. "Fucking cock tease." He knelt next to her. "And dad would have let her go. Been polite. Sat there with a hard-on and apologized while the bitch led him on, shit all over him and then just walked away."

"For real?" Brody said.

"Yeah, for real. But she forgot who she was fucking with. Thought I was, I don't know, weak or something." He stood and looked down at her. "It would have been easier if she'd just stayed."

"Was she even anybody, man?" Brody said as he crossed his thick arms over his massive chest.

"Naw. She was a nothing."

"I'm gonna hit it, man." Brody said, standing, his hand gripping his crotch.

"Fuck you. It's not yours. It's mine."

Brody sat. "What-the-fuck-ever, man. Like you said, bitch was nothing anyway. Just like you," he then said, his eyes on him, a small grin on his lips.

⁂

He'd first seen Tits in the park. Far from the crowds in a quiet alcove shaded by trees, she'd sat with a book on her lap. He'd just left behind Giggles, a girl with wide hips, small eyes and a clumsy mop of black hair. The first time they met, day before yesterday, she was sweet. An easy smile. A tendency to blush when he winked at her. His taking her hand resulting in a fit of giggling.

EIDOLON AVENUE—APARTMENT 1C

So, Giggles it was.

But unlike that first day, this time she sat too close. Leaned in too quick. There was a whiff of desperation, of blatant need. When he went to hold her hand, she placed her palm on his upper thigh, without his invitation, her fingers inching way too close to his dick, and, with a breathy "Oooo, such big muscles," had squeezed.

And like that, he was done. Stood. Walked away without a word, content Giggles would be left confused and hurt. Would be heartbroken and unwilling to trust the next guy who gave her the time of day. Would be emotionally scarred and riddled with doubt for years. Would be eating her emotions within the hour.

Served her right. He didn't like them too easy.

He was in charge. Always.

New girl. Fresh beginning. The blonde with the fake tits sitting out of sight and alone, her nose in a book. He approached and asked if he could share her bench.

"Yes," she said, her finger bookmarking her space. She glanced around.

"I'm not bothering you, am I?" He sat forward, ready to leave.

"No, no, not at all." The book opened and then closed, and opened again. Her legs crossed and uncrossed. "It's just . . ."

"What?" He smiled. One of those full-bore turn on the charm-type of deals that always made hearts flutter and panties drop.

"I mean, you know, you're you—I mean, I know who you are, of course—and, I don't know . . ." The book set aside, she folded her arms over her ample chest and then took them away, her hands landing in her lap where the fingers laced, the knuckles turning white. "And so I'm, like: Why would he want to sit here?" A weak smile.

"It's just sitting." A kinder, gentler smile this time. "We're not getting married or anything." A small laugh. "You haven't even kissed me yet!" A sly wink.

She laughed. "I'm sorry. I just don't . . . I'm not . . . Oh geez."

He heard her take a deep breath as she looked to the fountain and then to the great stone arch in the distance. The students milling about in the last of the summer sun. A couple sitting on a far bench, his arm around her, her head resting on his shoulder. The lithe blonde in the sundress strolling in the distance, her eyes catching theirs for the smallest of seconds before looking away with the smallest of grins. "I'm not like you, Mr. Colton Carryage," she finally said, her voice quiet.

"I know. I've seen you. I've watched you." The lie being said, he shifted, facing her, his knees now pointing toward hers. "And that's why I'm talking to you now. You seem unlike anyone I know. That's why I'm intrigued. Why I want to learn more about you." He paused the eyes looking up at her, shy and vulnerable, the lips lifting in a light, embarrassed grin. "If you'll let me."

She smiled. "Of course. I'm sorry. I'm just . . . Ugh, whatever. Please, just ignore me, or something." An embarrassed laugh.

Another full-bore smile from him.

They spent the next hour talking. About school. Classes. Teachers and tests. Her dorm. His small first floor apartment a block away on Eidolon.

EIDOLON AVENUE—APARTMENT 1C

"I'm happy your dad got out," she said before offering an embarrassed shrug. "I mean, I try not to pay too much attention to it, but, still, for what it's worth, I'm glad everything's okay, I guess."

He sat back, his long arms spanning the length of the bench as he stretched out. His fingers sat close, almost too close, to her shoulder, her soft hair, the back of her neck. "Well, you seem to be the only one to feel that way."

"People can be cruel." She leaned forward. He moved his fingers back, the tips caressing wood instead of skin. "I wouldn't pay any attention to what they're saying online or anything," she said. "I mean, I refuse to believe someone can just buy their way out of Federal prison, right?"

"I wasn't even aware they were talking about it online." He turned to her. "Do I *want* to know what they're saying?"

She chewed her bottom lip, her hand flying to her book, and then to the hem of her thin cardigan, and back to the book again. Finally, she shrugged.

"Ah, I thought not." He gave a light laugh.

"So," she said, "it must be a lot different coming here. I mean, we're not exactly Ivy League."

"The people here are better." His fingers moved from the bench, the tips finding her and picking an imaginary piece of lint off her shoulder. "Sorry. Lint." A small smile, his hand returning to the bench. "Anyway, I'm happier here."

"Why'd you leave?" She turned to him. Her legs crossed and then uncrossed, her hands first in her lap and then rubbing her arms. "We could never figure that out."

"We?" He offered a tight-lipped grin.

"Oh, my friends and me." Her arms folded over her chest. "No biggie."

"You seem uncomfortable."

"I'm sorry." She uncrossed her arms, her hands once again in her lap. "It's not you."

A dramatic sigh of relief. "Oh thank god." A smile. "Had me worried there for a sec." A brief pause. "Want to talk about it?"

She shook her head. "No, I can't."

"Of course you can." A slight furrowing of the brow. "Maybe I can help." A small playful pout. "Please?"

"You're here studying to be a doctor, right?"

"Right," he said, wondering where in the hell she got that idea. "Have one year left and then, you know, probably some more after that." Another small grin.

"I can only imagine."

"Yeah, I know, right?" A shake of the head. "So, you know, we doctors, or doctors in training, in this case, we're pretty good at keeping secrets."

"Oh, I don't know . . . "

"Doctor/patient confidentiality and all that stuff." A wink. "C'mon. I'm all ears."

She paused. "Okay."

He leaned forward, his hand dangerously close to hers.

She stared at his hand near hers. He could see the tears begin to well in her eyes. "It's these," she said with a glance to her chest.

"Your—?" He indicated her obviously fake breasts. For someone with her small frame and delicate limbs, the two swollen melons jutting from her chest were a jarring sight. A look that belonged on someone much more daring than the little mouse tucked in the shade of a great tree, a serious tome balanced on her knees.

She nodded and then sighed.

"What about them?" He inched his hand closer.

"They're not me." Her eyes closed and she shook her head. "I hate them. And they hurt. Like, all the time. It's hard to close my arms or run or, I don't know. I just don't feel like *me* anymore."

"Why, then?" He moved closer, their knees touching, his hands not yet holding hers. "Why'd you get them?"

"Mom and Dad thought it'd be a good graduation present." She shrugged. "Thought it'd give me a lift in life, so to speak. Help me find a great husband or a great job or have a great career or something. I don't know." She turned away, her eyes once again on the students, the arch, the trees. "They always said I was too shy. That I read too much. Never had a boyfriend, or whatever."

Perfect, he thought. There would be curiosity. The rush of her body discovering passion, need. The excitement of his touch. The predictable fear of something new as she opened to him and readied herself for that first stab of gentle pain. There'd be hunger and need and want. Even love. Maybe first love.

Perhaps even surprise and bliss followed by regret and shame when I leave without a word? Just like with Giggles?

Ha! Didn't get better than that.

"And you said they hurt?" Trying not to smile, he leaned a little closer. "How?"

"The scars, they're not fading, and sometimes they kinda sting or itch or something."

Jackpot.

"Have they been looked at?" He leaned closer still, his eyes looking into hers. "You should have someone look at them just to be sure everything's okay."

She shook her head. "No way. Because A: I can't afford a doctor on my own, and B: if I went to our usual doctor, my parents would find out and that would *so* not be a good thing, if you know what I mean. It's like they think I'm some ungrateful little something-or-other *already*, so, like, you know, to *complain* about these? Ugh. I can't imagine the shit fit they'd have."

"I know what you mean." A rueful grin. "So, listen, I could take a look, if you want. Scars are scars, regardless where they are, and you can usually tell from the smallest of peeks whether or not something needs attention. A peek in the most professional of ways, of course." A sudden laugh. "You know what? No. I'm sorry. That's just . . . that's a dumb idea. Forget it. What was I thinking?" More laughter. "You must think I'm some pervert now. I wasn't thinking. Forget it. We'll, uh, we'll find you a doctor. Someone affordable."

"No, no, no." She'd turned to him. "As a professional, or an almost-professional, you'd do that for me?"

"I don't know. It sounded good in my head and my first inclination is always to help, you know. I try to be a nice guy. It's how I was raised and it's just who I am."

"Of course—"

"But wouldn't it be weird me seeing you . . . you know, so intimately so soon?"

"Maybe." Her fingers gripped the edge of her book. "But it'd be just a peek, right?" Her eyes found his.

EIDOLON AVENUE—APARTMENT 1C

"That's all it'd have to be, generally speaking." He looked away. "Strictly professional. All about the scars. Their color. Are they raised? Blistered? Are there signs of metacarxolottalatedsipsis?"

"Metacarxolottalata-what?" Her eyes grew wide. "That sounds horrible."

"Oh yeah." A serious look for the made up word he'd already forgotten. "Nasty stuff. Too complicated to explain, of course, but *definitely* needs a trained eye to spot." A look away. "Anyway, it was a dumb idea. I was just trying to help. We'll figure something else out."

"Okay."

"You know, I might know someone. A girl in one of my classes. Really nice. Maybe she could talk with you and perhaps—"

"No, you." She stood, her book clutched to her chest. "Let's do it. I mean, this has been bugging me and it hurts, like, right now and, heck, you're right here and you're free, so . . . let's just do it." She bent to lift her canvas bag from the ground. "Okay?"

He stood, moving close to her. "You sure?"

She nodded and then turned to walk away. "My dorm room is this way."

"My place is this way, over on Eidolon. More private, I think." He took her hand, the two of them leaving the anonymity of the shade. "Don't worry. It'll be quick."

<hr />

"She was the first." He traced his finger over the web of red stealing from beneath Tits' armpit.

"Liar." Brody still sat at the window, arms crossed, eyes narrowed.

"The first here on Eidolon, I mean."

"You were too quick, amateur," his bro said.

"Yeah, I know." The *click* had happened too fast, his impatience stealing the joy of the experience. Her bra barely fastened before his hands were on her neck and her fists were gripping his wrists and the blubbering began as the tears fell while confusion fought fear, fear turned to realization, realization turned to terror, and terror tried to scream before he snapped her quiet with a *click*.

And then, moving quick, he'd dragged her off the couch, her broken neck cracking against the wood as she landed on the floor. Her skirt lifted, her cotton panties dragged down and wrestled from her ankles and, his dick out, he was on top, moving inside her. She was still warm. Still smelled alive. Still yielded to the weight of him. The thought that somewhere her spirit stood watching, confused and filled with regret for a life unfinished, for a trust betrayed, excited him even more.

This is what worked for him. With her quiet and still, he could do what he wanted. It could be too fast and finish too sudden and she'd show no disappointment or judgment. There would be no laughter. No loose lips sinking ships as she ran home to whisper to her friends. He could be cruel and she wouldn't wince or cringe or beg him to be gentle or go slower. No quiet "ow" to kill the mood.

He could move her any way he wanted, bend her this way and that, slap and punch and, driven by passion, rip her hair out, if he wanted, and she'd never complain. Bite her flesh and hear nothing but silence. Lick the tears still staining her eyes and feel no reproach. Use her again and again and again and never hear "no."

The first time with these anonymous playthings was always quick. Staying in them, staying on them, he could finish, rest, and then move slow, finding his excitement again and build to a second time before things became unpleasant.

"You know she's gonna shit and piss, right, bro?" Brody lingered, his eyes on Tits on the floor, her arms to the side, legs spread, her body dead. "And her skin's gonna turn grey and get tight and shrink."

"I know."

"Her lungs will, like, breathe out some noxious shit, man."

"Yeah."

"It's gonna make you blow chunks, bro."

"Dude, stop."

"And her eyes are gonna go into the sockets or something."

"Yeah, yeah, yeah. And she's also going to blister and swell and her skin's going to tear and turn blue and red and purple and black, man. I know, so just chill, 'k?"

"Fuck that, man." Brody walked to the door. "You gotta stick her with the ice cream. Or the meat."

"I'm on it."

Brody walked to the door and stopped "We need a walk-in, like back at school." Leaning back, he crossed his arms. "Remember that, bro?"

He did.

"What do you need with something like this?" the delivery man had asked as he'd plunked the jumbo-size, industrial strength deep freezer in the middle of his bedroom weeks ago.

"I'm studying to be a chef," he lied, Tits sitting seven steps away in the closet, tied tight and bundled in a laundry bag, three days after the *click*. "Have to buy meat in bulk. For class. Save more money that way. Ran out of room in the other fridge."

"Yeah, yeah." The handsome man in the blue work shirt nodded, his eyes trying not to linger on the hunky frat boy in front of him. "Those freezers with the fridge, they ain't big enough, are they?"

"Not for what I'm doing." A flirtatious grin as he'd shaken the man's hand, the small smile soon a full-bore assault of white teeth as he gripped the man's hand a moment longer than necessary.

The delivery man ushered out the door, a business card with the besotted stranger's cell scrawled on the back slipped in Colton's pocket, and Tits shoved to the bottom of his new toy, he turned it on, listening for the familiar pings and knocks and whirs as it revved up, breathing clouds of frost. "This is fine. It'll work."

"Always has," Brody said with a shrug.

And it did this time, too. Well enough for him to retrieve her at night and lie with her, his fingers caressing her thawing flesh as he kissed the white of her lips.

Then, when her hips could bend and open, he'd take her. The silent body offering no complaint, no hesitation. A willing receptacle bearing the brunt of his rage while accepting the darkest of his desires.

"Notch in the belt, son." Brody said, stifling a yawn.

A month later the frozen flesh had started to tighten, the nails were coming loose, the eyes had

EIDOLON AVENUE—APARTMENT 1C

shriveled and sunk, and the barest hint of marbling appeared from her armpits and around her neck.

"Fuck, I told you, man." Another shrug from his bro.

His plaything had become unpleasant.

"Ditch her, dude." Brody's eyes met his.

The next day, he'd met Teeth.

"Sweet," said his friend with a grin.

○○○

Unnecessary lay sprawled on the kitchen floor.

She must have fallen at some point, he thought, landing with her arms reaching, her feet under the chair, her dress shifting and now thankfully providing her more modest coverage than before.

He paced the small kitchen, bottled water in hand, the bending and popping and snapping of Tits as he'd forced her into that damn laundry bag exhausting and tedious. But moving full bags of laundry to his SUV at the end of the day was a lot less noticeable than dragging three bodies along the sidewalk and tossing them into the back.

"These bags are kinda genius, dude." Brody said from the bedroom.

He chuckled and looked at Unnecessary.

Her face was tilted to the side. The broken bone in her neck pushed against the flesh, wounding it three shades of red in an island of dark blue. At a certain angle, it looked like she'd tried to crawl along the floor. Her fingers digging into the boards, her feet pushing against the wood. He considered kneeling next to her, perhaps feeling the soft skin on the back of her leg, but thought of the two bodies left to pack and the sweat already staining his brow and dripping down his neck.

Maybe I should pick her up and put her in the chair, he thought as he walked to the bedroom.

"Fuck her, man," bro called out.

Yeah, he needed to focus. Teeth and Freckles. Or Freckles and Teeth.

Although he'd met Teeth first, Freckles had been the next *click*.

And he needed to do this in order. Besides, he wasn't ready to touch Teeth yet.

She, like Unnecessary, had been different than the others.

Two months ago, they'd met. The weather had turned, the summer sun replaced by the crisp bite of Fall. Clouds hanging low in what was once a blue sky. The park empty save for those few souls who preferred the cold sting of rain to the warm comfort of overpriced lattes in a cafe.

Which, debit card in hand, is what he opted for.

Small and meek, she'd stood at the counter, clutching a steaming mug, scanning the room for an empty seat. He'd caught her eye. Smiled. Indicated the free chair opposite him.

A smile in return, her lips parting to reveal teeth that were too white, too flat and too big for her mouth.

Yep, he thought. Already got a name for this one.

She came over to sit.

"Thank you." She introduced herself, but to him, she was already Teeth.

"No problem." His smile in return not yet full-bore, but close.

She looked away, the cup brought to her lips for a sip. "I've seen you around." The cup back on the table.

He leaned forward, struggling to remember if he

EIDOLON AVENUE—APARTMENT 1C

saw her before. He didn't think he had. "Why didn't you say hi?"

"Because you were untouchable. Part of the cool, better-than-everyone-else crowd. No one but your douche bag bros—you know, Clay Fitzsimmons, Trent Whitehall, Brody Howard-Meister *the Third*, thank-you-very-much—could get anywhere near you back at your old school. Them and all those other upper class crème de la crème tight ass high and mighty bourgeois arrogant insufferable bitches and pricks."

He laughed. "Ah, so you went to—"

A nod from her. "Left right before you did."

He glanced around the crowded cafe, the doubts about his decision to consider targeting her growing as the conversations rose and fell, laughter here, silence there. Too many eyes, he decided. "Nevertheless, it was nice to meet you." He belted back the next to last swallow. "I really should—"

"I admire your courage," she suddenly said.

"My what?" The cup returned to the table.

"To go through what you've gone through, the embarrassment, the shame, the utter hatred, and still come out in public, go to school, try and have a life, it's impressive." Her eyes watched him. "I don't know if I could do it."

"I try not to pay attention."

"How could you not?" A small, quick laugh. "On every front page. On every blog and website. Trending on Facebook and Twitter. Seriously, you'd have to live in a cave or something to not know how much you guys are hated. Your dad landing that Presidential pardon, benefits restored, pension, restitution?"

"My dad's not who everyone thinks he is." He

paused. Gathered his thoughts. "He's a nice guy. Too nice, I think. He just doesn't *think* sometimes, you know? And he gets trapped and then tries to make things right."

"Right." She took a sip of her coffee. "So he's innocent? Especially after what he did? With all that evidence?"

"There's more to it than people know."

"Please." She leaned back, her coffee in hand. "Anyway, all I'm saying is the fact that you're still standing and working to have a life. Like I said, I'm impressed. Really." She lifted her cup in a toast then took a sip.

"You find all of that impressive?"

She shook her head. "No, I find you carrying the burden of your father's sins impressive. Making yourself an easy target simply by being alive and trying to accomplish something. *That* I find impressive. What he did?" Her arms crossed, her elbows on the table. "That's disgusting and illegal and, because he's a Senator—or at least *was* a Senator—completely predictable."

"Again, it's more complicated than people think. And it wasn't his fault. Truth be told . . . " He took a deep breath. "It's a parental thing, I guess. And that's all I can say." He shrugged and belted back his last swallow.

She smiled. "I'm sorry. Give me a soapbox . . . " A shrug.

"You know, he might be innocent."

"And you could be a blushing Boy Scout who still hasn't popped his cherry." Her eyes caught his. She was teasing him, challenging him.

EIDOLON AVENUE—APARTMENT 1C

"Have dinner with me." He returned her stare. Teased her. Challenged her.

"Why?" She held his gaze.

"Because as strong as someone is, he still needs a friend now and then, wouldn't you say?"

"Yeah, that must've hurt. Your bros suddenly forgetting you were alive. Clay? Trent?" She glanced around the room and then looked back at him. "Must have been brutal how they dropped you like a bad habit. As if you'd never existed. That must've sucked. Seriously." Her gaze held him. "I'm sorry. Really."

He broke the stare, his eyes returning to his fingers circling the empty cup.

There was a long moment of silence. The memory of his friends' betrayal hanging in the air. The wound of that still bleeding and raw, ripped open and weeping.

"No. Not dinner." She offered him an easy grin. "What I will do, though, if you want, is give you my cell and, I don't know, maybe meet you here again. And we can talk some more. Or walk around the park or something when the weather clears. But dinner? Not yet."

"Not yet?" He tried a smile, but, damnit, this sudden pain was too real. It came off more like a grimace.

"It's too much like a date, Mr. Carryage." Her hands gripped her cup. "And, let's face it, I'm not anything like the supermodels, cheerleaders, beauty queen society bitches or whatever the hell you usually go out with."

"You're saying it's a no, but also a not yet." Catching her eye, he moved closer to a full-bore smile, driven to change her No into a Yes. "So there's hope."

She nodded. "But not right now. Not today." Reaching low, she brought her oversize purse to her lap, her hand disappearing to rummage before emerging with her cell and a textbook. "I have studying to do." A moment later, her eyes found his as she waited, ready to give him her number, her cell phone in hand. "Keep your eye out for me. We'll run into each other. I'm sure of it."

For the next week, all he could think of was Teeth. Tits lay ignored in the deep freeze. The work of lifting her out, letting her thaw, wrapping her up, elbows snapping, knees popping, and driving her to the pit he'd dug deep in the woods an hour out of town seemed like too much to do. All he wanted was to meet for coffee with Teeth, talk with Teeth, listen to Teeth, discover who Teeth was.

He kind of wanted to date Teeth.

And then end it with a *click*, of course.

"That's what Teeth told me," he said, pacing, his arms crossed, his hands gripping his elbows. "That's what she said . . . fucking bitch."

"I hear ya, man." Brody, back to the window, dragged deep on another joint.

"But she was right, though. Clay, Trent, man, fucking punk-ass, piece of shit pussies. Put you to shame, my man."

"Bro—"

"Seriously! It *was* brutal." He could hear his voice rising. He stopped. Took a breath.

Exhaling a cloud of blue smoke, his bro leaned his head back, the lit joint in his fingers ignored as he closed his eyes.

"Whatever," Colton said, looking away. "I'm over it."

EIDOLON AVENUE—APARTMENT 1C

So, he reached out to Teeth again and again. And nothing.

For a week, his texts went ignored, his emails getting no response. For a week, she kept him waiting and hoping on the verge of frustrated anger. For a week, he'd swing by the cafe several times a day and glance in, hoping to catch sight of her.

For a week, she was nowhere to be found.

The rain continued, the clouds refusing to part.

"Bitch's dropped you like a Taco Bell baby, bro," Brody said with a chuckle.

He grew angrier, stalking his apartment like a caged animal.

"I'm gonna fuck her up, man."

"Do it."

"She thinks she's gonna fuck with Colton fuckin' Carryage?"

"Hell no."

"It's gonna be rough and mean and cruel. She's going to suffer."

"Fuck yeah."

"And you know what? She's gonna *know* she's gonna die."

"That's dope."

"Serves her right for making me wait, making me . . . I don't know, man."

Silent, Brody stood in front of him.

"You hear me, Brody?" he said. "She'll be alive and know what's happening. She'll feel every single fucking thing I do to her. And it's gonna fuckin' hurt, man. Like hell. And you know what, bro?"

"Shoot."

"She won't be able to do a damn thing to stop it."

"Sweet," Brody said with a laugh.

It'll be perfect, he thought later as he cut through the park, the rain pelting his head and bouncing off his coat. He couldn't wait.

And turning the corner, he discovered Freckles.

"I'm Mrs. Butterworth," she'd said from beneath a green frog umbrella. Her speech was stilted, her words careful, her thoughts slow. The sound of thick congestion stuck in her throat and bubbled through her nose with each breath.

He'd stopped. They were alone. She was young with brown hair that fell down her back, thick glasses, skin covered in dark freckles, and her chunky body and wide hips stuffed into a bright red raincoat. "What do you mean?" He took a step toward her.

She stepped back. "I'm waiting. I'm not supposed to talk to strangers." Another step back, her pink mittens clutching the green handle of her umbrella.

"You're not going to tell me why you're called 'Mrs. Butterworth?'" He took another small step her way.

"I know who you are, Mister." She sniffled. "I saw you on a magazine once."

"On a magazine?" Another step closer. "Or in?"

"You look like a prince." She brought the umbrella down over her face.

"And you look like a frog." He smiled and took another step toward her.

From beneath the green plastic, she giggled. "In. It was in."

"In what?"

"The magazine! In. On a page." She lifted the

EIDOLON AVENUE—APARTMENT 1C

umbrella, her eyes finding his. "There were words. I didn't read them." A loud sniffle, the snot bubbling in her nose as she breathed in. "I have a cold."

"I'm sorry." A small pout, his brow furrowing for a brief second. "So you know my name?"

A nod from her. She glanced up at her umbrella.

His eyes followed hers. "I like it." He gave her a small grin. "It's cool."

"It's because I'm slow. I talk slow. My head is slow. Like the syrup. That you put on pancakes. With butter. But not too much 'cause you'll get a tummy ache. And be *sick*." She twirled, swinging her hips, and then took a step toward him. "Mrs. Butterworth. *See?*"

"Very clever."

She grew silent for a moment. "I'm waiting. In the *rain*. My tutor, he's late. He's *always* late." She took a big step back.

"You go to school here?"

She shook her head. "One class. A special class." Looking to the side, she stopped. "I'm not supposed to talk to strangers." The umbrella dropped low again.

"But you know me."

She raised the umbrella a bit, peering out from beneath it.

"You said yourself that you saw me in a magazine." He smiled.

"On a magazine. I said on. Not *in*." She cleared her throat. "I shouldn't say what the words said."

"In the magazine." He shoved his hands in his pockets.

"You're bad. That's what the words said. What he *told* me they said."

"Who?"

"My tutor." A step back. "He said you were cute." She glanced to the street, the sidewalk. "He's late."

"Do I look bad?" A step toward her.

"You look like a prince. From a book." A pause, the umbrella covering her face again. Through the green plastic and large googly frog eyes, he could see her chewing her lip.

"What'd he say, your tutor?"

"That you killed a girl. But your dad was the king with a ton of money he *stole* so you never got in trouble and that girl's family still cries because they miss their princess."

"Wow—"

"And *that's* why you had to leave the fancy school and *that's* why you're here and *that's* why he went to jail because he *forced* people to give him money in *secret* and *paid* everybody to SHUT UP and let you go."

"That's not entirely true." The rain fell harder, pinging off the cheap plastic of the green frog and running down the back of his neck. "Can I see your umbrella?" He moved toward her.

"It's a frog." She lifted it a little higher, her head turning up to see it.

He moved quick, snatching it from her.

"No!" She put her hands over her head. "It's mine! I'm getting wet! Give it back! It's not yours, it's mine!" Her face turning red, she started to cry. "Give it back."

The umbrella over his head, he turned toward Eidolon. "Come and get it."

She stumbled after him, the sound of her red rain boots heavy on the concrete. "I. Said. Give. It. Back. NOW!" She lunged for him.

EIDOLON AVENUE—APARTMENT 1C

"I will," he said, dodging out of reach. "All you have to do is follow me and you get it, okay?"

"No! It's not okay!" She'd stopped. Her face was still red and running with rain, her arms at her sides, her hands balled into angry fists. "It's mine. I'm getting WET!"

The umbrella over his head, he skipped down Eidolon. She followed, her hands once again over her head, her steps lumbering and slow, her breathing heavy. Onto the curb, past the corner store and the snapping, flickering neon of the local dive, they approached his building.

She stopped. He crossed the street and turned, waiting at the front door.

"C'mon," he shouted to her across the street. He opened the door and held the umbrella out to her. "You can have it back now."

Her eyes watched the building. "What is that?" She fought to catch her breath.

He twirled the green frog. "He misses you." He smiled. "Come in. You're getting wet. I have cocoa. Hot cocoa. With marshmallows."

She ignored him. "That thing, there." She pointed toward the top of the building. "It's too dark. I've never seen that. I don't like it. It's . . . wrong."

"What?" He stepped onto the sidewalk and looked up. There was nothing but low clouds in the sky, wet brick, dirty windows, and rain hitting his face. "There's nothing there, Freckles. C'mon." He crossed the street. "You hear me? I have hot cocoa with marshmallows inside." He grabbed her hand. "Let's go."

He dragged her behind him, her eyes never leaving the building as her heels dug into the concrete. "No.

Who are all these people? I can't, I can't, don't make me, I can't," she said as she fought.

He stopped.

Under the awning outside the corner store, she stood. The blonde in the sun dress. She stared forward, down the street, and then turned, her eyes not on him, but on the building, the windows, the top where the rain hit the roof.

It made his skin crawl.

Moving quickly, he pushed Freckles into the empty hall, slamming the door behind them. "No, it's too crowded." She wrestled away from him. "There are too many people. I don't like it. Let me go." She scrambled back to the door. "It's going to eat me. I hear it. It's breathing."

"There's no one here." He grabbed her around the waist and lifted her to the stairs. "You're coming in."

She suddenly gasped and grew tense, her arms reaching to the walls, her legs stretching out in front, her neck bending back to rest on his shoulder as her jaw clenched. "Oh my god," she whispered. "I'm sorry." And then she grew limp.

So, step by step, he carried her up to his apartment. Setting her down in the hall while he fished the keys out of his pocket, she leaned against the wall, quiet and still, her breathing shallow, her eyes fixed to the ceiling above.

He hip checked the door open and, taking her hand, led her into the apartment.

She stood, her eyes above him, to the walls, the ceiling, as he unbuttoned her rain coat and dragged it away from her shoulders. "Who are they?" she said.

"Huh?" He threw her coat in the hall. "Who? That's just Brody. Relax."

EIDOLON AVENUE—APARTMENT 1C

"Who?"

"Brody. Brody!" He watched her. "My bud Brody. He's cool. That is who you're talking about, right?"

"Fuck, dude, you tapping the bottom of the gene pool now?" Brody said with a laugh from the bedroom door.

"Shut up!" he said.

"What?" Freckles pushed back against the wall. "I'm confused. Who's—"

"Ignore him." He pulled closer. "He's nobody."

She shook her head. "No, there's a lot of . . . I don't know." Her breath grew ragged. "There's more than one. I don't like them. Their eyes, they're dark. Like people, but not people. And their fingers are like scary claws. And the *smell*, they smell, it's—" Her cheeks blushed as she fought for breath, her chest rising and falling in quick jerks. "I don't . . . I don't like it."

"I'm telling you, man," Brody said. "She's fucking loony tunes."

"Hey, hey, hey," he said, ignoring Brody. He cradled her face in his hands. "Relax. You're okay. We're just getting out of the rain for a minute, alright?"

"I can smell that *thing*. Can't you smell that thing?" Her eyes rolled back in her head as her chin titled up. "Oh my god, Mom, Mom? Help! This is wrong, wrong, wrong, wrong—"

"Yo!" He gripped her face tighter. "Hey! What's wrong?" He gave her a quick, violent shake. "Freak! Yo! Answer me!"

"It won't . . . stop . . . *breathing*." She screwed her eyes shut and started to cry.

"That's you." She shook her head. "You're the one breathing, okay?" He stopped her. "You need to settle down. You're fine." He lifted the umbrella. "You want this back? Here you go. See? I promised. Take it."

She opened her eyes, her cheeks stained with tears. She ignored the umbrella.

"You can't leave." She sniffled. "It won't let you."

"You said I looked like a prince, remember? Remember that?" He forced a smile. "Wanna kiss a prince?"

She shook her head. "I want to leave."

"Aw, c'mon." He moved closer, pressing his body against hers. "Just one kiss? When have you ever gotten to kiss a prince? One time shot, right here." A smile. "Yeah?"

Another shake of the head, this one slower, more careful, her eyes on him. She started to cry again, her nose leaking thick streams of snot, her shoulders rising as she hiccupped and sobbed.

"Shhh, shhh, shhh." He traced a tear with his thumb, rubbing it into her cheek. "Relax. It's okay. I'm not going to hurt you."

She caught her breath, her tear-filled eyes watching him. "You lie."

⁂

Taking a break from the impossible act of stuffing fat dead Freckles in the laundry bag, Colton headed back to the kitchen for another swig of water.

"You gonna cut her down, man?" Brody called out from the bedroom. "Slice the blubber off her ass?"

"Do you *not* see the packing boxes, shit head?" The knife was a good idea, but every damn thing he owned was balled up in bubble wrap, crammed in a box and taped up tight. "Can't get to shit, man. Besides, I don't have time."

EIDOLON AVENUE—APARTMENT 1C

"Riiiiiiight. They're throwing your broke ass out, ain't that right, loser?"

"Fuck you." He opened the fridge and, the cap unscrewed and the bottle to his lips, turned to find Unnecessary in the chair in the living room.

Outside, the heavens opened with a flash of lightning and a thunderous crack, the rain smacking the window with a sudden ferocity.

Unnecessary sat with her legs open, the sundress wrinkled around her hips, her hands dangling at her sides. "That's right. I moved her to the chair earlier. She'd fallen." He stopped, searching for the memory of gathering her from the floor and lifting her and placing her there, in the chair. "That's right, right, man?"

No response from the bedroom.

He looked at her. Her head had snapped to the side, the jagged edge of the broken bone threatening to poke through the flesh. A trickle of blood, a thin faint pink, had seeped through to wander down her shoulder and onto her chest.

"I gotta move her in with the others."

Still no response.

"I almost don't want to move her." He came near. His hand reached out to stroke her face, the fingers moving lower, tracing the lips, the chin, the neck, and lower still, to slip beneath the thin cotton and lay flat against the gentle slope of her breast.

He caressed a large nipple. "Yo, Brody! You see these, man? Fuckin' weird nips. Huge monster big and shit. Like the buttons on one of my old cashmere coats or something. They're freaky."

His bro refused to answer. Fucker probably dialing his plug for more weed or something.

He closed his eyes, thinking how the sight of those large nips had made his throat tighten and his stomach clench. He released the flat nub of flesh, his palm rubbing the skin instead. If he didn't have the disastrous mess that was Freckles and the lingering disappointment that was Teeth to attend to, he'd lay Unnecessary flat, shove a pillow under her ass, force her hips open and take her again.

He felt a stirring. A longing for release, for attention. I could take her quickly, he thought. Before she's too cold and her body sighs clouds of disgusting gas and her skin pulls tight and grey.

Lightning flashed and another deep rumble of thunder rolled through the sky to shake the room.

He glanced toward the window. The rain was falling so thick he couldn't see outside; his view a distorted waterfall rushing over the pane. The reality of what waited beyond hidden by this sudden, almost violent torrent of brief chaos.

I need to focus, he thought. Freckles and Teeth waited.

He turned back and took his hand away. Unnecessary's head had swiveled while he was looking away, her eyes finding him. Cold and dead and lifeless, they stared, unblinking. He smiled, wondering what she saw. Was it dark? Was it empty? Was her spirit trapped somewhere, standing near, enraged and resentful?

"I hope so, you stupid bitch." He paused. "What is it with me and these stupid bitches, man?" He turned, looking for Brody.

Right. Dude was scoring a blunt.

Asshole.

EIDOLON AVENUE—APARTMENT 1C

"What-the-fuck-ever," he said as he turned to grab the baseball bat from the corner. "I got work to do." And, swinging it over his shoulder, he walked to the bedroom.

Unnecessary's head swiveled to follow him.

◆

"Two hours, Freckles." Still too frozen to move, the corpse of Freckles laid on the floor.

Weeks ago, she'd died.

Reaching down, he spread her legs apart. He slammed the bat down on the dead girl's knee. It broke with a crack.

"You're hurting me!" she'd screamed weeks ago as he pulled her from the door and thrown her on the ground.

"Had I waited just two hours . . . " He paused, kneeling down to move the shattered joint, forcing it into a cleaner break that would bend and fold. "None of this would have been necessary." He stood, focusing on the other knee.

Brody sat near the window rolling a joint from his new bag of weed.

"You good, Brody?" he asked as he held the bat.

His friend sparked it up. "I will be, man."

Dead Freckles at his feet, he gripped the bat.

Brody inhaled, holding it in. "This was the slow chick, right?" he said through gritted teeth.

"Where the fuck have you been, man?" he said.

"Short bus doesn't do it for me," he said, exhaling a cloud of blue.

"Fucker." Colton lifted the bat.

Brody put the joint back to his lips. "So, you gonna do this or what?"

"Please don't." She'd tried to crawl away weeks ago, her knees pushing against the floor as he'd grabbed her ankles. *"Stop!"* He'd dragged her back.

The bat bouncing back with a deep thunk, the second knee snapped with a jarring pop.

"Nice!" Brody said with a chuckle.

"Don't," she cried weeks ago as he'd forced her on her back. His hands pawed at her clothes. Fabric ripping. Seams tearing. Buttons popping. *"Stop!"* Her large breasts exposed, she tried to cover them with her hands. *"You're not supposed to . . . I don't want to—"* He punched her quiet, his fist falling one, two, three, four, five times. Her nose had split, blood cascading down her lips, her cheeks, into her mouth.

Crouching next to the body, he tested the second knee. Although broken, it was still stiff, the joint refusing to budge. He stood, the bat lifted high.

"Help." Weeks ago, her hands pushed against her bloodied nose, her palms dripping red. *"I'm bleeding."* She struggled to turn over onto her stomach, her lips smeared crimson. *"I can't breathe."*

"Don't be a pussy, man," his bro said.

The bat fell. The corpse's knee split. He reached down.

"Ow, ow, ow," she'd said as he grabbed her hair and lifted her off the ground. *"Come with me,"* he said. He dragged her into the bedroom, her rain boots stumbling across the floor, and thrown her against the freezer. Her face hit the metal, her front teeth popping loose as she fell to the floor.

Bending and folding, the broken bone moved, the flesh tearing where the shattered knee peeked through.

EIDOLON AVENUE—APARTMENT 1C

"Ow," she said, her hand to her mouth, her palm discovering fresh blood where nuggets of white used to be. She cried again. *"My teeth."*

He grabbed her by the hair and lifted her to her feet. Pushed her against the deep freezer. *"Open it."*

He bent the knees, out and in, out and in. Yeah, nice and easy.

"It gonna fit?" Brody said, looking at the bag.

"Yeah, I think so." He reached up, testing the arm. It moved, the shoulder rotating, the elbow bending. "It'll be fine."

"Still . . ."

"I'm on it," he said.

"Fuck, yeah!" Brody said.

"No." She'd stood in front of the hulking white of the freezer, her clothes torn, her large breasts dangling, her pudgy stomach exposed, her flesh smeared with blood. Her words bubbling and wet with running red, the sound awkward as her tongue discovered the missing teeth. *"Why?"*

Catching his breath, he lifted the bat.

"Just open it," he'd said to her.

"I don't want to." She stepped back. *"What's in there?"*

He reached forward and, working the latch, lifted the lid. *"You tell me."*

"Dumb as shit slow chick," he said. The bat fell.

"A doll?" She glanced in to see the bent, broken body of Tits. *"A really big doll? She's naked. Why is she naked?"*

Missing the shoulder, the bat bounced off the front of Freckle's head with a crack. " 'Why is she naked?'" he said, mocking her.

"Why do you have a nasty doll?" She'd turned away. *"That's weird."*

He grabbed her by the neck. *"Look again."* He forced her to turn back. She screwed her eyes shut. He smacked the back of her head with his hand. *"Open your eyes."*

The shoulder snapped as the bat slammed into it.

"Bottom of the fucking gene pool, my friend," Brody said. He sat, his back to the wall.

He bent over to test it. Yanked the arm up and wrenched it to the side. Easy-peasy. No resistance. Yep, broken. He stepped over the body, his feet on either side, straddling it.

"I mean, c'mon." Brody crossed his ankles, his legs stretched out.

"What do you see?" He gripped her hair in his fist. *"Tell me."*

"It looks like a girl," she said. *"Sleeping. She's sleeping. I don't know."*

"Going for those easy pickings." Brody adjusted his crotch in his jeans and then folded his hands in his lap.

"No, no, you're right." He moved behind her. *"She's a girl. And her eyes are closed."* He still clutched a fistful of her hair. *"What else do you see?"*

He looked down at the body.

Weeks ago, she shook her head. *"No."*

"Tell me." He punched her. She cried again. *"Is she pretty?"* Holding her steady, he reached low to undo his belt buckle.

She hiccupped, her sobs catching in her throat as she gripped his fist, trying to take it out of her hair.

"Is she pretty?" he asked again, his voice dropping to a thick whisper. She shook her head.

EIDOLON AVENUE—APARTMENT 1C

"Seriously, dude, short bus," Brody said with a laugh.

"No. She's not," she'd said as large bubbles of snot ran down her lips and dripped onto her chin. *"She's too white. She's sort of blue. And her boobs don't look right."*

"Really?" He unzipped his zipper and stood behind her, her hair gripped in his fist. *"How? Tell me. How do her boobs look? What's wrong with them?"*

He caught his breath, the dead Freckles waiting between his feet.

Weeks ago, she fought. He clutched her hair tighter. She gasped. *"Ow!"*

"Do you know her?" His pants open, he pressed close behind her, smelling her hair, her neck. Pulled her head back so he could drag his cheek and lips and nose through the blood staining her face. *"Do you?"* She paused, silent. He tightened his grip. *"Are you sure?"*

"I don't know dolls. Dolls aren't real." She inhaled sharply, the snot sucked back into her nose. *"I can't breathe. Ow. That hurts."* Her hand returned to the fist in her hair.

"Is she a doll?" He smiled, his free hand caressing the hardness in his briefs. *"Are you sure she's a doll?"*

Now, on Eidolon, he stood, straddling the dead Freckles,

"Do it—" Brody said.

lifting the bat high—

"Do it—"

and aiming for her second shoulder.

"DO IT—" Brody said, his shout shattering the quiet of the room.

"Ow. Stop." She'd gasped as he snapped her head forward. Her eyes fell on Tits laying in the freezer, naked and pale and wounded. *"What else would she be? This is a freezer. It's dangerous. It's not a toy."*

The bat fell, bouncing off the collar bone with a sharp crack.

"Nice!" His bro clapped his hands.

He lifted it again.

"If the lid closes, you can't breathe, so you shouldn't put people in—" She'd started to move, then, weeks ago. Her feet turning to walk, to flee. Her hands pushing against the freezer, backing away. Her panic growing, she turned and pushed against him. *"Let me go. Let me out. I have to go. My tutor, my mom—"*

He grabbed her and forced her back to face the freezer. *"Do you want to go in there? Huh? Do you?"*

She was hyperventilating by then. Her breath difficult to catch, her fingers pushing the freezer away or wrestling with the fist in her hair or still trying to cover her breasts. *"I want to go home. I want to go—"*

"Look at her. Watch her." His knees forced her legs apart, a sharp blow with the elbow making her arch her back, his pants pushed around his knees as he shoved himself deep while pinning her against the freezer. He ignored her scream and how she stood on her tippy-toes as if moving away from the sudden pain of the unexpected invasion. Ignored how she went silent as she fought for breath while he roughly pounded, skin slapping skin. Had finished quickly, his teeth sinking into the meat of her shoulder as he pushed deep one final time, and held still, the feel of her flesh in his mouth, the fold of her skin in his teeth, the taste of her blood on his tongue.

EIDOLON AVENUE—APARTMENT 1C

He slammed the bat down on the second shoulder.

"You took her, man." His back still against the wall, his friend shrugged.

And then again.

"Owned that fucking bitch." Brody's hand reached low to adjust his crotch again.

And again.

"Just a nobody who meant nothing." A smile on his bro's handsome face.

"Will you be my princess?" he'd said as he hoisted her, still alive and wounded and panicked, into the freezer, her limbs flailing as she awkwardly tumbled with a thump face-first onto Tits. She gulped and gasped, her hands pushing away the dead girl as she scrambled to her knees and tried to turn over. To lift and rise and stand and escape as she found her breath, found her voice and found her scream.

"Shhhhhh, you need to cool down," he said as he dropped the lid with a

click.

⁂

He'd waited until Freckles grew quiet in the freezer. He checked his watch. Ten minutes. Damn. New record, he thought. And then he left, heading to the bathroom to wash Freckle's blood from his hands, his face, his dick.

"She's got an hour or two before the air runs out." He said as he stood in the living room that day, his eyes on the bedroom door. "Maybe I should grab some lunch."

The room was silent.

"Yo, Brody!"

Nothing.

"I'm hungry."

Fucking friend probably already chowing down at Taco King or something.

Asshole.

So, alone, he stayed, watching the hulking white of the freezer. Kneeled and pressed his cheek close to the metal. Listened to the low hum as the cold air cycled in. "You hear that?" he said as a series of clinks and pings and clanks rattled through the walls as the freezer turned on and then off and then on again. "That's so cool. You think she's still alive?"

There was no response.

"She's just cooling off."

Still nothing.

"You think she hyperventilated herself to death?"

Silence.

"I hope she doesn't have a fear of dead people."

Fear of dead people, he thought. Ha! Good one. He laughed thinking of Freckles, battered and bruised and bloodied, huddled up next to Tits.

His phone buzzed, then. A text.

From Teeth.

DINNER? it said.

He stood and opened the door. "Hey." Freckles sat, breathing calmly, her back pushed against the end, far from Tits, her knees angled away, her hands clutching her shins. She was alive and shivering. He gave her a quick shake. She was cold. She looked at him. The tears were still there. "Look." He showed her his phone. "She texted. We have a date."

Leaning against the edge, he hit Reply, and then stopped. "What should I say?"

EIDOLON AVENUE—APARTMENT 1C

"What? Who?" Freckles tried to stand. He put his hands on her shoulders, gently holding her down.

"Hey, wait." He flashed the phone in front of her again. "Hello? I need to reply, here. What should I say? Thoughts?"

She sniffled and started to cry. "To who? I don't—"

"To my girlfriend." He held the phone, the blinking cursor in the reply box annoying him. "Yes? Should I just say 'yes' or, I don't know, 'sure' or something?"

A nod from Freckles.

He giggled and texted

SURE :)

"This is so exciting." He smiled at her.

She smiled back, the gesture slow, perhaps unsure. "Can I go now?" Rising, she'd started to stand again.

"Come here," he said as he helped her up and drawn her into a big hug, squeezing her tight. "I just got so angry she hadn't texted back and I hadn't heard from her and I couldn't find her, so I took it out on you. It's just that I've been left before. By people I trusted. Friends. Good friends. Just dropped and ignored and, you know, it hurts. You know?"

She nodded, her chin against his shoulder.

"So, hey, I'm sorry, okay?" he said.

She pulled away and watched him. "My tutor is—"

"I know, I know." He laughed. "He's waiting."

Her hands gripped the edge as she started climbing out. He'd stopped her. "Hey, hey, hey, hold on, wait a second." She paused. He shook his head. "I'm saying I'm sorry. You get that? It's important to apologize. To make things right." He moved to hug her again, bringing her too close and squeezing too tight. "When someone has hurt you, it's important for them to acknowledge that. Make it right. So you don't carry that anger with you."

"I'm not mad," she said. Her hand patted his back as he squeezed again.

He pulled away, his hands on her shoulders. "Why would you be?"

"I dunno," she said with a shrug.

"Right!" He grinned. "So, little froggy, we good?"

A second nod.

"Yeah?" He looked at her, his grin growing to a friendly smile.

A small grin from her.

"Good! Because I have a date."

And then he snapped her neck and let her dead body fall next to Tits, the door dropped and locking with a

click.

⁂

Brody still lingered, eating a bag of chips. Unnecessary still sat in the living room. The rain still pelted Eidolon outside.

And dead Freckles, hips and knees broken and bent, arms bashed and popped from the socket and crossed over her chest, a tuft of hair peeking from the top where he'd pulled the drawstring tight, was finally stuffed in the bag, feet first.

Taking a breath, he laid down exhausted next to the dead Teeth.

Brody waited behind him. "Is that the one?"

He nodded. Thank god her shoulders were loose and her joints bent. "She's loose, man. She won't need me to break her."

EIDOLON AVENUE—APARTMENT 1C

"Damn," Brody said, disappointment in his voice.

"No, man, she's too good for that," he said, looking at her. "I really didn't want it to go there, you know. It would've felt wrong or something."

He pulled Teeth near and snuggled up close. "She was kinda awesome, you know."

"They always are in the beginning," his bro said from behind him.

He sighed. Her skin was still cold. Thin threads of red and black and purple crept along the white flesh, mere whispers of the decay to come. The finger nails were white, but not yet falling loose, and her lips were no longer the pink he'd dreamt of kissing. "You know, I considered not ending this one like this."

His hand snaked below and snuck between her legs. Her secret place, though frigid, was still soft, still welcoming. He pried a finger inside. "But this one," he said, brushing his nose against her neck as a second finger joined the first, "this is the cat curiosity killed."

⁂

He'd handed Teeth a beer, his fifth, her third. Second date, three weeks ago. She'd finally agreed to join him in his apartment for a drink after dinner. He sat next to her on the couch.

"You've got quite the cloud hanging around you," she'd said.

"How so?" He took a long swallow.

"Oh please. Don't pull that crap with me." She smiled. "You know damn well what I'm talking about."

"But you know me. You know that all that stuff back at the old school, what they said I did, all that *stuff*, none of it's true."

"But I *don't* know that." Her knees touching his, she turned to him. "Listen, what I do know are the facts and they are what they are. They're indisputable. Fact: your dad did a dipshit, despicable thing. Fact: there was enough anger over what happened in your dorm room that night, and the emergency room later, before Brody and—

"Naw, Brody's good." He shrugged. "What they said about him, that wasn't . . . it's just not right."

"Brody's good? Is that what you just said?" She put her beer on the table. "He was a serial rapist. A disgusting exhibitionist. Hot as hell and hung like a horse, yeah, but he was cruel. He was a pervert. He was dangerous. Every girl, every guy, everyone I knew *knew* not to get caught alone with him." She leaned in. "He'd fuck you, then fuck you up, and then trap you in the walk-in freezer. Beat you, tie you up and then leave you. Seriously. People almost *froze* to death, Colton. All because your boy, Billion Dollar Brody, thought they needed to 'cool down' or something."

"But you don't *know* that, do you?"

"I saw it with my own eyes!" She sat back. "What about that blonde girl? Second year? Right before classes started? You know about that, right?"

He shook his head.

"Gorgeous girl. From the South. Sweetest thing in the world, I've been told. Found in sandals and a sun dress in the walk in freezer. Was *last* seen with good ol' Brody. She'd been raped. And cut, if you know what I mean. Butchered, actually, in a very delicate place. Or so they said. I don't know. It was covered up, of course, and never talked about again."

"For real?"

EIDOLON AVENUE—APARTMENT 1C

"Yeah, 'for real.'" She sighed, her shoulders falling. "This was your boy, Colton. He was bad. I mean, c'mon. Like, *legendary* bad. He was infamous for making people do things they wouldn't ordinarily do. He'd link up with someone weak, maybe even, you know, a little off, if you know what I mean, find their Achilles' Heel, and then just strum that baby like a banjo until it snapped."

"Someone weak."

"It was kind of common knowledge." Lifting her bottle, she took a swig. "It's also common knowledge that the girl in your dorm that night wasn't with you. She was with *him*."

"Are you saying she wouldn't have wanted to be with me?" He could feel his cheeks flush.

"No—"

"That they'd want Brody instead of me?"

"Colton—"

"Because she *was* with me, okay? *Me*. Not him"

"And she ended up with a broken neck. In your bed. Next to you. Both of you naked."

He grew silent.

"What was the knife for, Colton?" She waited.

Finally,

"That was Brody, not me." He looked at his hands. His finger tips were buzzing, tingling. He made a fist. "I don't know what he was thinking. He said he was curious or something."

"Curious about what?"

Another shrug from him, his forehead feeling warm.

She sighed. "Which took the whole thing from some fucked up weird shit to a fucked up weird shit felony. And from there, the dominos fell."

The room felt hot. He wanted to open a window. He shifted in his seat. "Listen—"

"No, you listen: these are the facts: Brody sold you out. Pointed his arrogant finger and put it all on you. He was never really there for you, okay? He was not a friend. He hung you out to dry when the shit hit the fan. Your dad, this nice guy, or at least that's what you say—"

"He's weak. I said he's weak. Not nice." He watched her before looking away. "I'm nothing like him, you understand?"

"Whatever. He played the system, got you a nice Get Out of Jail Free card, got busted, went to jail *himself* and then called in favors and, they say, spent a shit ton of money, most of it not his, by the way, to get himself out. And right now the whole world thinks the Carryage family makes the Borgias look like frickin' shit stain wannabes on Amateur Night."

She placed her hand on his, the warmth of her touch feeling like a silent apology. "No matter what you say or what you believe, those are the facts as everyone sees them. Okay? And, I don't know, I kinda think it still bothers you that your dad took the fall and you *still* ended up losing it all and paying the price, here on glamorous Eidolon."

"Is that really what you think?"

"Does it matter?" She pulled her hand away, her fingers wrapping around the cold beer perched on the table.

"Yes." He waited. The seconds ticked by. He could feel her watching him and then felt her look away. Could sense her eyes scanning the small space on Eidolon he called home.

EIDOLON AVENUE—APARTMENT 1C

"How different this must be from what you know. From where you dreamt of ending up." She stared at one of the many stains creeping from the ceiling to wander down the wall. "Not exactly 'The Manor,' is it?" She turned to him with a gentle smile. "And it certainly isn't the White House."

"You didn't answer my question." Another long swallow of cold beer. His stomach rumbled and he swallowed back a belch. "Is that really what you think?"

"About what?"

"The girl in the dorm. Brody. My dad." He felt sick, his face flushed, his skull, the top of his head, warm. "Is that what you think?"

"I don't know. But I'm here, aren't I? That's something, right?" A long pause. "Do you really want to know?"

He nodded.

"I'm trying to like you . . . *less* than I do." She turned, her eyes on the closed bedroom door behind them. "But, c'mon, a girl, someone I knew, a classmate, is dead because of you."

"Wait, you *knew* her—"

"Yeah. She was paralyzed, her neck snapped or something, and, they say, she'd been raped repeatedly over the last twelve hours." She turned back to him. "The girl you insisted was *yours,* not Brody's, by the way. But I already knew that she'd been with *you*. You want to know why?" She looked at him. The bottle in her hand trembled as it rested on her knee.

He nodded. His thoughts felt slow, his head thick. Too much beer, he thought.

"Because she blinked twice for yes when they

questioned her in the emergency room." She took another long drink. "Do you want to know what the question was? What they asked? What your thousand dollar an hour lawyers shot down on a thin-as-air technicality as any type of evidence that could be used against you?"

He counted his breaths. Fought to remain calm. His stomach grumbled again, his guts shifting and dropping.

"The question was 'Did Colton Carryage do this?' and 'Did he rape you?' That's what the question was." She closed her eyes. "And here I sit, sharing a beer with you. I'm just . . . I'm just trying to understand. For me. And for her, my friend." A quick shrug. "That's all, I guess."

She pulled another long swallow from the bottle. "I thought for so long it was Brody, not you. But now . . . " She paused. "I'm drunk. A little." She lifted her bottle in a toast. "Lucky for you she was found dead in her hospital room hours later, right? Lucky for her, too, I guess. To have to live like that . . . " She sighed. "But at least you're alive, right?"

"What do you mean?" His stomach lurched. His head throbbed.

"Colton . . . " She paused, her eyes on him. "It must have been horrible. I'm sorry."

"What?" He shifted on the couch, his shirt suddenly tight. "What are you talking about?"

"Brody. The dorm room? You were there that night. You were there when he fell out the window. Or at least that's what the official report said." She leaned in close. Placed her hand on his leg. "But that's not what *they* said, Colton."

EIDOLON AVENUE—APARTMENT 1C

"What do they say?" His heart thumped in his chest. He couldn't breathe. He blinked back tears. "I mean, what . . . what *did* they say?"

"That you were arguing with him and you moved toward him. He moved back. You moved forward, he moved back. Then back, back, back until he tumbled out the open window to land fifteen floors below." She stopped and took a long swallow of her beer. "To have Brody dead, like that, I can't imagine what . . ."

He watched her. Watched her speak. Watched her lips move, the words lost in the rushing in his head, his mind a slow chaos of lazy fireworks popping and snapping in muted bursts of light. His thoughts moving too slow as she talked and then sipped her beer and then, the bottle perched on her knee, talked again, the words circling him, but not hitting his ears.

"What?" he finally said. He closed his eyes, his forehead feeling warm.

"No, I'm sorry," she said, turning to him. "It's just that what they said . . ."

"No. No, no, no, no, no. Not at all. Not true." He stood. "No."

"Colton, I'm sorry." She started to stand. He held her down.

"Stay, no, it's okay." He took his hands from her shoulders. "My stomach . . . my head . . . I need to . . . would you excuse me? I'll be right back."

A nod from her. "Okay." The bottle back to her lips.

"Don't move." He forced a smile.

Her eyes on him. "Why would I?"

"Curiosity," he said as he pressed close, snuggling again with the dead Teeth, the laundry bag waiting, his tongue sliding forward to lick the flesh below her ear, his teeth snapping in a gentle bite. "And lies."

⸺⸺

Steps away, on the other side of the bathroom door, Teeth sat in the living room with her beer, waiting on the couch, whispering lies. Outside, rain slapped the window.

Here, in front of the mirror, he counted his breaths and steadied his heart. He felt his forehead. Hot. Too hot. His ears were ringing. The tips of his fingers buzzed and tingled. The dark behind his closed eyes still sparked with bursts of light. And his thoughts, they jumped, leaping and darting, impossible to catch.

That night Brody left. Yes, the night she'd mentioned. Yes, he'd argued with him. In the dorm. And, yes, yes, yes, he'd approached Brody. Yes. The window was open, he thought. The night was cold and the breeze made him shiver. He wanted to close the window, had asked to have the window closed, but the mountain that is—

was

Brody stopped him. The jock with the dangerous temper that is—

was

Brody wouldn't let him. The friend that Brody is—
was
despite the lies and the leaving and the window and the
click.
Fuck. He put his hand on his forehead, the palm cool against his skin. He fucking hated the
click

EIDOLON AVENUE—APARTMENT 1C

that robbed him of his thoughts. That painted a ravenous black hole where memory should be. The
click
that snapped between his eyes, the warmth stealing in from his temples to snake over his forehead. That crept over his skull like a gentle wave to slide down the back of his neck. The
click
as Brody had neared the window. The drop in his gut as he'd closed his eyes, not having the heart to watch Brody slip out the door unseen.
Or so he thought.
But the sudden silence of the room followed by the screams far below and the flashing lights and the police standing in front of him with their note pads and questions. The blanket warming his shoulders as the
click
crawled down his back and reached around to cradle his heart as someone somewhere spoke of Brody's blood on the concrete, Brody's skull caved in, Brody's brains splattered—
But not *Brody* Brody, right?
No.
Never.
Fuck it, man, he thought as he closed his eyes. Bitches lie and Brody, his bro, his friend, his Brody, was hiding in the bedroom with the rest of the corpses.
Wait.
He stopped. Shut off his mind. Shut down his thoughts. He gritted his teeth, his forehead warm, the familiar tingle inching down the back of his neck as he swallowed and then swallowed again.

And, ignoring the obvious, he opened the door.

Teeth was shrugging her coat over her shoulders, her cell quickly shoved into her front pocket, when he came back in.

"What's up?" He'd walked toward her. "Leaving already?" His words felt thick, his head slow.

"Had no idea it was so late," she'd said, her eyes on her fingers as she struggled with the buttons. He glanced toward the bedroom door. Still closed.

"This seems kinda sudden. I mean, I was hoping to at least defend myself a little bit against what—"

"No, that's okay." She stopped, her hands still for the smallest of moments, and then started buttoning again. "It's done and in the past and . . . it's okay. Really."

"I just . . . " He ran his hand through his hair. "As weird as it sounds, I kinda thought we were having a good time, you know, despite—"

"No, no, yeah, we were. We were." She gave up on the buttoning the coat and made a beeline for her purse. "It's just I have a . . . I have studying to do—"

"We're on break this week."

A sudden laugh from her. It sounded awkward and forced. "Well," she said, "no harm starting early, right?" She pressed her lips to his cheek. A quick peck with her body moving to a brief embrace while her feet started for the door.

"Wait, wait, hold on." He grabbed her by the arm. "Talk to me. What happened? Are you okay?"

"No, really, I'm fine." She gently pulled away, but he held tight. "I'm just a little tired, that's all. Too much beer. Too many flowers. I'm allergic to flowers. They make me drowsy."

EIDOLON AVENUE—APARTMENT 1C

"Flowers?"

"Oops," he said as he looked at the dead girl next to him. The liar. The snoop. He moved to a crouch and grabbed the last laundry bag. Opening the hole as wide as it'd go, he drew it over her feet before bringing her arms across her chest and then, the knees folding, bringing her knees up. He looked at her, forced into a fetal position, the empty bag dangling off her ankles. "Think you'll fit?"

"Yeah." She'd stepped close that night three weeks ago, her purse over her shoulder, her fingers cupping his as she discreetly tried to pry them away from her arm. *"Gotta get home for a Claritin or I'll be sneezing all night."* Another quick laugh.

He laughed as well. *"Remind me to never bring you flowers, right?"*

"Ha! I know, right? Yeah . . . " She clutched his gripping fingers tighter, her smile plastered on her face as she discreetly fought to get her arm back. *"Anyway, it totally sucks. But, hey, could be worse, right?"*

"Yes, it could. Much worse." He gripped tighter, his eyes narrowing as he watched her. *"You know, I can't remember the last time I've had flowers in here."*

Unless you count the potted posies and pansies and whatnot in the bedroom to help hide the suspicious smell from the freezer.

"You lying cunt," he said as he wrapped the rope around Teeth's cold corpse. "Told you to stay still. To stay put."

"Can't trust 'em, man," Brody said from his place near the window.

"She said you were dead, man, you know?" He pulled the rope tight, watching as it ate into the skin,

Teeth's dead flesh puckering and splitting as he steadied her with his feet. "And then she said 'Not going anywhere', but she fucking lied, man."

"Tighter, man!"

He pulled the rope tighter, the dead girl's flesh weeping.

"She had it coming."

"Ain't that the damn truth." His fingers tied the ends into a knot, pulling it tight.

"I'm sorry," she'd said, her voice sounding desperate, a note of panic creeping in.

"No, you weren't." He turned her on her side and slid the bag up her dead white legs, her stiff hips, gathering it close and then tipping her so the body sat, squatting in the fabric, his hand steadying her.

"Now she is, right?" his bro said with a laugh.

"Yeah, Brody, I'd say she's sorry."

"For what?" He'd pulled her closer that night.

"Oh, you know, having to leave so sudden. Could you . . . ?" She'd patted his hand.

"My apologies." He released her. *"I don't want you to leave, that's all. It's so out of the blue."*

"I know. I'm sorry." Her hands pulled the flaps of her unbuttoned coat in close, her arms crossing and then uncrossing. *"I can just feel the sneezes coming on, though. And my eyes will turn red and ugly, and my nose will run, so . . . So, yeah, I'll just go ahead and—"* She turned to the door.

"Of course." He followed her. Her hand turned the knob. The door refused.

"Deadbolt," he said as he reached over to unlock the lock.

She chuckled. *"Can't be too careful, right?"*

EIDOLON AVENUE—APARTMENT 1C

She opened the door. It stopped, the chain lock at the top catching it.

"Whoops. Gotta do this one, too." He closed the door. *"Wait."*

He stopped, pausing, his hand resting near the lock.

"What?" she said.

There was a long moment of silence.

"Not even a hug goodbye?" His eyes met hers. She looks terrified, he'd thought. Her smile looked tight, her body language afraid. Her hand still clutched the door knob.

"Sure," she said.

He leaned in close, gathering her into his arms and squeezing her tight, his step forward pushing her away from the door. *"We didn't even get to kiss."* Still holding her, he pulled back, his face nose to nose with hers. Her heart raced against his chest. He grinned and then, nice and slow, pressed his lips to hers.

Winding the rope around the dead Teeth, he counted, his breath coming slow. His mind refused quiet, the memories rushing and tumbling. His heart pounded. He took his hand from the cold body. Stretched his fingers. They hurt, the tips snapping, buzzing. He closed his eyes, ignoring those fucking lazy fireworks popping between his eyes. Tried to focus. Had to focus.

The dead Teeth stared, her eyes still open. "Was that so bad?" he said to the corpse. "Our kiss. That wasn't so bad, was it?" The words sounded odd. Hollow and muffled. His hand still on her shoulders, he steadied her as she squatted in the bag. "Had it been that, had we left it at just *that*, man, I'd still be meeting her for dinner and coffee, you know?"

"I know, man," Brody said.

"I'd still be kissing her." He took a breath and drew the bag up around her. "Instead, I have to throw her in a pit out in the woods."

"Fuck, dude."

"No shit." He tied the knot tight, the hole closing over her head. "That's really, really gonna suck."

"For her, man, yeah."

"You're right," she'd said as she pulled away that night. His arms were still around her. *"It was nice. Very nice."* She patted him on the shoulder and tried to pull away.

"Not too shabby, if I do say so myself." He pushed his hardness against her.

"Okay, okay." She tried to pull away. *"I should go now."*

"Not even time for one more kiss?"

"I really shouldn't." She'd been pushing him away as she tried to step to the door. *"Next time, yeah?"*

"But it was nice." He stepped forward when she stepped back, frustrating her effort to escape. *"You said it was."*

"It was. I just really have to go." Another tight smile from her. He saw her eyes watering with tears then.

"Oh well." He grinned in return. *"I've had worse last kisses."*

Her laugh died in her throat. She swallowed. He stepped forward, pushing her back, the gesture cruel and impatient. She stumbled. Tried to say something, who knows what, the words lost as her heel caught and she fought to right herself.

EIDOLON AVENUE—APARTMENT 1C

"I didn't want it to be like this." He walked slowly, stalking her.

"I really didn't," he said as he looked at the body in the bag.

"I wanted a better end. One not so predictable." He moved close to her.

"We can . . . we can see each other again, you know." Her voice sounded scared. The kind of forced calm usually snapped by a panicked scream. *"Tomorrow. We can see each other tomorrow, if you want."* She was walking backwards, to the couch, close to the bedroom door. *"I'd like that."*

"I'd like that, too. But I want one more kiss. Because it was nice. You said so yourself. It. Was. Nice." He stopped. *"Just one more."* She had nowhere left to run, save for the bedroom. *"Can you do that for me?"*

She nodded, her lips in a tight grin. *"One more kiss."*

Coming near her, he held his arms out to embrace her. Her knee jerked up, narrowly missing his groin and hitting his thigh. He moved quick, his hands around her neck before she could scream, his lips on hers, his tongue invading her mouth as he cracked her neck with that familiar click and then held her as she fell.

Zippers pulled, fabric moved, cotton ripped, legs opened, he took her with a savage cruelty, her silence, her helplessness, her death exciting him as she tore and bled on that second date, three weeks ago.

"But they chose this instead." He stood, now, weeks later, allowing the body in the bag to topple over and lay next to its twins. Tits in one, Freckles in the other.

And now Teeth. "I don't know what they were trying to prove, man but they were wrong."

"Fuck yeah, man," Brody said.

"It's like they forgot who I am," he said, the familiar heat spreading down his neck.

"Who you were, you mean."

"Fuck you." He clenched his fists. "I'm Colton fucking Carryage. You don't get away with fucking over Colton fucking Carryage, you know? Ain't gonna happen."

He waited.

"Ain't that right, bro?"

Nothing.

"Bro!"

I've been waiting.

He stopped.

Forever.

The voice came from behind him. A new voice. Not Brody's. A girl's. From the door. The words recognizable, though they were slow and careful. The sound somewhat garbled, almost choked. And impossible.

He couldn't turn. His eyes stared at the floor. At the wood, worn by time and scuffed with the footfalls of countless strangers. The slight warp of the planks and how it all sunk in the middle as it rose toward the edges.

A *sigh* from behind him. At the door.

He ignored it, emotion and memory knowing what it was, who it was, but logic refusing to admit the obvious. He hadn't taken her off the floor to the chair, he realized. Had considered and then forgot. Had left her laying. Somehow she'd moved. On her own.

EIDOLON AVENUE—APARTMENT 1C

He focused on the base of the freezer. The lid was open, on the top. Propped up and waiting. I need to close the lid, he thought, suddenly aware how the powerful hum of the machine clicking on cut the silence of the room and how the clouds of frost billowing from the yawning oversized chasm made his throat tight.

"Bro, man, you there?" He hated how scared his voice sounded. He cleared his throat and swallowed.

It's a shame, came the voice at the door.

What would I find if I turned, he thought. A girl I thought was dead, who appeared dead, who somehow wasn't and was now, what, waiting? Half-alive and severely wounded?

Yeah, that's what I'd find. He was going to turn. After he closed the lid, he'd turn.

He heard a rustling from behind him. The sound of fingers scratching silk. Thick, durable silk, the insistent nails muffled in a swath of fabric tied with a knot.

Impossible, he thought. He smiled at his stupidity. At his weakness. His imagination. He laughed, the sound hollow and afraid.

A second rustle joined the first, this new one accompanied by a heavy sigh and the noxious smell of thawing decay.

He stepped toward the freezer. I'll close the lid, he thought again, this goal becoming something of a mantra. First I'll close the lid and then I'll unplug it and then I'll take a deep breath and then I'll turn. And there'll be nothing.

Am I wrong? said the voice still at the door.

You're dead, he wanted to say. But his throat was too tight. Too trapped. No words would come out.

What's it like?

He paused. "Where you at, man?" His words were a whisper. His heart thumped in his chest, beads of sweat running down his forehead, his cheeks, the back of his neck.

"Fuck, man." He laughed, this one loud. He clenched his eyes shut and shook his head. He hadn't eaten, so it wasn't food poisoning. And he wasn't using this week, so . . . what the hell was this? He ducked his chin to his chest and breathed in, nice and long, and then exhaled, nice and long.

Close the lid, he told himself. Close the lid and then turn and there'll be nothing there. Nothing but four nobodies no one misses and Brody—not dead, but alive, alive and fucking well—fucking with him.

Golden son of a favored Senator . . .

I know who you are, came a second voice. Not Brody's. This was from a bag. The words whispered as fingers scratched and tugged and pulled at silk.

"You're not real," he said, though he still refused to turn. "You're in my head or something. You don't talk unless I talk first." His stomach shifted and his bladder threatened release. "You don't do anything unless I . . . unless I allow it. Unless there's a lesson to be learned. So, this . . . this is . . . " He stopped.

God, what I wouldn't do for a piss, he thought. He clenched his fists and shook his head. "I'm tired, man," he said, hoping his bro would respond. "Tired and stressed. I could've used some help, you know?" He paused. "I just need to settle the fuck down." He exhaled, letting his shoulders drop. "Settle down. It's good. It's all good."

No response.

EIDOLON AVENUE—APARTMENT 1C

The sound of fabric rustling as a knot released and a bag fell to the floor filled his ears.

People can be cruel, said the second voice.

And the son's light dimmed, answered the voice at the door.

The second bag, still plagued with the desperate scratching of insistent nails, fell over with a thump as well. And then a sigh followed by

Ow.

This was crazy, he said to himself, his hands rubbing his arms as he bounced on the balls of his feet. Calm down and close the lid and go.

I just don't feel like me anymore, whispered the second voice.

Is that why you're leaving? said the voice at the door.

I should just go, he thought.

You can't leave, said the muffled voice still pawing at the bag.

"This is stupid," he said.

He turned.

Unnecessary stood, blocking the door to the living room. A shoulder strap had slipped, almost revealing her breast. And her head tilted to the side, resting squarely, her ear to her shoulder, the flesh weeping where the broken bone pushed and poked and prodded against the skin.

Her eyes watched, but not him, her stare moving to the wall, the ceiling, out the window. She took a breath, her shoulders rising as her hands gripped the door jamb.

On the floor near the wall, Tits squatted in the bag, the knot untied and useless, the fabric pushed down past her knees and hips to land in a crumple by her ankles. The not-dead girl turned this way and that, the ropes binding her scraping the skin and digging into the flesh as she wrestled them from her arms, her wrists.

Next to her, the second bag laid on its side. The silk moved as nails fought and fingers reached, fists punched and feet kicked. The knot strained and then unraveled. The hole at the top opened, the dead Freckles climbing free as if sliding from the womb.

He closed his eyes. He took a deep breath, and then another. It's not real, he said to himself. This isn't happening. It's stress or too much tap water or something. I just need to stop and relax. They're dead. They're forgotten. They need to be carried down and loaded into the SUV. Driven into the woods and dumped in the pit by the tree. Far away from the road. Dug deep enough where they can rot in anonymity.

Brody and me, man, that's what we gotta do. This shit, it's not real, he thought again, knowing it was somehow a lie. But it couldn't be. Brody was here. He hadn't walked back, back, back to the window. Hadn't fallen. Hadn't tumbled to the pavement fifteen floors below.

The heat in his head was there again. It was growing. He blinked. Took a breath. Steadied himself, his eyes still closed. Those lazy fireworks a slow storm of snapping light in his own private darkness.

And then he heard the clicking. The rapid chattering of bone on bone. Muffled and quiet, but not. It was loud. Too loud. Over the breathing, the disgusting, stench-filled breathing, of those three impossibilities standing in the door or resting on the floor surrounded by laundry bags, he could hear it.

EIDOLON AVENUE—APARTMENT 1C

It was inescapable, this rhythmic, persistent sound of
Teeth.
He opened his eyes.
Nothing had changed. Unnecessary stood. Tits squatted, the ropes peeling her flesh as she shimmied them free. Freckles, her limbs broken, laid on the ground, her head rolling as she tried to move, to crawl, to draw near.

And the third bag, the one with Teeth, leaned against the wall.

His guts dropped, his hand raced to quiet his scream and he took a step back.

"Man, where the fuck are you, man?"

The bag moved as her fingers poked free to pluck at the knot, her mouth pressed to the hole.

"Brody—"

Sold you out, the voice said from the third bag. Her large teeth caught the light as they started to chatter and click and clack again. *He left.* A moment later, the knot came free, the silk fell and Teeth stood, the ropes binding her falling to her feet.

Her head turned and she found him. *He was never really there—*

"No, man. That's not true." He took another step back as his heart pounded and his bladder gave out, drenching his legs with hot piss. "Fuck—"

A charmed life. Unnecessary took a step forward, her neck cracking as ear pressed against shoulder, the bone peeking through as the skin ripped.

Another step back. "Man, where the fuck are you, man?"

The scars, they're not healing. Tits stood, the ropes

shrugged free. Her arms, her wrists, her legs, slashed with weeping canyons of scraped and wounded flesh. She watched him. She stepped forward.

"You can't be real." He wanted to shout. As if shouting would somehow break whatever nightmare this was. "You're not real!"

I'm slow. Freckles snaked along the floor. Her arms gripping the wood as, elbow after elbow, her eyes on him, she dragged her broken legs behind her. *I talk slow. My head is slow.*

"Please." He was sobbing now, his hands trembling. He clenched them together, the fingers lacing, the knuckles white. "I'm sorry. Oh god, help me. This is crazy." He hiccupped. "Holy Christ, I've pissed myself."

Like Mrs. Butterworth. Freckles threw her arm forward and pulled herself closer.

He took another step back. He'd be pressed against the freezer soon, he thought. He'd have to move around it. Have to slip within their reach. The tears came harder. He wiped them away with a shaking hand.

In fact, his whole body was shaking. He couldn't stop it. He was pathetic. He was covered in piss, he had snot running into his mouth, he was crying like a little girl. And his whole body wouldn't stop trembling.

His hand reaching behind him, he took another step toward the freezer.

Making yourself an easy target. Teeth said, stepping out of the bag and away from the wall.

"I'm not . . . I'm not weak . . . I have . . . fuck, man, Brody—"

Brody's dead. Teeth moved forward.

EIDOLON AVENUE—APARTMENT 1C

"No, he didn't. He—"
Left you out to dry
She came closer.
when the shit hit the fan.

"I can pay." He inched back, his hand still searching for the solidity of the hulking, humming white behind him. "My dad, he can . . . oh Jesus."

Dipshit, despicable thing. Teeth took another step closer.

"No! Stop!" His legs shaking, he considered falling to the ground. Just kneeling. Giving up. "Please stop." The words fought their way through a chorus of sobs and hiccups and more tears. "Just stop it. Please."

There's a cloud hanging over you. Teeth paused, her eyes, like Unnecessary's, not on him, but to the wall, the ceiling, out the window. On something not him.

That thing, there. Freckles paused as well. Her face lifted, black mucus falling from her lips and staining her chin. *It's . . . wrong.*

He tried to catch his breath. He couldn't breathe. He couldn't think. And he couldn't stop shaking. "I don't . . . you're not making sense. Oh god, this is FUCKING CRAZY."

They just feel weird. Tits waited. Her gaze, like the others, beyond him and above him and past him.

"What?" His voice was quiet. "What are you talking about." And then he started to laugh, his body trembling so hard his teeth chattered.

It won't . . . stop . . . breathing. Freckles blinked and looked at him. *It won't let you leave.* She pulled herself forward.

He thought of running, but couldn't. His hand

moved behind him, feeling for the edge of the freezer. It wasn't there.

I hope they show up soon. Unnecessary moved from her spot near the door. She stumbled, her footsteps large, her head snapping forward. She stopped. Her hands moved to return her head to her shoulder. The rip on her neck was now a violent gash, the snapped edge of white bone peeking through.

His stomach dropped and the taste of sick crept up his throat.

You moved forward. Teeth took a careful step.

He shook his head. "Jesus Christ!

He moved back, back, back, Teeth said.

"This is . . . I don't know what—" He fought to catch his breath.

You know damn well what I'm talking about. Teeth's eyes found him. She jerked forward, her foot slapping the wood. *The question was 'Did Colton Carryage do this?'*

"No—"

You killed a girl. Freckles inched forward. *It won't let you.*

Lucky for you. Teeth took a step forward.

He walked back, back, back.

And fell.

The pit was deep and covered with clouds of frost, the walls around him the white of the freezer, the floor beneath concrete slick with splattered red, the lid open and waiting high overhead. Too high.

The ceiling on Eidolon was gone. The familiar dingy yellow. The dusty broken ceiling fan. The rust-colored stains dripping along the edge. All gone.

Instead he saw dark clouds heavy with rain. The

EIDOLON AVENUE—APARTMENT 1C

tops of massive trees listing in the wind. And, soaring high above, the dorm building. A memory of brick and mortar climbing fifteen stories into the night sky. "What the—" He jumped and then jumped again, but he couldn't reach, his hands touching nothing but air. Cold air, the sides too smooth to grip, to climb.

The impossibility of it hit him. His body started to violently shake. He slammed his head against the frigid wall. He screamed. And then he laughed. "This is fucking crazy. Impossible. It's impossible. It's not real." He closed his eyes and slammed his head against the wall again. "Wake up, wake up. C'mon, fucker, WAKE UP!" He opened his eyes and looked up.

Four faces looked down at him. Unnecessary, Tits, Freckles and Teeth.

"What're you gonna do now, huh?" He jumped and landed with a thud. "What the fuck you gonna do now, you stupid, worthless, piece of shit bitches?"

Let's just do it. Tits squatted, her arms bleeding purple and black where the ropes had rubbed the flesh raw. She looked to Freckles.

If the lid closes, you can't breathe. Freckles looked at Teeth.

The burden of your father's sins. Teeth turned to Unnecessary.

You and your family. Unnecessary looked down at him.

Above them, the black of the sky dipped low. Like a tear drop. Hanging and dangling, slowly dripping, it gathered itself from the edges like a living thing. The clouds rippling as the tear, this thing, pulled together to draw closer.

He pulled away. Sat down. Drew back.

The tear came closer. As black as night, it paused above the heads of the four as they watched him. Turning their faces, they looked up at it.

"So, Brody's dead. Smashed his skull on the concrete? Big fucking deal!" He glared at the four above him. "You got your necks snapped? Your pathetic lives ended? Big fucking deal! Life sucks! My family, my money, got me off ? Got me a Get Out of Jail Free card? BIG FUCKING DEAL! That's life, bitches. That's POWER!"

He caught his breath. "I'm Colton fucking Carryage," he said, clenching his fists.

It looked at him, then, a nose and two eyes pushing from the black. A mouth stretching too long and too wide, the lips moving as an unseen tongue ran along a row of hidden teeth.

A moment later, he smelled the noxious air as it opened its mouth and sighed.

"What the . . . " he said as he stood. He had to get out. "No, wait!" He jumped again, high, landing hard, stumbling, the freezer jumping as the lid above knocked loose and slammed shut with a

click.

APARTMENT 1D

ANNIVERSARY

Monday, 3:24 PM

"WE ARE A walking history of our failures," Marta said as she snapped the napkin open and laid it across her lap. "A stumbling catastrophe of unbelievable screw ups that, as you can plainly see, screwed us up." She laughed, the tight smile on her gleaming lips held a moment longer than needed. "Really, it's just been an endless array of aborted endings. Until now, I mean." Her pudgy hand lifted her champagne glass—her sixth, but who was counting?—in yet another toast to the elegant man seated to her side. "And for that, we thank you, Mr. Peabody."

"I promise, this time we'll get it right," the stranger said with a small nod.

Even here, surrounded by the decay that was Eidolon, he seemed to fit. Untouched by the yellowing walls and the splintered baseboard, the brown stains running from the ceiling or the thin windows that rattled when the wind blew and rain pelted the glass, as it did now, this Peabody was neither tall nor short, neither handsome nor plain, neither this nor that or even the other thing. He just *was*.

Minus the saddlebag hips and flabby middle, she saw herself in him. Kind face. Easy smile. A steady gaze. A someone who was anonymously forgettable in the most wonderful way. So forgettable in fact, she imagined that, if he wanted to, this man could probably kill in broad daylight and still escape the recollections of even the most ardent witnesses. Because who expects something that evil from someone who's such a nothing, right?

But right here, right now, seated at the long table, a modest buffet waiting, a candle flickering in the center, he was here and he was perfect. The answer to all she wanted tonight to be. Peabody and a bottle of champagne: the perfect combination, she thought as she took another long drink.

She looked at her beloved Benji at the other end of the table. He sat quiet, riddled with the wounds of his mistakes. Their mistakes. So very far from the man she'd married fifty years ago tonight, he was darn near unrecognizable. Their life since coming to Eidolon like a long, slow circling of their graves.

But now Benji's handsome face was gaunt and pale, thin wisps of white clinging to his scalp like squatters on land that hadn't yielded a crop in years. His scrawny shoulders were still square, though one sat higher than the other, and his head tilted ever so slightly to the side giving him a lopsided smile. His bowl of broth sat untouched in front of him, his remaining fingers—three on one hand, two on the other, the thumbs still intact—looking much too thin as they rested on the white tablecloth.

Red wine dribbled from his lips. "Sweetie," she said as she gestured for him to wipe his chin.

He ignored her, his gaze fixed to the ceiling above her head.

Sighing, she struggled to rise, the napkin clutched in her hand.

"May I—?" Peabody rose as well.

"No, no, no. I'm fine." She winced, her left leg

dragging behind as she took the seven steps to Benji's chair. "I've been lugging this old thing around for, oh, I don't know, forty years now?" Dabbing the napkin with her tongue, she bent forward to rub her beloved's face. "Isn't that right, sweetie?" she said to Benji. "Dead as a doornail from the knee on down, it is. Foot's still wood, though the rest is some fancy plastic or heaven knows what." She folded the napkin, tucking the stain inward, the clean corner moistened with her tongue. "That was the tenth year anniversary screw up, I think. Yep. That's right. I lost a leg and you . . . " She stopped, her eyes on her silent beloved as she cradled his chin in her palm. "What did you lose?"

He sat, his eyes still on the ceiling at the other end of the room. A thin river of red slipped from his mouth and slid off his lip. She wiped it clean with the napkin. "Well, I do know it wasn't as horrible as losing a leg from knee to foot. Or as annoying. Even now, after all these years of taking the leg off, wiping the stump, cleaning away the scabs, massaging lotion on the skin that's worn red from rubbing and then, next morning, having to strap the dang thing back on all over again, it's still exhausting. Simply exhausting. That's for darn sure."

"Perhaps it was." Peabody watched as she pivoted, leaning on the table as she paused to catch her breath, the carpet beneath worn thin in a familiar trail of shuffling feet.

"What was?" She steadied her breath.

"The thing he lost." Peabody's eyes caught hers. "Perhaps it was horrible and exhausting. Just in a quiet, less dramatic, noticeable way."

"I suppose." Gripping the table's edge, she hoisted

herself back and plopped down into her chair with a deep sigh. "That makes more sense." The thought rolled through her mind as she reached for her champagne. "Oh, that's right. I remember. He took a bump to the head, quite a big one, now that I think about it, and knocked himself cold as a cucumber for, oh, how long was it . . . " A glance down at Benji. "Something like two or three weeks, wasn't it, dear?"

He ignored her, his eyes on the ceiling above.

"What do you think he's looking at?" Peabody said.

She looked back at him with a shrug. "The stains, the decay. The general ugh of this . . . *place* we could never quite call home."

"You can't leave." The tall man watched her, his hands resting in his lap.

"Ha! You're telling me!" She laughed. "And it's not like we could, mind you. What, with my leg and Benji's . . . whatever, it's a bit like the lame leading the blind when we find the strength to venture out. But it follows, this Eidolon. Like finding yourself stuck in a heavy smelly winter coat with a busted zipper in the middle of a sudden summer's day, this place just *sits* on you, swallowing you. Until you can't breathe."

She paused, her eyes still on her beloved Benji. "But, anyway, trust me, it was two or three weeks. The bump on his head. For two or three weeks, he just lay there in the hospital bed, dead to the world and snoring like a lumberjack. Took his darn sweet time waking up, too, I gotta say. Found myself envying him toward the end. And then he woke up and . . . " She shrugged. "Life went back to being life and we went back to messing it all up, time and time again." She paused. "Though he did seem . . . I don't know. Off, I guess. Or somehow different in some way after then. Just not the same." A small grin for Peabody as she sipped her champagne. "I guess that's what falling off a cliff will do to you."

"But that wasn't the first time," Peabody said as he placed the champagne back on the table and pulled his salad bowl near.

"Oh no, no. Not at all." Fork in hand, she tucked into her bowl of watercress. "Now, remember, that was the ten year anniversary. We'd had, oh, I don't know, maybe . . . " She stabbed a piece of lettuce as she thought. "I'm not sure, but definitely a few, if not several, tries before then." She shoved the lettuce in her mouth.

"Really. Several?" Peabody swallowed a bite of salad and then sipped his champagne.

She nodded. "Absolutely. You see—and I was twenty-eight by this time, mind you, so in the world's eyes, and that of my family, I was darn near a spinster and utterly without hope—I met my beloved Benji one month, married him the next, and then we spent the following fifty years happily trying to kill each other. By choice."

"By choice."

"Of course." She returned the champagne flute to its place near the untouched glass of chardonnay. "Murder/suicide pacts. One after the other. All of them sincere. All of them determined and, one would hope, well thought out. And all of them ending either dismally or disastrously, take your pick." She dabbed the napkin to her lips. "Never could get it right." Napkin in hand, she put her elbows on the table and leaned forward. "And when we got it wrong, boy howdy did we get it wrong."

"So now it's Mr. Peabody to the rescue?" The affable stranger, the napkin covering his lap, speared another piece of lettuce.

"Well, it's a necessity, don't you think? Because, try as we might, we can't do it on our own. And lord knows we don't have the strength for anymore oopsies." She paused, elbows off the table, fork in hand, a leaf of watercress impaled on the tines.

"But do you still want to?"

"What? End it all?" She nodded, taking a quick bite of the green. "Of course," she said, chewing. She swallowed, her napkin revisiting her lips for a quick dab. "When it comes to leaving, as we talked about, the only way that's *really* going to happen is if my Benji and I are shoved, piece by piece, if need be, into body bags. And that's fine.

"Listen," she said, the fork at rest near her plate. "I knew the moment I met him that I wanted to marry him and I wanted to live with him and I wanted to die with him. That whole 'till death do you part' thing hit me very hard in a very deep, dark place. Those words, that promise, resonated. Like the rolling of thunder."

She stopped. "I—well, we—couldn't imagine a moment without the other. Our greatest fear, my greatest fear, would be to see the other perish and be left alone to live without them. Without him." Her elbows on the table, she leaned forward again, her eyes shining with quiet tears. "And, not being the most patient of people, we just decided to get a jump on things." She looked down the table at her husband. "Isn't that right, sweetie?"

Benji didn't respond. Red wine dripped from his lips.

EIDOLON AVENUE—APARTMENT 1D

"Darling," she said as she indicated he wipe his chin.

He ignored her, his eyes on the ceiling.

She waved him away. "Eh, he's having a quiet night, I think." She offered Peabody a tight grin. "He eats less, and what he does eat is tossed into the blender and ladled into bowls."

"That's unfortunate."

"You're right. It *is* unfortunate." She glanced at Benji again.

"What do you think he sees when he watches like that?" Peabody said.

"I'm not sure." Her fingers moved the cutlery into place, lining up the spoon with the fork just so.

"Have you asked?" the stranger said with a small smile.

"I have not." She left the cutlery to linger, perfectly aligned and just right. "Let's just say the twenty year anniversary was truly disastrous, so . . . his words, they're sometimes . . . you know." She kept her eyes on her beloved as her fingers fiddled with the edge of her napkin. "And he drinks less. But heaven knows most of that ends up down his front or on his lap, so it's probably best." She gave Peabody a quick grin. "I'm not a fan of doing the laundry, if you know what I mean. But who is, right?"

Her eyes back on Benji, she hesitated. "He talks a lot less, too. Which I miss." She paused, a small smile on her lips. "There was nothing more lovely than hearing my beloved Benji read the paper after dinner, he armed with his gin and tonic, me sipping my seltzer through a straw." She sighed. "Oh, I don't know. I guess it's inevitable, those things we lose, what with time and age and—"

"The living wounds of fifty years of failure." Peabody, elbows on the table, watched her. "Tell me about the first time."

"Our first failure, you mean." She took a deep breath. "Well, that'd be the night of our honeymoon."

"Your honeymoon?"

"Like I said, we didn't want to wait. Still don't, as a matter of fact. And so it was a very quick 'I do' with a Justice of the Peace—"

Glancing down the table at her beloved Benji. "Remember him, sweetie? He was so mad, probably because we'd pounded on the window like guttersnipe hooligans. The two of us standing there, me, damn near a spinster and dangerously loose with my skirt way too high above my knees, and you looking like an undertaker in your Woolworth's suit and bow tie, all dapper with your hair slicked with pomade and parted on the side." She stopped, her eyes still on the silent man sitting at the other end. "You had a small daisy tucked in the buttonhole of your lapel and I had a flimsy cheap corsage of something bland and forgettable on my wrist. Remember?"

A moment later, she turned back to Peabody. "Anyway, this poor man, this Justice of the Peace, I think he'd been eating lunch. Still had bread crumbs on his chin, his belt was damn near undone with his gut spilling out of his shirt, and his breath smelled like a bargain basement gin and tonic." She giggled. "Lunch indeed," she said with a wink. "Point is, our life together began with a very quick 'I do' followed by a Blue Plate special of biscuits and gravy and then Benji off to the Rexall around the corner for sleeping powder and furniture polish."

EIDOLON AVENUE—APARTMENT 1D

Her hand darting to her mouth, she gave a quiet belch. "Excuse me. 'Tis the champagne, me'thinks." A small smile. "Down went the powder in a glass of water followed by a healthy glug of furniture polish. And, oh my stars, did we end up sick as sin that night before we went out like lights. Just poof! Like that. So quick!" She laughed. "Any-hoo, came to a day or so later, half on the bed, half off, pools of sick on the carpet, our skin hurting, our jaws aching and our stomachs swollen and hard as rocks." She shook her head. "Lived on Saltines for awhile after that. Saltines moistened with water and mashed into bowls, isn't that right, Benji? Oh, and neither of us could poop for a week." The champagne to her lips, she took a sip.

"Sleeping powder and furniture polish. Sounds like a lethal combo." Peabody put his glass down, his fingers resting around the delicate stem. "Not sure how you could mess that one up."

"Well, if we're being honest here, and we are, of course, it was Benji who messed it up." She glanced at him sitting at the head of the table. "I'm sorry, sweetie, but it's the truth. Wouldn't be polite to lie to Mr. Peabody, now, would it." She glanced over at Peabody. "I swear, my Benji can squeeze a nickel so hard the buffalo poops. And when you're buying sleeping powder and furniture polish, you can't go cheap! Only the best will do. And this was far, far from the best. So . . . here we still are."

Her eyes scanned the plates—the good china, of course—lined up and waiting with anniversary food. "Well, I don't know about you, Mr. Peabody, but I'm done with this rabbit food. On to the next course?"

With a smile, Peabody nodded with a glance toward Benji.

Benji sat silent, red staining his chin, his eyes on the ceiling above Marta.

And Marta, ignoring the chaos that was Eidolon, reached for the cheese plate.

―――

"It may not seem like much, but we cleaned out our cupboards for tonight. Even emptied the fridge and took everything out of the freezer. Not that it was going to be too fancy to begin with." She leaned in close to Peabody, her voice dropping to a whisper. "I also maxed out the credit card—shhhhhh—and closed the bank account. Couldn't afford any of this extra stuff if I hadn't, but, hell, what are they gonna do? Dig us up from the grave and put us to work in some debtor's camp?" She laughed. "Listen, you, we've earned it. We deserve it. And after the lifetime of darn near comical disasters I've endured at the hands of my beloved, cheap Benji, why not go out on top, right?" She sat back. "Right."

Peabody folded his hands over his lap. "Buying inexpensive sleeping powder and furniture polish on your honeymoon hardly counts as a disaster, I think. Unfortunate? Yes. Uncomfortable? Absolutely. But a disaster?" He shrugged. "I don't know about that."

"No, I'll tell you what a disaster is," she said between bites of cheese and cracker. "The tenth anniversary at, oh, where was it?" She looked down at Benji. "Dear, where'd we go for the tenth? The tenth anniversary, I mean. Where was it?"

Getting nothing from Benji,

EIDOLON AVENUE—APARTMENT 1D

"Oh, who the heck can remember? Some godforsaken State park in the middle of somewhere. Nothing but steep mountains, deep ravines, trees and allegedly heart-stopping views of yet more mountains, ravines and trees." Another bite followed by more crunching, a smattering of crumbs landing on the table beneath her. "All you need to know is it was an unmitigated disaster."

Though Benji'd said nothing, she shot him a look. "Didn't I ask if there was a ledge below, Benji? Yes, I did. And what did you say? 'No, no, dear. No ledge. Nothing but a steep drop into the ravine far below.' And, boy howdy, were you ever wrong."

"This was in the State park?" Peabody said as he gathered the cracker crumbs from the table in his palm and wiped them onto his plate.

"Yes, our tenth anniversary. A steep hike, a long hug, a quick kiss, and then, hand in hand, a jump off a cliff. Should have landed with a splat of broken bones and bashed in heads deep down far below, our mangled bodies dragged into the forest by god knows what." She shrugged. "To be honest, I was perfectly fine ending up lunch for some bear or antelope or wild cougar or whatever. It just made sense, somehow. Circle of life or something, you know. But nope, not a chance. That simply wasn't to be."

"So there was a ledge." Peabody spread cheese onto a cracker.

"Boy was there ever!" She popped a cracker in her mouth and chewed. "A nice big one." A lone finger rose, indicating Peabody wait while she swallowed. "Hard to miss, unless you've forgotten your glasses back at the lodge and you can't see two feet in front of you without them." She shot a quick look at Benji. "Isn't that right, darling? Forgot your glasses, didn't you?" Her eyes met Peabody's as she dusted the crumbs from her hands. "He said he didn't need them. He promised he was fine without them. Insisted on his dear mother's grave that he could see perfectly well, thank you very much." A quick dab at her lips with the napkin. "He lied."

Her fingers toyed with the stem of the champagne flute. "And that's how I ended up losing the foot. And the rest of the leg, from the knee down. Hand in hand, we jumped . . . and we fell. I was told later that we probably hit some of the wall and a few branches on the way down, though of course I don't remember that part. And that we probably bounced and tumbled and probably with a *horrifying* crunch—or at least that's how I imagine it—landed on the ledge below." She laughed. "Leg cracked on a big rock and dang near split in two. Arm popped out the socket at the shoulder. Poor Benji conked his head and darn near broke his neck. He did break his collarbone, though, and his pelvis. Or hip. I forget which." She sighed. "But we only knew all of that stuff three days later when they found us."

"Three days later." Ignoring the champagne, Peabody reached for his chardonnay.

"Yes. Took the dang fools three days to get their act together, realize we weren't coming back to the lodge, and then set out—in a helicopter, no less—to learn what the heck had happened to us." She took a sip of her chardonnay. "Oh, that's nice."

"So you waited on the ledge for three days."

"Yes! Just plunked there, suffering in agony and

EIDOLON AVENUE—APARTMENT 1D

basically alone since the husband was off in dreamland. And I knew he wasn't dead, by the way, because I could see the dang fool breathing. So I sat there, shooing away ants and other creepy crawly critters with my one good arm, my shin bone poking through the skin of my leg, the whole thing becoming horribly infected and swollen and yellow with pus."

She shook her head. "I remember hoping to god that death would come before the buzzards did." She leaned in close to Peabody. "Of course, I don't know if that park even had buzzards. But I'd read once, or Benji had, anyway, that those ugly things will actually start pecking at you before you're even dead and that's the last thing I wanted."

She sat back. "Can you imagine? Sitting there still alive watching yourself get eaten by some horrible creature? No thank you."

From the other end of the table, Benji moaned.

"What's that, dear?" She shook her head and glanced at Peabody. "The history of our failures weighs a bit heavier on him than it does me." A sigh, her eyes back on Benji. "Do you need something, hon?"

"I think he does," Peabody said.

She glanced at the various bowls in front of her beloved. "Hasn't even touched his anniversary dinner, poor dear."

"Tonight really is all about putting him out of his misery, isn't it?"

She paused and then nodded. "Yes, it is, Mr. Peabody. Like an old hound who can no longer hunt, his best days are behind him and it's time to head on out to the woods and end it." Her eyes found Peabody's. "And that's what we're going to do, yes?"

The elegant stranger gave a nod. His head turned from her, his eyes on Benji sitting, wounded and lost.

Peabody smiled.

⁂

Red wine dribbled from Benji's mouth. He did nothing, his hands and remaining fingers resting on the tablecloth, his dinner untouched.

"He doesn't eat much, does he," Peabody said as he wiped the cracker crumbs from his hand onto the empty plate in front of him.

"Not much. It's hard to, I imagine, what with the lower part of his jaw, there on the left side, as you can see, basically gone." She pushed the finished plate of crackers and cheese away.

"Another screw up?" Peabody eyed the remaining plates. The jasmine rice. The bow tie pasta drenched in a lemony butter sauce.

He reached for the pasta.

"The twentieth anniversary screw up." She speared a bow tie with her fork. "Why on earth I thought it'd be a good idea to give that man a gun, what with his history of disasters, is beyond me."

"You're not saying he missed shooting himself in the head, are you?"

"No, no, I'm not. Actually, truth be told, that was my fault." She sighed. "We'd practiced on tin cans and old tires, out back in the old place. The place with the field and the trees, far, far from town. Too nosey, those townsfolk. Couldn't stand them. And so it seemed like an easy thing to do, shooting a gun. And it was."

She looked back at Benji. "And had you not flinched and ducked and moved your head, you'd be

EIDOLON AVENUE—APARTMENT 1D

dead right now, wouldn't you? And we wouldn't be sitting here, in pain, stuck in this rat trap on Eidolon discussing all this with you and your blended food and the red wine falling out your mouth and your jaw half-missing, would we?"

She turned to Peabody. "I put the gun to his temple and I counted back from three as we agreed—you know, three, two, one—and on one when I was supposed to pull the trigger, he flinched and moved and reared back." A shake of her head. "Well, that scared me near half to death and the gun went off and struck him in the side of the face, at the bottom. Darn near took that side of his jaw clean off." Another bite of pasta. "And I sat there for what felt like forever with him lying in my lap, holding what was left of his dang jaw in place until the ambulance showed up." She swallowed, her lips wiped clean with a quick brush of the napkin.

"So instead of ending my days with a gunshot to the head, I just sat there, my hands covered in blood, with my beloved Benji in the back of the ambulance. Spent that anniversary explaining to the doctors, nurses, cops and anyone else who felt the need to butt their big bazoos in how my dumb-as-a-duck husband had accidentally fired the gun while cleaning it, or something." A small shrug as she took a sip of chardonnay. "Small town cops. Couldn't care less as long as they didn't have a murder on their hands. I'm guessing that would have been too much paperwork."

"That was your mistake, then." Peabody placed his chardonnay back on the table. "Not Benji's."

"That's right. I meant to make that clear."

"No, no, you did. I was just clarifying." He stabbed

a bow tie with his fork. "Are there other mistakes we should talk about?"

"This whole fiasco has been one whole big Benji mistake after another."

"What about your mistakes?" Peabody watched her.

"Other than the gunshot, I've been as clean as the Sunday wash."

"Yet your hands are still stained with his blood."

She looked at her hands. They were red, the stain sitting squarely on her palms and creeping around her fingers. The red even sneaking around the heel of her hand to sit on the top in a series of drops and specks and splatters. "This?" She laughed. "Oh no, no, no. This isn't the gun. My goodness, me, that was some thirty years ago." She held up her hands, the palms facing Peabody. "This is tomato sauce. For the spaghetti and meatballs."

"Meatballs." Peabody leaned forward, his elbows on the table, his long fingers resting on his forearms. "Sounds good."

They looked long, she thought, her eyes suddenly captured by how elastic and pointed his fingers seemed. Although she couldn't place it, there was something off about them. "It's not ready yet," she said, her eyes closing as she turned her head away. "Soon, I think."

She shook her head, banishing the image of Peabody's odd fingers from her mind. "Honeymoon, tenth anniversary, and then twentieth. That's what we've covered. We should talk about the thirtieth now."

"No, no. Let's talk about the last one. Last year."

EIDOLON AVENUE—APARTMENT 1D

With her eyes still closed, Peabody's voice sounded far away. A whisper shouted from the end of the longest hall. And she could smell the room. More than just the mold and the damp, there was the slight stench of decay. Of death. Unwanted death. From somewhere. Perhaps the tiny skeletons of rats piled behind the walls. Or of beetles and bugs and snakes resting, molded and forgotten, under the floor boards beneath her feet. For a moment, just a moment, the air, heavy and hot, seemed to sigh with that final exhalation of unexpected darkness.

Had these anonymous corpses, like her, found themselves stuck? Had they, too, searched for a way out only to stumble, exhausted and beaten, to fall in battle?

In what? She stopped with a light laugh. "That last year?" she said, pushing away the thought of battles that didn't exist. "The last one?" She took a breath. "Okay."

Opening her eyes, she looked back at him. Peabody waited, a small smile on his face, his gaze steady.

"Go ahead," he said. "Let's go back."

⁂

She had one plate left. Fork and knife in hand, she absentmindedly arranged the slender bites waiting in front of her before tucking in. "We had just moved to Eidolon. We knew this would be our last year, our last everything, really, and, honestly—" She glanced around the room, taking in the yellowing walls, the splintered baseboard, and flecks of ceiling dropping from overhead. "Can you think of a more fitting place for a couple of old fogies limping their way toward the Great Beyond?"

Peabody sat, the place before him empty, save for the glass of chardonnay. "The last anniversary. Tell me about it."

"What can I say? It was nothing."

"Tell me."

"Why? It was a non-event. It was embarrassing." She gripped her knife and fork, her swollen knuckles turning white.

"How so?"

"The toaster bouncing off the side of the tub? Dang cord popping out of the wall? Stupid thing landing in the water with barely a spark? Please." She stabbed the slice of meat on her plate and sawed it in half. "That's not even worth revisiting."

Peabody's long fingers toyed with the stem of his glass of chardonnay. "Oh, I believe it is. And I suspect it's worth talking about."

"Oh, I don't know." She shrugged. "Like I said, it was a non-event. And it's not like I didn't feel a little twinge of something maybe a little dangerous. But obviously it wasn't enough to do us in, so why waste our time?" She shoved the fork in her mouth, struggling to bite the undercooked piece of meat as it squeaked against her teeth.

"But what happened after that?"

"After what?" She considered spitting the dang thing out, but decided to choke it down. The last thing she wanted was to look rude in front of Peabody.

"The toaster in the bath."

"Nothing. Just nothing, all right? Nothing happened." A quick pause, her stomach feeling nauseated. "I got up, got out, dried off and made dinner. Big deal."

EIDOLON AVENUE—APARTMENT 1D

"And felt nothing?"

"Yeah, I felt something." Her throat felt tight. She swallowed the sick creeping up her throat. Ignored the smell of hidden death in every breath. "I felt tingly and my heart was pounding like I'd just ran a marathon or hustled into bingo late. And I saw spots, little flashes of light, for a few days. So what? Does it matter?"

"And the headaches began, correct?"

"Yes, the headaches began. And I started seeing you. Finally admitted that, yes, I need someone to talk with and confide in. I need someone to help me get to the end of this epic comedy of errors." Her eyes on Peabody, a second slice waited on her fork. She inched it past her lips and chewed.

"That's why I'm here." Peabody nodded, his gaze holding hers. "That and your spaghetti and meatballs." He smiled.

She coughed, the meat catching for a quick moment before sliding down her throat. "They're almost ready."

"Your hands are still red."

"Damn tomato sauce won't come clean," she said as she lifted her hand and looked at the deep red staining her palms, her fingers, the flesh under the nails. "Like the stains on these dang walls, it just lingers, refusing to leave." She hid her hands in her lap. "Need a nice long bath. After this, that's what I'll do. Have a nice long bath." She stopped. "Oh wait. I'll be dead." She laughed.

"How's Benji?"

Looking down the table, her beloved still sat, still quiet, his eyes still fixed on the ceiling above her head, red wine still slipping from his lip to his chin.

"Sweetie," she said, indicating he needed to wipe his mouth.

"He can't hear you." Peabody watched him as well. "He looks so lost and wounded." He turned toward her. "Go. Help him." He paused. "For the last time."

She nodded and struggled to stand, the back of the chair creaking beneath her weight as she leveraged against it to rise. Seven painful steps later, she stood in front of Benji, her napkin moist with spit.

Wiping his chin, she noticed the bowls of blended food untouched, the glass of clear, pale chardonnay and golden champagne sitting in front of him, ignored. "Huh."

"What's that, Marta?" Peabody watched her carefully.

"He seems to have misplaced his glass of red."

She left him, pivoting to lumber back to her chair. Her head had started throbbing. An insistent spike of pain thumping in her temples and digging behind her eyes. The sharp ping making her think of miners with pick-axes attacking a wall of stone in search of buried treasure. Or freedom, the tunnel having collapsed, oxygen running low. This repetitive stab of agony their only chance for safety. For a way out. Away from all that rotting, anonymous death.

"Huh." Her eyes closed, she rubbed her temples with her fingers.

"Talk to me." In the dark behind her eyes, his voice, as it had earlier, sounded far away. Muffled and strange.

"I just thought of miners with pick-axes digging their way to safety." She chuckled. "How strange."

"Your face is turning red."

EIDOLON AVENUE—APARTMENT 1D

"My what?" She opened her eyes. She took her red, sticky fingers away from her temples. "Dang." The stained napkin in hand, she wiped her face. "I didn't think."

"Where's Benji's red?"

"Hmmm?" She rubbed and rubbed, the napkin useless, the red spreading across her temple down to her cheek. She'd never get the napkin clean, she thought. And then realized she'd be dead anyway, so who cares?

"The wine. Where's Benji's red wine?" Peabody had leaned forward.

"I don't know." Her hands paused. The pain in her head spiked. She winced.

"How's your steak?"

"It's too raw," she heard herself saying, but her eyes watched Benji. The undertaker from her wedding day had become a corpse. The lips turning blue. The color gone from his cheeks, his hands, his fingers. The eyes fixed to the ceiling were becoming pale and glassy. And he hadn't moved the entire dinner. "It's undercooked."

Peabody said something, though she didn't know what. Her eyes were on Benji. Something was wrong. She gasped, the miners slicing her forehead, the pain blinding her for a moment, her wince turning into an obvious gritting of teeth. "Dang!"

"Look at it," he said.

"Look at what?"

"The steak on your plate. Why is it so raw?"

"I didn't pay attention. Took it away from the broiler too soon. Too impatient. I've always been too impatient."

"From the same stove the meatballs are cooking on?"

Yes, she wanted to say. But she couldn't. Benji's mouth was moving as he mouthed words. Words he couldn't say. But he could speak. Even with the jaw hollowed out on one side of his face, he could still form words. Clumsy and thick, he could still speak. But not now.

"Benji?" She considered standing and moving close, but the pain, the pain in her head, it was a full-throttle attack on her skull now.

"There's nothing on the stove." Peabody's voice sounded strange. She wanted to shake her head, perhaps rub her ears. She swallowed again, the dreaded burn of vomit lingering at the back of her throat. Maybe she was getting sick? Why else would it sound like Peabody was whispering in the dark?

She looked to the kitchen. Peabody was right. There was nothing on the stove. No pot bubbling away. No meatballs. No spaghetti.

"You're right," she said through clenched teeth. She just wanted to lie down. Rest. Take a bath. Surround herself with the smell of soap and steam instead of whatever was rotting behind those gosh dang walls. Considered suggesting that Peabody do them in later. When she felt better. "It's in the oven. The meatballs. Keeping warm."

She looked at her hands. They were still red and sticky. The fingers still stained. Her palms tacky with . . . something. "I need to wipe them clean." She lifted the napkin, snapping it out and bringing it to her palms. But it was useless. There wasn't even a clean corner to wipe the red from Benji's lips.

"Your plate. Look at it." Peabody's voice had grown deeper. More serious. She thought of remarking on it.

EIDOLON AVENUE—APARTMENT 1D

But couldn't. Not with the pain and the stain and Benji mouthing words he couldn't say, the wine now a river running down his chin.

"Why?" was all she could say.

"Because that's how this begins, Marta."

She dragged her eyes from the ruined napkin to her hands and then to Peabody, her head moving slow, her thoughts moving slow, the world now an endless stabbing of spikes drilling behind and around and over her eyes and down into her teeth, her jaw, inside her ears, down the back of her neck, inching down her spine.

Peabody waited, his eyes on her plate.

She turned from him to Benji. He had slumped in the seat, his head back, his mouth a stream of running red inching down his neck to his shoulders and his scrawny arms.

Then she looked at her plate.

Smack dab in the middle of her good china sat her beloved's tongue, raw, sliced thin, and swimming in a pool of blood.

She crawled on the floor, her hands and knees sloshing through a fetid swamp of steaming vomit. Her stomach clenched. She swallowed and then swallowed again. Her hand, dripping with sick and splattered with chunks of half-digested tongue and bits of cheese and cracker, pressed against her lips, closing her mouth. But it was no use. She gagged, her throat opened, another geyser of yellow and red shooting down her front and onto the carpet. Exploding from her mouth. Squirting from her nose. Tears burning her eyes and falling down her cheeks.

Stopping, she turned back to Peabody and Benji, her wounded, beloved Benji. Her back against the wall, she sat, facing the table. The carpet squished beneath her. She didn't care. She didn't care that her fingers had balled into steamy, slimy fists. She didn't care that every rancid breath made her want to gag. And she didn't care that her tongue tasted sour, the inside of her mouth burned, and she could feel flecks of vomit dotting her teeth. She didn't care.

"What have you done?" She looked at Peabody.

He was gone.

"Hello?" She rose to her knees, bubbles of puke squishing from the carpet. Her stomach clenched and the miners swung their pick-axes. Their blades ripping bloody gashes in her brain and knocking chunks off her skull as they stabbed again and again.

"Hello? Mr. Peabody?" She looked at the table. Two place settings remained, one at each end. As always. Benji's bowls and her plates. Her champagne and chardonnay. Benji's untouched champagne and chardonnay. No third place setting in front of that extra chair. Nothing indicating her guest. "Peabody?" she said again, her voice sounding small and weak.

Her stomach rumbled and then spiked with a sharp stab. Her head, my god, her head. She closed her eyes, the thumping now a constant drilling. Like a saw. The kind of circular saw she'd seen on TV. The ones used in emergency surgeries to cleave the skull in two so they can rip out the brain.

The pressure in her throat built. She swallowed and then gagged. Bending forward, her stomach spasmed and her throat stretched as she vomited.

Out came Peabody.

EIDOLON AVENUE—APARTMENT 1D

Very small and much too tall and horribly, impossibly thin, he crawled from her, his fingers inching from between her lips, his elbows jabbing at her cheeks, opening wider as his head pushed out. She felt her jaw pop and crack as he angled his shoulders past her teeth, the heels of his expensive loafers pushing against the sides of her throat as he climbed. His bony knees digging against her tongue until he tumbled free, dripping in spit and strings of errant sick.

His body stretched and grew. Joints popping. Bones cracking. The neck rolling as his head expanded like a balloon filling with helium. Still on the carpet, his long fingers stretched and reached and found hers. His body lifted as he rose to kneel before her, nose to nose, his eyes blinking to open beneath a layer of dripping goo, his gaze steady.

She couldn't breathe. She couldn't move. She couldn't think. Her bladder gave way, the sudden flood a noxious pool of hot liquid drenching her backside and soaking into the already ruined carpet.

Peabody's face was no longer plain and forgettable. It looked waxen and strange. The gaze neither gentle nor kind, it was unblinking and intense. Too intense, the eyes now dark and deep. The lips too thin, the smile stretching too far from cheek to cheek. The eyebrows like strips of cheap plastic stuck to his brow. The flesh of his forehead, his cheeks, his chin, shiny and smooth and stiff.

She couldn't speak. The words wouldn't come. She had thoughts of food poisoning. Or of bad wine. Champagne past its Best By date, if champagnes even had a Best By date. Did they? She had no clue.

And then she thought of the helmet of spikes squeezing her head and pummeling her brain. The team of miners digging their way to safety, desperate to escape the collapse before the air ran out and the forgotten dead woke to crawl and slither and bite. She thought of how she really couldn't think straight. She blinked and tried to breathe. Tried to quiet the panic.

Peabody spoke, the voice deep and quiet, the words whispered through lips that didn't move. The message a secret only she could hear.

There he sits. The monster's head swiveled to face Benji.

His head, it was wrong, she thought. It didn't turn. It was hard to explain. She closed her eyes for a moment, a brief moment. Caught her breath. It had swiveled. She knew that. Yes, that's the right word. Or pivoted. Like a doll's head, it had pivoted, the neck not moving.

Is this what you've done? His eyes were back on her now though she couldn't remember the face pivoting again.

She clenched her teeth. He's going to stand, she thought. Please don't. Please, please, please don't. Don't stand. Please. Don't.

His smile still locked in place, his eyes unblinking orbs of black, Peabody stood.

And then, his feet not moving, he slid back, his heels gliding along the floor, his shoes parting the ocean of puke without leaving a trail. Like a ghost, he moved, floating through the table to stop where he'd sat that night.

And every night since your first anniversary here on Eidolon. He opened his arms. The gesture made her think of the first hello with a long lost friend. The first embrace as you reconnect with that missing part of yourself.

I'm the toaster that bounced off the edge of the tub. Peabody smiled. *I'm the tingle you felt.*

She shook her head. "No. You're new to me," she managed to say. Her tongue felt slow. Her thoughts felt slow. Her words, her reasoning, even the reality around her, this nightmare that couldn't be, felt slow. Time plummeting into a sudden, unexpected crawl.

I'm the spots of light you saw. He watched her. *I'm the drilling in your brain.*

She took a breath and focused. "I met you tonight. You're a stranger."

I'm a secret. He brought a frightening, long finger to his lips. *A secret you kept even from yourself.*

He grew, the room darkening into shadow as his neck craned and bent, his shoulders rising, his head ducking as it touched the ceiling. His legs lengthened in a chorus of ominous pops. With a deep crunch, his waist extended, his chest, his ribs, his hips cracking as they widened. He opened his arms, his hands, with the fingers that were too long, opening and flexing like greedy paws.

Somewhere behind the walls, the dead woke, responding to the silent tune of Peabody the ghoulish Pied Piper. Beneath her feet, under the boards, the dead stretched. And above her, somewhere, she could hear the quiet dead reach to find and grip and hold.

Peabody's fingers grew longer, the arms grew longer. From where he stood, this Peabody's reach seemed inescapable, spanning wall to wall, the fingers much too long, the palms larger than her biggest serving platter or frying pan.

Moving slow, he brought his arms in. The unwanted embrace of a long lost friend you'd hoped to never see again, she thought. She backed against the wall. Clenched her teeth. Tried to move away from the inevitable.

Do you want to see what you've done? His elbows scraped against the walls on either side of the room as his fingers drew close. Like the bars of a cage, they closed in.

She shut her eyes and shook her head. "I haven't done anything."

Marta, he said as those too long fingers found her flesh, the icy skin ensnaring her from the bottom of her chin all the way around the top of her thumping, throbbing skull. *This is what you've done.*

The honeymoon. Half-awake, she saw herself spooning furniture polish into the open mouth of her beloved Benji as, sleep creeping near, he, unaware and trusting, had mouthed "No" before swallowing. Her "I do" earlier that afternoon the key that locked the door and this, spoonful by spoonful, her desperately digging her way out.

"That's not how it happened." She tried to move, but Peabody held her firm.

The ten year anniversary. Hand in hand, her pulling a frightened Benji off the cliff as he'd shouted "No!" And later, barely conscious, her crawling to Benji as he lay bleeding and motionless. And, rock in hand, hitting the back of his head again and again and again. Wanting him dead, wanting him gone. Wanting this end, there, on that ledge, to be her path to freedom and a safe exit.

"I'd never want him dead!" she said. "Never."

EIDOLON AVENUE—APARTMENT 1D

Peabody's lips pulled into a wide grin of vicious white.

The sound of tiny feet scurried in the walls, the floor, the ceiling as all those forgotten dead woke and stretched and reached.

The twentieth year anniversary. She saw herself, gun in hand, aiming for her beloved's face, and pulling the trigger as he'd begged "No" before ducking. But she'd known he'd survive, incapacitated and helpless. She'd hoped his agony would balance the suffering. Hoped he'd know, with each painful day, what she'd endured. Hoped to find peace in his silence. And then sitting enraged as the blood had flowed over her best skirt, his shattered jaw in her hand, her Benji still a burden.

"No, no, no. That's not how I remember it." She started to cry, Peabody's fingers a cold cage, much like Eidolon itself, she couldn't escape from. "It's not."

The anniversary last year, the first on Eidolon. The bath, the toaster. Her refusing to allow Benji to sit in the water. Wanting his punishment to be a life without her. Always taking care of him. Always at his beck and call. Always doing, doing, doing. From sun-up to sundown, doing. Him fighting her over the toaster, insisting "No" as he'd tried to take it from her. And the slippery metal falling and bouncing and landing, unplugged and useless. Her plan for it to fall and spark and free her from this cage her beloved Benji had built around her another failure. Her hopes that he'd be left alone to stumble, wounded and lost, without her, his heart broken, dashed.

"That's not me," she said. "I wouldn't do that."

But it is. Peabody pulled her close. *This is who you*

are. His eyes held hers. His breath filled her nose, each inhalation that dense fog of rotten, forgotten, molding things. *This is who you became.* His lips moved near hers. *Who we became.*

Earlier tonight.

There she stood, her beloved Benji awake and aware as she prepared his dinner. There she stood, her beloved Benji innocent and trusting as she dropped a handful of blue, red, yellow pills into the blender and whirred them into oblivion. And there she stood, her beloved Benji sealing his fate with every bite she fed him.

And she waited as he grew quiet. Counted the seconds one, two, three until his eyes grew heavy, the minutes until his head ducked chin to chest. Counted the footsteps four, five, six as, her best butcher knife in hand, she lumbered her way toward this man, her prison.

There she was, bent over the man she'd called husband and friend for fifty years, her fist shoved down his throat as she counted, sawing at the slippery root of his tongue. Until, with seven, eight, nine, she'd straightened up, the treasure gripped in her fist, her palms and fingers stained red with her beloved's blood.

And she saw herself later, her flesh shining with sweat, her smile too broad, her eyes too wide, her best butcher knife in hand, the weeping tongue bleeding red onto her best china.

Now here she sat, Peabody's shadow darkening her world, Peabody's cold fingers singeing her flesh, Peabody's cruelty—her cruelty—opening the door to their end. Her end.

"I'm a monster." She closed her eyes, her breath strangled by sobs.

EIDOLON AVENUE—APARTMENT 1D

You are perfect. His fingers trapping her head, he drew close, the movement too quick, the arms shortening. *You're exactly what Eidolon needs.*

She glanced toward Benji, not wanting to see Peabody's waxen face or unblinking eyes or ghoulish grin.

He stood, her beloved. His body abandoned and forgotten, the memory of who he was waited, his eyes on the ceiling.

All those failures feeding your shadow. Peabody's breath was cold against her cheek as he smiled, his eyes, too, lifting skyward to the dusty, dingy, yellow stretch above. *And now, your trip into forever.*

And against all reason, her thoughts too slow to stop her, she looked up.

On the ceiling above, the dead lived. But not the rats and beetles and bugs and snakes she feared waited in the hidden spaces of Eidolon. No. This was a seething swarm of human souls fighting what felt like a never-ending war.

Half-formed and steaming red, elbows knocked out teeth. Fingers poked out eyes. Teeth bared and snarled to bite and tear. They twisted and turned, feet kicking, arms reaching. Souls screaming for release, for escape. For safe passage. Their backs arched and their knees bent, pushing as yet more punched and gripped and pulled and ripped. More red ignoring the laws of gravity to spill and spread in a wandering sea along the ceiling as ephemeral skin tore in jagged gashes.

Peabody's arms circled her. A predator to her prey, she found herself thinking as they rose.

"No," she'd tried to say. But the word had been

stolen by chaos as she ducked her head, chin to chest, and screamed as she and Peabody lifted, his mouth stretching wide to swallow the souls in one greedy gulp, as they ascended into hell.

⁂

The memory of her stood outside. The building on Eidolon sat in front of her. It was raining, the water racing through the cracks on the sidewalk.

She closed her eyes and bent her head back. She couldn't feel the rain on her face. Couldn't feel the chill of what she was sure was an endless dark. Her body felt light, the aches and pains she'd associated with life gone. She took a deep breath and then exhaled.

She opened her eyes.

The sky was a twisting, turning storm of black and grey. Clouds folding and dipping only to reach through their brethren and dive back again. It was monstrous. What evil would look like, she thought. But there were no swarming, fighting bodies. Thank god.

Her eyes caught the building.

She stopped.

Peabody squatted on the top. Impossibly large, he waited, his elbows out, his too large hands gripping the edges, his feet planted on the opposite corners on the back of the building. His body no longer thin and elegant, it was bloated and round. As if he'd feasted. A still hungry spider with a belly full of flies.

His head swiveled, searching the street below. Seeing her, he stopped.

In a breath, the feet had moved and the hands had reached, the round stomach sliding over the windows

EIDOLON AVENUE—APARTMENT 1D

and scraping against the brick as he'd skittered down the building.

Now he paused in front of her. His mouth opened, the jaw popping wide, the rows of sharp, tiny teeth glinting yellow and red in the dark. With a belch, it opened wider, an avalanche of souls spilling forward to land on the avenue in a jumbled, twisting tumble of arms and legs and skulls cracking against pavement.

At once, they were on her. Teeth biting, elbows knocking, fingers gripping and fighting to tear and shred, Eidolon now a battlefield. A living nightmare of snapping bone and the wrenching of flesh against flesh. The constant crashing of waves. A howling of wind. A deep rumbling of earth.

Her knees bent, the weight of them forcing her down. And as the crowd covered her, she heard him. Her beloved Benji. Somewhere safe. Somewhere far from the fight, from the storm. Somewhere where elbows wouldn't jab and jaws wouldn't bite, Benji's voice, though small and without hope, screaming

"NO ... NO ... NO ... NO ... "

APARTMENT 1E

UMBRA

There was something living in the walls.

Still wearing her only black dress, a rose taken from the cemetery in one hand, her bright pink backpack in the other, she'd watched the stain in her new bedroom. Round and raised in the middle, like a bubble, it was different than the others.

And it was alive.

She'd known it the moment she'd walked in. Had felt it as she'd turned to put her backpack on the creaky bed. Had expected, when she first saw the stain two weeks ago, to see a face, two eyes, lips, a nose and cheeks and teeth, pushing from the wall.

But there'd only been a wide brown circle. A stain that wasn't a stain. One that wasn't long and dark like the others. One that hadn't dripped from the ceiling to the floor. One that sat alone, removed from the others. Just like her.

"What kind of name is 'Umbra?'" were the first words Gran had said when the big lady with the onion bagel breath first dropped her off. The State had decided this was where she had to be. With her dad as flat as a pancake under the car in the garage and her mom, after belting back her fifth Jack and Coke of the morning, shredding her throat by eating the glass, she'd had nowhere else to go.

"Worthless cunt never could hold her liquor," Gran had said with a laugh.

Had she known there'd be a new home, a new

school, new classes, and new kids, all making fun of the skinny girl with the boney knees who walked too slow and read too much, she wouldn't have sorta accidentally wished her folks dead.

Which, by the way, she had *huge* questions about. Because *everyone* knew it would suck to *not* have a mom and a dad—even her mom and dad—so why would she *do* something like that? And *could* she even do something like *that*?

Because you know what? If she could do something like that, she *definitely* would have done things differently. If she could.

This was before the stain that wasn't a stain. Before the police came. Before the ambulance with its flashing lights.

This was when she was little and dumb, before the State decided where she'd live.

The big lady had given her a nod and a push forward, her teeth clenched in a tight smile. So she'd trudged to her room as Gran had signed her name on the dotted line while she and the stranger from the State had whispered about "adult things."

And in the safe quiet of her new room, in this stain that wasn't a stain, she'd found a friend.

"So," Onion Bagel Breath had said as she'd stood in the doorway, "everything okay?" She'd looked at the woman doing her best to ignore the stains, the dirt and dust, the peeling wallpaper and cracked window.

And she'd forgotten it all. Didn't worry about the smell and the way the bed creaked. Or the thin mattress and scratchy blanket. Had no longer felt trapped by the low ceiling and the wind sneaking past the cracked window to lift the torn curtain. The stain

EIDOLON AVENUE—APARTMENT 1E

that wasn't a stain had helped her feel welcome. Safe and secure. Protected. No longer alone.

"Yeah," she'd said to the woman who'd already left. "It's okay."

But before that, before dad getting smooshed and mom freaking out and the big lady from the State, before the funeral and all those super-simple cheese sandwiches with Gran, before the beginning of the end on Eidolon, there was Miranda Jacobs.

"You gonna cry, baby?" The little girl kicked her in the shin. "Huh? Gonna cry for us, *baby?*"

Umbra stood with her arms crossed over her chest, her head ducked. She could hear the silence all around her. No one was playing on the monkey bars or throwing the ball against the wall. No one was running or chasing or play fighting. Although she wouldn't look, although she *refused* to look, she could *feel* everyone looking at her. Watching her.

"Huh?" A mean push, Miranda's friends laughing as they stood behind her. "What's that? Can't talk, baby?"

Umbra bit her lip and shook her head.

A second kick to the shin. "Don't know the words?"

Slap, slap, push, slap, punch.

Kick.

She felt her face grow hot and her eyes water with tears. Her neck and cheeks turned red. She prayed the bell would ring soon. She prayed recess would end and everyone would have to stop looking and she could get back to her desk and her books and her very sharp pencils. She was tired of her shins bruising and her chest feeling tight. She was tired of gritting her teeth and clenching her fists. She was tired of living with a target on her back. At home. At school. Always the one kicked or poked or pushed or slapped or smacked or yelled at or punched.

And she was tired of praying.

Another kick. Another push.

She prayed Miranda would stop. That she would stop and shut up and just die and leave her alone. Just leave her alone so she could escape to the library. In her heart of hearts, she prayed that this mean girl would hurt. Hurt like she was hurting. That her throat would close and her heart would swell and blood would explode in her chest and rush through her body and gush out her eyes and nose and ears and mouth. That there'd be so much blood she'd shut up and go away and leave her—

A moment later, the screaming began.

"Are you sure you didn't do anything?" Miss Hessler leaned in close, her elbows on the table. "Anything at all? Think!"

She *was* thinking and she knew that if *she* put her elbows on the table her teacher Mr. Peters would yell at her. But obviously if you were an *adult* you could do anything you wanted.

"Umbra? Sweetie?" The woman waited, her fingers squeezed together so tight the skin was turning white.

She was doing her best to listen to the principal sitting on the other side of the big desk. She really was. But the woman looked tired. Her hair was brown with bits of silver peeking through. Her eyes were heavy and had dark, puffy circles under them. Her face was pale, the pink blush on her cheeks and the red smeared on

EIDOLON AVENUE—APARTMENT 1E

her lips reminding her of those clowns she'd sometimes see in her books. The creepy ones. Even the sweater with the thread coming loose around the neck and the dried ketchup stain on the sleeve looked tired and old and finished. "I told you I didn't *do* anything," she said.

"Now, Umbra—"

"*I* was the one getting kicked. *I* was the one getting pushed. And *punched*. I *told* Mr. Peters and he told me to ignore it. And I did. I *ignored* it. And I didn't do *anything*!"

Miss Hessler sighed and closed her eyes, her fingers rising to massage her temples.

"But it was the truth," she said later that night as she sat in front of the stain that wasn't a stain. "Like I *meant* for all that blood to come out? Like I somehow *meant* for Mean Miranda to stand there like an idiot as it shot from her mouth and her nose and her ears and her eyes and everything? I just wanted her to shut up and *leave me alone*. That's all." She stood and faced it. "I was just as shocked as everyone. Honest!"

She sighed. She'd rather be sitting in front of it, but it was too high to see clearly from the floor. She'd wanted to bring one of the kitchen chairs into the room so she could look at it face to face, but Gran wouldn't let her. Especially after she explained why.

"What on earth do you mean 'Can walls talk?'" Gran had said as she'd dragged her eyes away from the TV. "What kind of question is that? Of course they can't talk!" The old woman smiled. It wasn't a nice smile. It made Umbra feel stupid and small. Like a baby.

"I just want to read to it," she'd said.

"Why on earth-" Gran had laughed, the sound sticking in her throat. The laugh becoming a cackle and then a cough, her skeleton fingers dragging a crumpled wad of tissue from her sleeve as the green spittle sprayed from her lips to land on her chin. "Dumb as shit and crazy as a loon." And then she'd laughed some more.

She'd slunk back to her room.

"You *can* talk, though." Umbra stood and pushed close to the stain. "I *know* you can. All I have to do is listen. And read you books. So you can learn words. And I'll tell you about me. Whatever you want to know." She placed her hands on the brown circle, her fingers feeling the slight bubble in the middle. "Then you'll talk. I know you will."

She sighed. Her head hurt and her eyes were sleepy and her shoulders felt tight. She'd walk to bed, but her legs were heavy and, right now, it felt like too much work. She just wanted to stay with her friend. She swallowed a yawn and looked over at the digital clock. The one that clicked when the minutes changed.

It was late. Too late. She had school in the morning and she should be in bed. "I hate school." She closed her eyes for a moment. "And I hate Gran. She smells weird. She smells old." She closed her eyes really tight. She didn't want to cry. "I miss Mom and Dad, even though they were horrible sometimes. Even though they yelled. And slapped and punched and kicked me. Like Miranda. But I miss them. I do." She fought back another yawn. "Except Mean Miss Miranda. I don't miss her. Not even one little bit."

She pulled close. "And I like you, I do, but I don't like it here. If I knew they'd put me here, I don't

EIDOLON AVENUE—APARTMENT 1E

think—" She stopped. "I would have been more careful with my wishes."

She leaned her forehead against the wall. "Because you know what?" She pressed her lips to the stain. "Because I wanted them to die. I know it sounds awful. I do. But I did. And Miranda, too." Her heart thumping, she took a deep breath. "I just closed my eyes and really hoped they would go away and die and they did. I did that. With my head. With my prayers. Maybe even with Jesus." She stopped. "Is that wrong?"

She rested her cheek against the stain. "I'm afraid I might be bad." And even though she was tired and didn't want to, even though no one was around and no one cared, she cried, her tears smearing the circle of brown.

This was when the stain responded. This was when the bubble grew and the edges spread, the circle larger. As if it had felt her sadness. Had heard her. Liked her stories. Or fed on her guilt. Or enjoyed the fact that she had secrets like it did. Dangerous secrets. Wrong secrets. Or was happy that she wished for death and that her wishes had power.

"I just wish I knew you." She wiped the tears from her cheek and, her hand wet, laid her palm flat over the breathing bubble clinging to the wall. "Like, *really* knew you. Will you tell me who you are?"

The stain deflated. The breathing stopping. Whatever had come to life suddenly went quiet. The brown circle on the wall went back to being nothing but a brown circle.

"I'm sorry." She stepped away. Watched it. Hoped it'd do something. Anything. "Someday you'll tell me. Someday you'll show me." She turned and crawled into bed, pulling the thin blanket up to her chin. "I hope so."

And, alone and friendless once again, she fell into a quick sleep.

～⚭～

The room dark, her eyes on the TV, Umbra took a bite of her cheese sandwich. Gran was ignoring her. Still. She'd tried to talk about her day, but Gran wouldn't respond. It was like she didn't even exist. If she'd ever wondered what it was like to be a ghost, now she knew.

She didn't like it.

The old woman coughed, her fingers diving into her sleeve to get the balled up tissue and hold it to her lips. A minute later, the coughing stopped, the wheezing grew quiet, and Gran went back to staring at a TV that stayed forever mute.

Umbra focused on her sandwich, chewing quietly. Tonight Gran's coughing and wheezing and sniffling seemed worse than usual. And, from what she could catch, Gran had been "healthy as a bleedin' horse" before moving to the one bedroom on Eidolon. But now she was very skinny and very pale and her skin was covered with red circles of icky, flakey skin that sometimes bled if she moved her arms or stretched her legs to go to the toilet. The thin hair on her head had turned snow white and her breath wheezed sometimes, especially after she coughed. Which she did. A lot.

Dressed in the same old housecoat—faded flowers stained with soup and spit and sick and blood—she sat in the same chair all day every day, the TV always on and always on mute. No longer saw her friends for

EIDOLON AVENUE—APARTMENT 1E

whatever the messages on the answering machine invited her to do.

"Carol? It's Joan," the lady in the voicemail had said. "Are you okay, hon? Betty, Ruth and I are looking for a fourth for bridge this Friday. We'd love to see you. Call me, okay? Okay." But Gran never did. She just sat in front of the TV, her bowl of soup sitting ignored beside her. The used tissue balled in her fist or pressed to her mouth as she coughed and wheezed and gasped.

"Oh, for Christ's sake." Gran looked at her. Her eyes were small and dark. And her lips were curled. Almost like she was trying not to laugh. Or like she was just *waiting* for the moment to say something cruel.

"I dunno." She shrugged and, feeling small and stupid for the millionth time, wanted to hide. But she was curious, again, so she'd asked if walls could talk. Again. "Why wouldn't they?"

"Walls would have to know *words*. You think walls know *words*?" Gran said. "Of course they don't. And how in the goddamn hell is a *wall* supposed to speak if it doesn't know *words*. Or have a mouth. Or a soul." She dragged the tissue across her runny nose, her lips in a sneer. "Of all the idiotic, worthless, stupid things to say . . . " And then she laughed as Umbra sat quiet.

"It's okay," she said, swallowing the last bite of cheese and bread. "I was just asking. That's all."

More laughter as Gran pressed the crumpled tissue to her lips. "That's *all*?"

She shrugged. "It's just sometimes I feel—"

"You *feel*?" Gran struggled to catch her breath. "Oh, just shut the hell up. The last thing I want to hear about is how you *feel*. Goddamn, girl, you always were an odd one." She drew her housecoat in, wrapping her arms around her chest and hugging tight, her hands rubbing her arms. "Just . . . strange. The way you sat there, in your crib, staring at the ceiling. Or stood in the front yard looking at the house. Like there was *something* there to *see* when it was only a goddamn ordinary piece of shit rental. But you kept *looking* as if it was something *other* than a house." Gran shook her head. "Stone cold weirdo. That's what I told your mother, the stupid bitch, and that's what you were. What you still *are*." She sighed and looked over at her. "The way you stared. Holy hell. At me, at what's her name, your mother. Even your father. *That's* what made me sit up and take notice. It was like you were looking *into* us. Not at us. *Into* us. Mother of god, that made my skin crawl."

Gran leaned forward and grabbed the remote, changing the channel, though the TV stayed quiet. "That's one of the reasons, hell, that was the *main* reason, truth be told, I never came over. That and your mother, of course. But the both of you? Together?" She shivered. "Holy Christ. Gave me the goddamn heebie-jeebies. How your father put up with you, god only knows." Her eyes stayed on the TV. The room was quiet. Too quiet. A long moment passed as Umbra sat, wondering if Gran was finished being mean.

"You don't remember do you?" Gran cleared her throat.

"Remember what?" She sat, her cheeks flushing red. She thought of *thinking* about considering different ways to get this mean old woman, this *bitch*, as Mom used to call her, out of her life. And then, not wanting Onion Bagel Breath to move her around again, decided it'd be best to do nothing. "I dunno—"

EIDOLON AVENUE—APARTMENT 1E

A cruel laugh from Gran as her hand rummaged in the cushion of the chair. "Of course you *dunno*, dumb as shit *Umbra*. You *dunno* anything." A fistfull of new tissue in hand, she wiped her chin and her top lip as her breathing steadied. "You were, what, three, maybe four? Still shitting in a diaper, for Christ's sake. Took forever for your mom to fix *that* little problem, but there you were, sitting in shit, out in the front yard playin' in the dirt. Remember?" Gran looked at her. Her eyes grew small as she watched her. "Hmmm?"

She shook her head.

"Poor Señor Sanchez." Gran grinned, her thin lips smirking in the flickering light from the TV. "No one could ever figure out what happened to him, the pervert. Disappeared just like *that*," she said with a snap of her fingers.

Then Gran leaned forward, coming close to her, the smell of pee and bad breath and sticky, sweaty skin hitting her in one big breath. "But I know what happened. I *saw* what you did." She drew back, tugging her housecoat close around her. "I couldn't believe it, but I *saw* it and it scared the ever-loving shit out of me. That's why I never came back."

Gran paused. Glanced at the TV. "If it wasn't for the State kicking a little extra into the kitty each month for taking care of you, there's no way in holy hell you'd be here." She gave a quick laugh. "Got me off of cheap gin, let me tell you. Nothing but top shelf from here on out." She pointed her long, skeleton finger at her. The nail was long and sharp and sorta yellow, the skin wrinkled and old. "It was you, *Umbra*. That day with Señor Sanchez. It was all you." Gran turned away from her to look at the TV. "I could not believe my eyes. I wasn't lit and I wasn't drunk, but I saw what I saw and I heard what I heard."

In the light of the TV, Gran looked at her again, her eyes narrowing. "You know what you did. Yes you do. You asked for forgiveness from God. Later that night. I heard that little girl voice of yours whispering or whatnot. To God." She turned her head away. "But *you* did that, you'll *never* escape that, and it's something *you* need to live with."

Umbra sat there for a long moment. She bit her lip and sniffled. There was a *something* in what Gran was saying. A *something* that said . . . she didn't know. *Something*. But it was horrible and bad and super-secret and sat in her tummy like a rock and made her eyes hurt like she was going to cry. Again. But she couldn't. She wouldn't. Not in front of the old woman.

She looked at her. Gran didn't say a word, her attention on some stupid sitcom still set to mute. So, feeling like a ghost again, Umbra stood and gathered the crumbs in her napkin and headed to the kitchen.

She stood at the counter for a long moment. She missed home. If she were home, she'd be in the kitchen, like now, but she'd be cleaning mac & cheese off her plate instead of dusting the crumbs off a napkin from yet another cheese sandwich. Or maybe there would have been Hamburger Helper. Or tacos. She loved tacos.

If she were home, dinner would be done, Dad would be in the chair watching TV with the sound on and Mom would be out on the back patio drinking as the sun went down. It would be like it always was. At least before Dad died.

She squeezed her eyes closed, real tight. She was

EIDOLON AVENUE—APARTMENT 1E

tired of crying. She was so done with tears. Maybe it wouldn't be so bad if Onion Bagel Breath came back and took her somewhere else? Somewhere away from Gran?

But her friend. The stain that wasn't a stain. She took a deep breath. No, she was where she needed to be.

Besides, she had no idea who Gran was talking about. Señor Sanchez? No idea. She folded the crumbs in the napkin and threw it in the trash. Besides, she didn't remember playing in the dirt when she was a baby. Babies are babies. How are *babies* supposed to remember what they do, you know? But she kinda wished she could, even though it already felt like something wrong or bad. And, if that were true, she didn't want to.

She did remember her mom that last morning in the kitchen though, and that was enough.

Mom sitting at the table in a dirty T-shirt and her underwear, so skinny and already "sloppy drunk and mean as a skunk" as her dad used to say. Remembered trying to ignore her as she'd slurred "Comere." Remembered her mom getting mad and yelling at her as she'd tried to sit there quietly and eat her cereal *without* milk because they didn't have any. "I'said comere!" The table jumping as mom's hand slapped it. Tried to forget the sick feeling in her stomach as Mom tried to stand, and then lean across the table to grab her, her hand swiping nothing but air until, losing her balance—probably because she was too drunk to stand *again*—she'd sat back down. The table thumping when her fist pounded it.

She didn't want to remember the thoughts she'd

had in her head. The dreams. Her mom peaceful and calm, healthy and happy. Her eyes bright and her smile real. Her arms not flapping around and her feet not stumbling as she tried to stand or move or walk.

Her dream of a morning where no one fought, no one screamed, no one drank. Her dad in a happy mood as he joined them for cereal. Him kissing her on the cheek or the forehead or the top of the head as he sat, the whole family finally together at the table.

She didn't want to remember how she'd always hoped for peace and quiet. How she just wanted to eat her cereal. With milk. How she wanted her mom to *not* drink. Or, if she had to, to not drink *too* much. Maybe even have her try to be normal or something. She didn't know what that was like, to have a nice, happy mom.

She remembered seeing out of the corner of her eye—it was best to never look at mom when she was like this—the glass with the brown liquid at the bottom rise into the air for another drink.

She'd hated that glass. Hated whatever was in it that made her mom mean and nasty and smelly. Whatever it was that made her angry and sad. And made her cry and hug and hold and then push away and punch and slap and scream.

She'd tried to forget that glass. And the sight of that glass touching her Mom's lips. And watching her throat gulp, gulp, gulp as she swallowed from that glass. She remembered wanting that glass gone. And wanting Mom gone. Of just wanting Mom quiet and *normal*. Somehow.

That's when it'd started. Mom belting back the last of her Jack and Coke. Mom smiling as she'd taken that

EIDOLON AVENUE—APARTMENT 1E

first bite of glass. The crunching as she chewed. And her sitting there with her cereal without any milk, not knowing what to do. Feeling like somehow this was, in some way, her fault, though she'd never ever imagined this. Never.

And then another bite, and another, mom's eyes wide, like she was confused. The broken glass cutting her bottom lip so bad that it peeled and hung there and swung, sticking to her chin. She remembered seeing her mom's gums and bottom row of white teeth because the lip had fallen away. She remembered how the pink had been stabbed by little shards of glass as she opened her mouth wide for another bite of glass.

She remembered how she'd sat there and felt bad. And then how she'd just finished her cereal. Almost like whatever had happened was a dream that was part of something else. Something she didn't quite know or understand yet. Like it was a *something* that came from her heart. A something that told her it was okay and this was right and everything would be fine. And so she'd said nothing and done nothing.

That, she remembered.

Now, in Gran's kitchen, she tried to forget the blood. All that blood. The sight of it, the smell of it. Even how she thought it must feel as it dribbled from her mom's mouth, onto her chin and down her neck to the space between her boobs. The red looking sticky and gross as it stained her shirt while she sat there, looking so confused and so helpless and *still so drunk*, biting and crunching and chewing and swallowing the sharp pieces of broken glass.

That, she remembered, too. That, she'd never forget. She took a deep breath and reminded herself that the *something* was a thing to trust. And she was trying. But this Señor Sanchez? This man Gran had mentioned? She had no clue.

She left the kitchen and, head down and as quiet as a mouse, tried to sneak past Gran's Lazy-Boy with the stuffing coming out of the rips and the arms wrapped with old pieces of duct tape.

"Ah ah ah." Gran grabbed her arm. "What do we do?"

Holding her breath, the smell of pee-pee and old sweat making her stomach sick, she pressed her closed lips to the old woman's cheek. "Thank you for dinner, Gran."

"You're welcome." Gran paused, her eyes narrowing as she looked at her, her thin lips curling into a grin as she grabbed her shirt in her fist. "Señor Sanchez. In the front yard. In the dirt. *In* the dirt, Umbra. Hmmm?" Gran dipped her head, tucking her chin to her chest as her eyes looked at her. "Think about it. It'll come to you. I know it will." She released her and gave her a small shove. "God help you."

⁂

"I think the words in this one are too big." She sat cross legged on the floor, a book on her lap. "Maybe I should just talk . . . or something. And you can learn words that way, okay?"

She'd been reading to it for weeks. Had gone to the library and scrounged around, finally finding those big, slender books that had page after page filled with large pictures and easy words. "This one?" the librarian had said. "This is much too young for you. You really should be reading at a much higher level by now, don't you think?"

EIDOLON AVENUE—APARTMENT 1E

I do, she'd wanted to say to the skinny woman with the white flakes in her hair and the glasses that slid down her nose. But this thing in my bedroom, it's learning, okay? It's new. It needs my help. And these little kid books are perfect, so just mind your own business, lady.

But she'd said nothing. Just shrugged and looked at the squished library card in her hand, wanting to hurry up and get home, have her cheese sandwich and teach her silent friend to speak.

And so, wrapped in her PJs, a blanket around her shoulders, her feet warm in a pair of socks, she'd read, her voice small in the low-ceilinged room, the rain pelting the window. For hours, she'd sound out the words, careful and slow as night fell and her bedtime came and went. Hoped that somehow it'd learn enough to tell her what it is and what it wanted and if it, like her, was lonely and sad.

"Does this story make sense?" She looked at the stain. Searched for a response. A sign that what she was doing was working. "Are you following it?"

It didn't respond.

She took a breath. She was being a grown-up about this. Nice and patient. Not like how she felt with Mom and Dad, or even Gran. With this, her friend, she was working hard and letting it take as long as it needed. "You know, learning words isn't easy," she said. "It took me a long time, too, way back when I was a baby."

It sat there, doing nothing.

"But my teachers were patient and sometimes nice." She gave it a small smile. "And I promise I'll be patient and nice with you, okay?" She closed the book and put it down. "We'll try again tomorrow." She stood and stretched. "I don't know you," she said. "But you don't know me either. Would that help? Knowing more?"

She drew near the stain and took a long look at it, wondering where to begin.

"My dad was an accident." She waited for some response. There was nothing. "I'll tell you about it, if you want. But know that it wasn't *supposed* to happen. I *kinda* thought of it and, I don't know, I guess it got away from me."

She stopped, wondering what it was hearing. Wondered if it heard anything. Decided it did. "I'll tell you, okay?"

She placed her palm against the wall. Near the stain, but not on it. "I've never told anyone. You're the first. You're special." She inched her fingers near the brown circle. "To me, you're special. Something I can tell my greatest secrets to."

A deep breath to calm down. "Okay, he was in the garage working on the car. Not our car, but another car. One he'd found in the junkyard that had no wheels or anything. And I sat there with my sandwich and watched him because Mom was 'sloppy drunk and mean as a skunk' and throwing things in the kitchen, and he . . . "

She was never quite sure what, exactly, had happened at this point. Whatever it was, though, it had made her uncomfortable and feel a little less safe. Like it was *almost* something that had happened *before* but it was all cloudy and weird. But she'd always felt safe with her dad. Had always had him as someone to run to when Mom got mean. So this, what she could remember, had always felt wrong.

EIDOLON AVENUE—APARTMENT 1E

"He saw I wasn't wearing, you know, my undies. I was wearing a dress, like, for the fifth time that week because *nothing* was clean and we didn't have the powder soap for clothes or even the squirty blue one for dishes. So I couldn't even *do* the laundry if I *wanted* to. And I wanted to because I had *no* clean undies." She felt her cheeks grow red. "I kept my knees together. I did, but I think I forgot for a quick moment and Dad saw my, um, you know, my um . . . " She cupped her hand around her mouth as she whispered. "My private place." A quick glance at the door. "I mean, I don't know, I *think* he saw and, anyway, he made fun of me being smooth like a tiny little baby."

That sick feeling in her stomach came back as she stood with the stain. The burn in her cheeks and that tight feeling at the back of her jaw that made her grit her teeth really, really hard. That feeling that made her want to go into a really dark corner where no one could find her and just stay there forever. "I didn't know what he meant. Really, I didn't. I still don't—"

She stopped and looked to the door again. She thought she'd heard something. Maybe Gran was listening in? Like way back when this stupid Señor Sanchez thing supposedly happened? She considered going to the door. Opening it. Making sure she was alone and not being overheard. But Gran wouldn't be there. She'd be in front of her TV watching a show with the mute on. She knew it.

"Honest. I didn't know what he meant, calling me a tiny little baby." Her eyes watched the stain as she moved closer and whispered. "I still don't. Honest. Even though Onion Bagel Breath tried to tell me when I sorta mentioned it which I should *not* have done, by the way, but he's dead anyway so it's not like it matters." She shook her head and closed her eyes real tight. "But she did say that what he said was wrong, though she wouldn't tell me why, exactly. Which was stupid. And that him peeking was wrong. But I already knew that. I knew it was somehow wrong and somehow mean, or something, and it was a thing he shouldn't be saying or doing or whatever." She shrugged. "Nothing *happened*, you know. It was like a joke or something. I dunno. I was just so embarrassed and so ashamed that my *one* pair of underwear was too dirty to wear and he'd caught me or something." She took a deep breath.

"And so I just . . . I just wanted him quiet. And I remember looking at the thingy-ma-bob holding the car up and seeing the car had no wheels, not yet, anyway, and I remember kinda thinking 'If that were to fall, he'd be flat as a pancake.' And before I knew it, that's what happened."

She felt her lip tremble. Her face started to flush. And her nose crinkled and was getting stuffy. Her throat felt tight. But she wouldn't cry. She didn't want to. She was tired of crying. Was tired of her throat hurting and her face feeling heavy. She swallowed and then bit her lip. Bit until it hurt, but it was too late.

The tears came.

"I didn't mean to do that. Believe me, I didn't. It was an accident." She was crying now, her voice hurting as she talked, her shoulders rising with hiccups as the tears ran down her cheeks and the snot dribbled out her nose. "I saw his insides. They smooshed out of him when the car landed. I saw his head split open and the big bone in the head, the skull,

EIDOLON AVENUE—APARTMENT 1E

like, crack open and I could see his brains. And all that blood and stuff, like green and yellow or something, all that stuff came close to me. Came close to my shoes." She wiped the snot from her top lip. "And I had to stand and go real quick through the kitchen and then out the back door to the neighbors, the ones with the loud dog on a chain that barked all the time at *everything*, and ask if they'd call 911 because my dad was dead. He was dead." The tears were so thick she could barely speak now. "And it was my fault. He left me alone with *her* and it was all my fault. I did it and I didn't even mean to."

She stopped and caught her breath. Wiped her face, wiped her nose again. Wiped her hands on her PJs. Took another breath. "I'm horrible." She sniffled. "You've probably never seen anyone as horrible as me. You probably can't even *imagine* doing something as horrible as I did. What I still do." She took a step back. "I'm sorry."

And having nothing more to say, she grew quiet, afraid she'd lost her friend.

"I didn't mean to do it. Really, I didn't."

She stopped and listened. Cocked her head and held her breath, sure she'd heard something again.

Was Gran at the door? She sighed and closed her eyes, hoping the old woman hadn't heard anything about her thoughts or her dad or what had happened.

The sound continued. And it wasn't the sound of someone listening in. Of someone shuffling near and leaning close, their ear pressed to the door. This noise was strange. And it wasn't coming from the other side of the door.

She turned from the stain and walked across the

room. Pressed her ear to the door. The sound was still there. But there was no one on the other side. Whatever it was came from farther away. From the living room. For a moment she thought Gran might be choking, but no. That wasn't it either.

She listened. It wasn't the wheezing of Gran's breath. She knew what that sounded like and this wasn't it. And it wasn't a cough. Or a sniffle. And she knew it wasn't the TV. It was something sticky and wet. And there were voices, too. A mumbling? A murmuring? Whatever it was, it wasn't a something that was quick, like Gran clearing her throat or coughing into her tissue. It was a something, a *weird* something, that wouldn't stop.

She opened the door and, because it was late and she wasn't supposed to be up, and she didn't feel like getting yelled at *again,* crept around the corner.

Gran sat sleeping in the chair, her chest rising and falling. A line of drool stained the side of her mouth, her lips spotted with flakes of dried spittle. Her thin hair stood in little tufts of fluffy white. In the light of the TV they kinda looked like the little devil horns you see at Halloween. But these were white. And hair. Old person hair. The picture on the screen—some stupid sitcom or something—jerked and bent and twisted as the signal struggled, their voices silenced by the mute button.

And in that jerking, bending, twisting light she saw them.

In what looked like a wispy cloud of cigarette smoke, *they* stood. Flashes of arms and bits of leg. Skinny shoulders and round stomachs. Gran's housecoat lifting and moving as these weird hands

EIDOLON AVENUE—APARTMENT 1E

touched her body. Her hair moving as fingers ran through it to feel her scalp. Mouths coming out of the air and pushing forward to press against Gran's forehead and cheeks. Pink tongues lapping at the smooth skin behind the ear and along the back of the neck. Lips kissing her temples and slobbering on her thin lips. The smoke showing the white of teeth tasting and nibbling and sucking. The sound very quiet and very wet. A greedy, hungry sound.

These *things* hiding in the smoke stood and reached, feasting on the body that lay trapped by age and sickness and sleep.

Umbra waited, quiet as a mouse, as they kneeled and bent. Steps from her, Gran's housecoat was lifted as they laid their hands on her body before more teeth bit and more tongues licked and more mouths sucked and more lips kissed. Her knees, her legs. The pale skin around her belly button. Her sagging boobies. Heads even pushing close to her super-duper secret private place. Lips spreading and jaws stretching and throats swallowing as her strength, her energy, her health was eaten. All she was, everything except her actual body, her life, being bit and crunched and chewed with the weird, soft sound of sucking and licking and savoring.

A moment later, these *things* lifted their heads, their eyes finding her as she watched silently. She breathed, nice and calm. Returned their gaze. Their lips curled into small grins, the lips wet with spit and the sweat from Gran's flesh.

As she stood there, *something* told her she would be okay. Both she and Gran. *Something* let her know that *they* wouldn't come close to her. *She* had nothing to worry about. Gran was who they wanted and they wouldn't kill her. No, there'd be no death. She *knew* that. No one would die. Not tonight.

A moment after that, the heads returned to the body. The licking, the tasting, the sucking and nibbling, the feasting, started again. Gran a buffet for the shifting, quivering, wavering strangers crawling all over each other as they fought through the smoke to crowd the old woman sleeping in the chair.

She moved away, nice and slow. Her feet feeling heavy and thick, she walked backward to her bedroom. Her fingers trembling, she turned the doorknob. Calmly, she went into her room and, once safe, closed the door. Tight.

Taking a deep breath, she looked to the stain that wasn't a stain.

And she remembered.

Señor Sanchez. Standing in front of her on a summer day as she sat outside. It was hot. And dusty. He was trying to give her ice cream. Or candy. He was big. This large dark thing blocking the sun as he squatted and tickled her ankle with his finger. She remembered his dusty cowboy boots. His shiny belt buckle. His tummy too big for his shirt and his moustache looking sweaty and gross. His face wrinkling as he smiled. His teeth big and yellow as he came close to her. Too close, his lips wet as he tried to press them to hers, his breath smelling like beer and cigarettes as he nudged his nose against her cheek.

Mi muñeca, he'd said, the words an urgent whisper. *Tan tierno—*

The ground moving. She remembered. It had lurched and shivered. Cracked in a cloud of dust. The sky blue, but black. Shadows where there shouldn't be shadows. And the ground *not* breaking as hands, like

EIDOLON AVENUE—APARTMENT 1E

old people hands, came and grabbed Señor Sanchez with his shiny belt buckle and dusty boots and his tummy too big for his shirt. She remembered how fast it was. And how skinny and dangerous the hands looked. The hands that grabbed him. They looked like claws, but only without fur. Like *human* claws. Like skeletons who lived under the ground had reached up, covered in dirt and vines and the roots of trees, to find him and and stop him and pull him down. The fingers skinny, the arms nothing but bones, the nails long and sharp and yellow. Like Gran's.

She'd forgotten this. She'd forgotten him. She'd forgotten how quickly the ground had swallowed him and his ice cream—yes, it was ice cream because it had melted and dripped on his hand and she'd thought that looked gross—and how the sky had gone back to being blue and the ground stopped moving and how she'd just sat there getting burned in the sun.

"Did I do that?" She stopped and looked at the stain. Saw nothing. No face, no eyes. No lips pressing forward to open and speak. "Not just with Gran, but back then? With this Señor Sanchez?"

Silence, the stain nothing but a stain.

"I forgot." She paused and tried to think. "I don't think I coulda done that. I was just a baby or something, you know?"

She watched the stain. "I've been bad a long time, I think." She traced it, running her finger all around the edge. Wondered if it tickled. "I can say that to you because you're a friend. I think that maybe sometimes I can be sorta bad. Sometimes." She thought again of Sanchez and stopped. "That there, outside in the living room, is it bad, too?"

Nothing.

"It can't be. Because if she dies, they'll make me leave. And I don't want to leave." She felt like moving close. Like pressing her cheek against it or kissing it or something. Anything to get it to listen. "Do you want me to leave?"

Again, nothing.

"I don't want to leave." She crawled into bed and lay down as the *things* in the wispy smoke on the other side of the door ate away at her last link to something normal and safe.

"I've told you all my secrets and you've told me nothing." She closed her eyes. "Maybe I should go. Maybe I don't belong. Maybe I'm wrong about you. About us." She sighed. "Maybe you're not a friend after all."

⁂

She was wrong.

Coming home from school, she'd turned the corner, her backpack slung over her shoulder, a new book from the library under her arm. Yet another she'd read aloud and hoped the stain would enjoy, as if it even cared. And in front of the corner store, she'd looked up and stopped.

And here she stood on Eidolon, still, across the street from the building.

They lived in what Gran called a tenement. But it wasn't like the others. Where the other buildings held each other up, the two walls smooshed into one, theirs sat separate with alleys on either side. If the grass wasn't so tall or the mud so deep, or if there weren't tons of flies buzzing around piles of empty liquor

EIDOLON AVENUE—APARTMENT 1E

bottles and poopy baby diapers, she'd be able to walk around it, her arms stretched, her fingers touching brick on both sides.

But today?

She was seeing the stain that wasn't a stain as it really was.

It sat on the building, this *thing*.

Like a blanket, it fell like a mist, but thicker. This darkness like a cloud that not even the wind could take. It was black and looked almost solid, but she guessed it wasn't. Shivering and shuddering, it swayed like fabric over all five floors, unrolling to rest on the sidewalk before spilling to the curb.

No one noticed it. No one stopped and looked and talked about the dark sheet hanging over her building. It was as if only she could see it. As if only she was special enough and trusted enough with this greatest of great secrets.

Standing there, she forgot she had to pee. Or that her tummy rumbled for dinner. Or that she was so very tired. She forgot that she was dreading climbing the stairs and walking into the smell of dust and old person and wet peppermint candy.

"This is you, isn't it?" She watched it breathe with the breeze. "You can tell me. I'm your friend. I love you. This is you, right?"

Yes.

She heard it speak. Heard it find the words it needed to talk with her. She closed her eyes. It was still her friend. She felt the tears come. But these were tears she wanted. Tears she welcomed. These were happy tears, her heart soaring, her smile the biggest it had been in what felt like *forever*. Despite the nights of silence, the days of quiet as she'd stood there begging it to speak, to trust her, to show her she was loved and that she mattered to someone, to *something*, now she knew without a doubt that it was still a friend and it loved her.

And she loved it.

Even from across the street, she could feel its pulse thump and its blood pump. Feel it turn its head and stretch its limbs. Caught its breath as it lifted her hair and cooled her face. Smiled when it kissed her cheek.

"I can *see* you." From beneath the dark blanket, it lifted its head. Turned to her. Like it'd heard. Like it'd followed her voice. Like it *knew* her. The darkness rose and fell as it breathed. As if it was waiting for her.

Her heart racing, her backpack lying in a puddle next to her feet, she watched it, trying to think of something to say, something to do.

"I *know* this is you," she finally said. "I'm coming." She shrugged the backpack over her shoulder and, the clouds in the sky rumbling with thunder, ran across the street to the door, her eyes on the darkness above. For a moment her vision dimmed as she passed beneath the black sheet. Her breath held, she paused.

There was another world here. Between the dark only she could see and the cold rain running over the brick. A world of hidden things. Of things that moved slow. Like her. A world of lost things. Lost dreams. Lost loved ones. Lost lives. Lost hopes. A place of regret and misery. A frightening world of shadow where things wandered and reached, always searching, never finding.

In this dark, lips whispered words she couldn't

EIDOLON AVENUE—APARTMENT 1E

hear. Were she to turn, she'd almost catch these strangers standing, watching, waiting, weeping.

"What is this?" She placed her hand on the door.

My skin.

She ran her hand over the metal, her fingers dipping into the dents, dings and scratches. Running over the thin iron bars that trapped the small window. Her hands even lying flat on the wet brick, the cold rain racing down her fingers, along her wrist, into her palm and past the sleeve of her rain coat.

She smiled. "This is your skin?" She pressed her face to the metal, the brick. Breathed in the cold and wet and rain. "And these people, these ghosts. Everyone here, are they you, too?"

My blood.

"They are your blood, the ghosts. And this, the door, the brick, the building, this is your skin." She slid her key in the lock and gently turned the knob. "I understand."

The door slamming behind her, she wandered down the hall past the mailboxes, her fingers tracing the dingy red tile on the walls. Her steps heavy and slow, she made her way to the stairs and, trusting her steps, trusting her friend to guide her, her hand gripping the wood railing, she climbed, her eyes closed.

"And this?" Pausing at the top on the first floor, she leaned into the smooth yellow wall. Felt how cool it was. Inhaled the musty smell. Didn't care that her cheek would come away dirty and smudged. "This wall, what is this?"

My bones.

She smiled. Staring down the hall, she saw the

apartments. Five on each floor. Five floors, five doors. The secrets of . . . wait, five times five equals . . . twenty-five . . . twenty-five strangers, maybe more, in this whole building, all opening with a simple knock. So many secrets, so many lives, so many mistakes. So much to learn.

"These walls, are all these walls your bones?" One arm holding the book to her chest, her backpack over her shoulder, she walked. "And outside, the building, the brick, that's your skin?" Her hand ran along the wall. "And the ghosts, their whispers, are they your blood?"

Her fingers inched over the walls, the doors, as she moved down the hall, her footsteps slow and careful, her body buzzing with excitement. A moment later, she stopped in front of her door.

The place where she lived.

The place where *it* lived.

The place where *they* lived.

She was home.

She snuck in. Gran sat snoring in her chair, the TV on mute, the cheap screen a glowing square of static. Her faded housecoat still stained with soup and spit and sick. Her thin hair still devil's horns of white standing on end. The lights on the ceiling flickered and popped.

Seven steps later, she was in her room. The stain waited on the wall. Backpack dropped by the door, the book, which felt kinda stupid now, tossed on the bed, her thin coat shrugged off, dropped and forgotten, she stood in front of it.

"Your skin, your blood, your bones." She laid her hand on the wall next to the stain. "This what you are?

EIDOLON AVENUE—APARTMENT 1E

This is who you've always been?" She moved near and closed her eyes. "So it wasn't me. Before. With Mom and Dad. With Miranda. Was it you? Is that how it happened? Was it *us*? Together?" She paused. She could feel its breath rising and falling. She breathed with it. Could almost feel it moving. Could sense the bubble in the middle expanding. "You can tell me."

It didn't respond.

"It'll be our secret. I promise." She waited, willing it to talk, afraid she'd lost it. The brown circle sat in front of her. She caressed it. "This brown stain, here, is it . . . ?" She paused as she tried to remember other body parts, other things it might be. "Is it your face?" Her mind flustered and her tummy grumbling, she gave up. "Please, tell me."

My heart.

"I like it." She smiled and pressed her lips to it. Waited for lips to kiss her back. Pulled away to look at the familiar round spot on the wall, but saw nothing. No face, no eyes, no lips.

"What do you want?" She waited, the minutes ticking by. From the living room the TV static crackled and snapped. The lights above dimmed and then grew bright. Somewhere on Eidolon a baby cried and a woman shouted and a horn blared as a car splashed the puddles on the street below. Gran snored and, waking quickly, cleared her throat. Distant thunder rumbled from the dark, heavy sky.

"You want something. I know you do." She traced her finger over the stain. Felt its warmth. Felt it buzzing and jumping with life. "What can I do to help?"

It grew quiet. She pressed closer. Took a deep

breath. Ignored the smell of dust and rotting walls. Tried to forget the sharp bite of the mold growing in the corners and the constant chill of the rain outside.

All she wanted was to hear it speak again.

"I'm your friend. And I love you."

Sudden silence. The baby quiet. The cars quiet. All of Eidolon quiet on this rainy Monday afternoon as she waited for this piece of the puzzle to snap into place. Hunger stabbed her stomach. She swallowed, trying to ignore her craving for a cheese sandwich.

It didn't work.

"I'm hungry." She leaned her forehead against the stain. "It's not even four o'clock yet, but I'm hungry." She wanted to eat, but was afraid to leave. Was afraid of losing it forever. "Are you hungry?"

Yes.

She breathed a sigh of relief and grinned. Her fingers stroked it, calm and gentle. The bubble shifted and spread beneath her palm. "You're hungry."

Her fingers ran over the stain as it split, the circle of brown opening with a gentle tear, sticky strings of something clear and white and pink stretching from the sudden wound. "Me, too." The tear became two lips. Thin and long, they pressed together as they moved and lengthened. Flexed and found themselves, bulging with the hint of a thick tongue running along a row of hidden teeth.

She traced the lips with her fingertips. Light and gentle. She wasn't afraid. She knew it loved her. And she loved it. She was safe. "You're safe," she said to the stain and then wondered why. Of course it was safe.

The lips stopped. Held still.

She took her fingers away and grinned.

EIDOLON AVENUE—APARTMENT 1E

Somewhere on Eidolon, the baby cried again. She listened, the sudden noise sounding far away and hollow. Like it was coming from behind a closed door at the end of a very long hall. She waited for it to grow quiet again. But probably hungry and maybe stuck in a poopy diaper, the baby cried louder, the noise becoming almost a scream.

The lips on the wall parted as the stain let out a sigh.

The crying stopped, the sharp silence almost shocking.

She looked back at the stain. Imagined the baby with a bottle shoved between its lips. "I need to eat, too. We should eat." She thought again of her cheese sandwich and wondered if it'd like some. "Can you eat?" Then she wondered if it actually *could* eat. "You don't have any hands or fingers. How can you eat? Do you need my help?"

The lips slowly spread in a dangerous baring of small, sharp teeth.

"Okay." She put her finger to her lips and kissed it. "I'll help you." And then, the little clock on her bedside table clicking over as the minutes changed, her finger lightly touched the teeth as she gave it a kiss.

"Let's eat."

Monday, 3:24 PM

If you enjoyed this book, I'm sure you'll also like the following titles:

Flowers in a Dumpster by Mark Allan Gunnells—The world is full of beauty and mystery. In these 17 tales, Gunnells will take you on a journey through landscapes of light and darkness, rapture and agony, hope and fear. Let Gunnells guide you through these landscapes where magnificence and decay co-exist side by side. Come pick a bouquet from these Flowers in a Dumpster.

Nameless: The Darkness Comes by Mercedes M. Yardley—Luna Masterson sees demons. She has been dealing with the demonic all her life, so when her brother gets tangled up with a demon named Sparkles, 'Luna the Lunatic' rolls in on her motorcycle to save the day. Armed with the ability to harm demons, her scathing sarcasm, and a hefty chip on her shoulder, Luna gathers the most unusual of allies, teaming up with a green-eyed heroin addict and a snarky demon 'of some import.' After all, outcasts of a feather should stick together . . . even until the end.

The Dark at the End of the Tunnel by Taylor Grant—Offered for the first time in a collected format, this selection features ten gripping and darkly imaginative stories by Taylor Grant, a Bram Stoker Award® nominated author and rising star in the suspense and horror genres. Grant exposes the terrors that hide beneath the surface of our ordinary world, behind people's masks of normalcy, and lurking in the shadows at the farthest reaches of the universe.

Little Dead Red by Mercedes M. Yardley—The Wolf is roaming the city, and he must be stopped. In this modern day retelling of Little Red Riding Hood, the wolf takes to the city streets to capture his prey, but the hunter is close behind him. With Grim Marie on the prowl, the hunter becomes the hunted.

The Outsiders Lovecraftian shared-world anthology—They'll do anything to protect their way of life. Anything. Welcome to Priory, a small gated community in the UK, where the only thing worse than an ancient monster is the group worshipping it. Is that which slithers below true evil, or does evil reside in the people of Priory? Includes stories by Stephen Bacon, James Everington, Rosanne Rabinowitz, V.H. Leslie, and Gary Fry.

Tales from The Lake Vol.1 anthology—Remember those dark and scary nights spent telling ghost stories and other campfire stories? With the *Tales from The Lake* horror anthologies, you can relive some of those memories by reading the best Dark Fiction stories around. Includes Dark Fiction stories and poems by horror greats such as Graham Masterton, Bev Vincent, Tim Curran, Tim Waggoner, Elizabeth Massie, and many more. Be sure to check out our website for future *Tales from The Lake* volumes.

Through a Mirror, Darkly by Kevin Lucia—Are there truths within the books we read? What if the book delves into the lives of the very town you live in? People you know? Or thought you knew. These are the questions a bookstore owner face when a mysterious book shows up.

Where You Live by Gary McMahon—Horror is everywhere, in the shadows and in the light. It takes on every shape, comes in every conceivable size. But most of all it's right where you live. With the WHERE YOU LIVE short story collection, Gary McMahon delves into the depths of dark and brooding horror in every day events, objects, and the ghost of human nature.

Samurai and Other Stories by William Meikle—No one can handle Scottish folklore with elements of the darkest horror, science fiction and fantasy, suspense and adventure like William Meikle.

If you ever thought of becoming an author, I'd also like to recommend these non-fiction titles:

The *Writers On Writing: An Author's Guide* Series—Your favorite authors share their secrets in the ultimate guide to becoming and being and author. With your support, *Writers On Writing* will become an ongoing eBook series with original 'On Writing' essays by writing professionals. A new edition will be launched every few months, featuring four or five essays per edition, so be sure to check out the webpage regularly for updates.

Horror 101: The Way Forward—a comprehensive overview of the Horror fiction genre and career opportunities available to established and aspiring authors, including Jack Ketchum, Graham Masterton,

Edward Lee, Lisa Morton, Ellen Datlow, Ramsey Campbell, and many more.

Horror 201: The Silver Scream Vol.1 and *Vol.2*—A must read for anyone interested in the horror film industry. Includes interviews and essays by Wes Craven, John Carpenter, George A. Romero, Mick Garris, and dozens more. Now available in paperback, as well.

Modern Mythmakers: 35 interviews with Horror and Science Fiction Writers and Filmmakers by Michael McCarty—Ever wanted to hang out with legends like Ray Bradbury, Richard Matheson, and Dean Koontz? *Modern Mythmakers* is your chance to hear fun anecdotes and career advice from authors and filmmakers like Forrest J. Ackerman, Ray Bradbury, Ramsey Campbell, John Carpenter, Dan Curtis, Elvira, Neil Gaiman, Mick Garris, Laurell K. Hamilton, Jack Ketchum, Dean Koontz, Graham Masterton, Richard Matheson, John Russo, William F. Nolan, John Saul, Peter Straub, and many more.

Or check out other Crystal Lake Publishing books for your Dark Fiction, Horror, Suspense, and Thriller needs.

BIOGRAPHY

In addition to Eidolon Avenue: The First Feast, *Jonathan Winn (Member, HWA) is a screenwriter and author of the full-length novels* Martuk . . . the Holy *(A Highlight of the Year, 2012 Papyrus Independent Fiction Awards),* Martuk . . . the Holy: Proseuche *(Top Twenty Horror Novels of 2014, Preditors & Editors Readers Poll),* Martuk . . . the Holy: Shayateen *(2016) and* The Martuk Series (The Wounded King, The Elder, Red and Gold), *an ongoing collection of short fiction inspired by* Martuk . . .

His work can also be found in Horror 201: The Silver Scream, Writers on Writing, Vol. 2, *and Crystal Lake's* Tales from the Lake, Vol. 2, *with his award-winning short story "Forever Dark".*

CONNECT WITH THE AUTHOR

http://martuktheholy.com
http://twitter.com/Jonathan_Winn
and
http://facebook.com/jonathan.winn.90

Connect with Crystal Lake Publishing

Website (be sure to sign up for our newsletter):
www.crystallakepub.com
Facebook:
www.facebook.com/Crystallakepublishing
Twitter:
https://twitter.com/crystallakepub

With unmatched success since 2012, Crystal Lake Publishing has quickly become one of the world's leading indie publishers of Mystery, Thriller, and Suspense books with a Dark Fiction edge.

Crystal Lake Publishing puts integrity, honor and respect at the forefront of our operations.

We strive for each book and outreach program that's launched to not only entertain and touch or comment on issues that affect our readers, but also to strengthen and support the Dark Fiction field and its authors.

Not only do we publish authors who are legends in the field and as hardworking as us, but we look for men and women who care about their readers and fellow human beings. We only publish the very best Dark Fiction, and look forward to launching many new careers.

We strive to know each and every one of our readers, while building personal relationships with our authors, reviewers, bloggers, pod-casters, bookstores and libraries.

Crystal Lake Publishing is and will always be a beacon of what passion and dedication, combined with overwhelming teamwork and respect, can accomplish: Unique fiction you can't find anywhere else.

We do not just publish books, we present you worlds within your world, doors within your mind, from talented authors who sacrifice so much for a moment of your time.

This is what we believe in. What we stand for. This will be our legacy.

Welcome to Crystal Lake Publishing.

We hope you enjoyed this title. If so, we'd be grateful if you could leave a review on your blog or any of the other websites and outlets open to book reviews. Reviews are like gold to writers and publishers, since word-of-mouth is and will always be the best way to market a great book. And remember to keep an eye out for more of our books.